CLEM'S CHANCES

SONIA LEVITIN

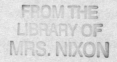

FROM THE
LIBRARY OF
MRS. NIXON

AN
APPLE
PAPERBACK

SCHOLASTIC INC.

New York Toronto London Auckland Sydney
Mexico City New Delhi Hong Kong Buenos Aires

This book was originally published in hardcover by Orchard Books in 2001.

ISBN 0-439-44054-8

12 11 10 9 8 7 6 5 4 3 2 1   2 3 4 5 6 7/0

Printed in the U.S.A.   40

First Scholastic paperback printing, November 2002

Designed by Rosanne Kakos-Main

The text of this book is set in 10.5-point Weidemann Medium.

Dedicated to Lloyd, my hero,
who has encouraged me
all the way

And for Dan and Shari
with love and thanks for
all the "nachos"

———◆◆———

Many thanks to
my dear friends
Clo and Ray Barnes
for their help
and inspiration.

CONTENTS

CLEM'S CHANCES

CHAPTER 1

From Graveyard to Graveness: How I Came to Meet Molly and Her Degenerate Brothers

S eems to me the beginnings of things are never so clear as when you look back. Then, it's plain as rain how one thing leads to another, and which trick of God or nature set everything in motion.

For me, it all started that afternoon at the grave of my mother and little Joy May, which was the name of my baby sister, only a year old and surely innocent. Not much joy had come into our house that winter, what with Pa gone to the gold fields. He'd left even before Joy May was born, needing to seek his fortune, but I'll explain about that later.

I see myself standing there on that little hilly spot where we put their graves. It was under the elm tree, where Ma used to sit and sew late afternoons, with Joy May swinging from a branch in the little seat I'd made. Surely those were happy days, but who counts happiness until it's gone? The fever came up so suddenlike. One day the baby was ailin', red in the face and croup-coughing, shivering in her blankets, and Ma tending her all night. It took but a week until both of them were down with fever, Ma praying and telling me the Lord would surely provide. Provide, He did, in His own wisdom, moving Ma and little Joy May to greener pastures. At least that's what the Pastor Blanchett told me when I ran over there to fetch help. Of course, the deed was done: Ma and Joy May were peacefully transported to that green pasture, and I was left alone with my future.

The first order of business was providing the funeral, of which I have had but little practice, being still alive myself. But Pastor Blanchett knew just what to do. "Ride on over to Thurstons' place," he told me, "and tell them to come up tomorrow, when we'll do a good and proper burial, followed by praises to the dear departed." Our neighbors would offer their sympathies and their services. Old Tom Thurston knew carpentry. He'd set to work building coffins. His neighbors would bring their shovels. Their combined passel of young'uns would love to bring news all over the township, their tongues wagging and flapping. They'd spread the word better than the newfangled telegraph machine that people were always talking about in town.

Pretty soon we were on the way to holding a real respectable funeral to give Ma and little Joy May a proper send-off. The problem was for eats. We had some pickles and prunes in the cellar, stored since last summer, and a sack of cornmeal for cakes. Pastor's wife helped me cook up a mess of corn cakes and syrup, and Scotty Lundgren, whose apples were seething in barrels since last harvest, could be counted on to provide applejack. Everyone knew Scotty's drink was so potent that it could burn a hole clear through the front of a man's shirt.

Lots of folks came to the funeral, there not being much in the way of entertainment in these parts. I went through all the motions a fellow is supposed to make, shaking hands, taking in sympathies and the tears of ladies who knew my ma from church. Some of 'em pecked at my cheeks and pulled at my hair until I thought I'd scream.

As the cider took hold, the men started swaggering and talking. They acted as if I was stone deaf, talking about my pa.

"That Pare Fontayne, sure was a study. . . ." They called him Pare, never having learned how to say his real name, Pierre. "Couldn't tell a sow from a cow!" Laughter followed. My face burned.

"It's readin' all them books, makes a man strange. I recall when we put up his barn roof, Pare hinged the doors on backward!"

"Where's he gone to, do you think?"

"Gone to the gold fields, with nary a pick nor shovel; he's prob'ly lost hisself in a patch of quicksand. Should of stayed in France, if you ask me, with those other Frenchies. Couldn't do nuthin' for himself. A drain on the community."

"Poor Pare, his wife and baby dead and gone. Guess he's sorry now, he run off that-a-way."

"Dogged if I'd leave my wife and kids, no siree, a man's got his duty." A chorus of cussing followed, such as made the pastor tuck his head further down into his collar.

Into this chorus came a new voice, as big as the frame of the woman who owned it. "Shut up, you vultures!" she called out, her chins and bosoms shaking hard. "You know better'n to speak ill of the dead!"

"Well, Pare Fontayne ain't dead; he's just gone to Californ-y."

"For all you know," retorted the woman, "he's dead and gone, and this poor boy is an orphan. We ought to show him some Christian charity instead of grieving him with ugly talk about his pa. I, for one, will hold no truck with doin's of this kind."

All the last weeks I'd been strong, bearing my cross as Ma would have said, but now, with this large woman taking up for me, I felt all weak and jellified, my eyes watering and my nose sniveling like a baby.

I turned away, to hide my weakness, and there stood a girl I'd never seen before, her hair wound around her head in two braids the color of shining molasses, and her eyes so blue it made me think about such things as the lake on a summer evening.

I thought about Pa, and how he sometimes read poems to Ma, and her cheeks would turn pink, her eyes misting over.

"Howdy," the girl said. She looked shy, but she sounded bold. "Sorry about your ma and baby sister. I'm Molly Warren. We live at the other side of town, you know, by Meakins' ranch."

"I know the Meakins," I said, "but I never saw your place. Of course, I've been occupied here, taking care of things."

I cursed myself right off for using that word, "occupied," such as nobody from around here—nobody except Pare Fontayne—would ever use. But Molly seemed to like it fine, for she smiled, showing a dimple at the side of her mouth, and her color brightened too.

"We only moved here a while ago," Molly told me, "from Ohio. You took care of this here farm all by yourself, Clem Fontayne?"

"Well, we had some help for harvest," I said modestly, "and our crop wasn't much to speak of." Then I added, "Next spring I hope to break some horses and sell them, and put in some hay, and of course a kitchen garden, maybe even strawberries."

Molly just nodded, and I stood there twisting my foot like a darn fool. Either I was talking too little or too much. I hadn't a clue which it was.

"They say your pappy's gone to Californ-y," Molly said, looking me straight in the eye in a way no other girl had ever done. "They say he's gone to the gold fields."

"He was headed that way," I replied. "Don't know whether he ever got there."

"But wouldn't he send a letter by stage? Or even by boat?"

"Letters can get lost," I said abruptly. "I'm sure he did write. My pa is good with words. He probably got held up there in Californ-y. Of course, he trusted me to take care of everything. . . ."

Thankfully Mrs. Warren came bustling up to take Molly by the arm, for it seemed like nothing could stop my mouth from running over. I was sorely embarrassed to be talking about family matters to a stranger.

"We'd best head home," said Mrs. Warren. "Now, Clem, if'n you ever need anything . . ." But her voice trailed off, and they were gone.

As folks were leaving, some of the women hung back, worrying.

"You gonna be all right out here by yourself? You have some stores set up?"

"Oh, I'll be fine," I told everyone, though in truth I didn't know what I'd do. Our crop was a dismal failure, and we'd run out of cash a long time ago. Ma did some needlepoint to sell in town, but folks didn't seem to favor her designs of little angels and daisies. All in all, my parents were ill suited for life on the frontier, which was what Missouri was called in those days. Ma had come from Wilmington, Delaware, where people sat on puffed-up chairs and talked in big words, telling politeness to each other, and the ladies stitched daisies onto napkins. She and my pa met at some lecture hall, introduced by folks who knew his cousin. He'd come from France a few years earlier, with a bundle of books all in English, which he had taught in France. He was tall and lean and good-looking. I had their wedding photograph, Ma looking so pretty and young it would make you cry.

Why'd they ever leave Delaware? I guess Pa was filled with notions from those books of his, determined to see the world. But reading is one thing, doing is another. They moved to Missouri so Pa could live off the land, like some squire he'd read about in the books he ordered from Boston and New York. That was part of the queerness of his nature, according to folks around here—spending money on books when he might have bought a bull instead.

As it was, we were the owners of a single cow, a few scratching hens, and a horse that some fellow caught in the wild and traded to my pa for an old camp stove. Pa turned the critter over to me, and in a month's time I broke him and we became friends. I named him Mr. Abe, meaning no disrespect for that statesman Mr. Lincoln. I'd read about Lincoln in the newspapers my pa brought home, him debating with a short little man called Douglas and winning everyone over with his wit and his wisdom.

This horse was lanky and big and wise in his own way. Mr. Abe and I had some long talks, and I found him sweet clover and pure water and licks of salt. When Pa left, he took Mr. Abe with him, and I'm shamed to admit it, but I think I missed that horse as much as I missed my pa.

Strange how as soon as the funeral was over, Ma and Joy May truly gone from my sight, they filled my mind more than in life. And the winter came on strong and sudden. The few vegetables we'd planted and canned were quickly consumed. I ate all the potatoes in the cellar, all the watermelon rind, and the last of the salt pork, and then I learned about the different types of hunger. There's the scratching hunger in the morning. At noon comes the yawning hunger. By late day the dizzy hunger, and at night the growling, gnawing I'll-do-anything-for-a-morsel-of-meat hunger, and the next day it starts over again. I ate some furry gray cheese I found wedged in the back of the cupboard and some dried corn kernels long forgotten in a sack. One day I shot three squirrels, but I was soon out of ammunition, and as the creek froze, the fish were hidden away. I trudged around to the neighbors, looking for work, but winter had come complete, and there was no work to be found. Besides, most of 'em had boys of their own to do what needed to be done. Nobody seemed inclined to feed an extra mouth.

I would have perished, except for the little milk provided by Belinda, the cow. I was considering ways to boil bark and leech acorns, when one day I heard a clattering outside. My heart did a skip. I thought it was one of the neighbors come to invite me for supper. But there stood a peeling, sagging wagon drawn by one sorry-looking horse, with two people inside leaning over to gaze at what was left of my homestead.

They got out of the wagon, and I saw my home through their eyes. The cabin roof was nearly caved in. The shutters flapped in the wind; the weeds blew and bent, brown and shriveled as the remains of last year's stubble in the field. Out in the yard Belinda moaned out her own complaints, a dreadful welcome for the Warrens.

In a moment they were out of the wagon and puffing toward me, Mrs. Warren thrusting out her chin and her ample chest with indignation. "My stars," she said, "this place is a wreck, and you are starving. This very morning I says to Hank, let us go on over and see how that poor orphan lad is doing. We would of come sooner, but we had stores to lay in, don't you know, what with our Molly and the boys to feed. You know what they say, the Lord helps those that help themselves."

I nodded and said, "Yes, ma'am," thinking how I *had* been trying to help myself, and then Mrs. Warren's eyes lit up like little fires when she saw Belinda. I was rightly drooling, expecting stew and biscuits and gravy to come my way, and thinking of seeing young Molly again.

"So I says to Hank, it is our Christian duty to look after that motherless boy."

Mr. Warren stood there, scratching his head. "You any good with critters, boy?"

"Very good, sir," I told him. "I broke our horse. I can mend fences too." Well, I thought he meant to offer me day work in exchange for food. My stomach churned in anticipation.

The Warrens walked around the place, nodding, inspecting. "They say you must speak the truth after the dead," said Mrs. Warren, "and it's God's truth that these folks never were much for farmin' or keepin' house."

"My ma kept a fine house!" I let out, alarmed.

"Aye, a fine house," said Mr. Warren, puckering his mouth.

"The way I see it, Clem," said Mrs. Warren, "you got two choices. You can stay here and let the walls fall down around you, or you can come and help us out at our place. We'll feed and shelter you. It's a good deed we're doing, not that we expect any glory for it, except in the Hereafter."

"And you can sleep in the dug-out closet off the cellar," said Mr. Warren.

"We'll rescue that sorry-lookin' critter too. C'mon, Hank, rope that cow to the wagon and we'll be on our way."

What could I do? I'd never make it on my own. So I piled a few things into a sack, slung the sack onto my shoulder, and was about to climb aboard.

"No, you'll walk," said the good Mrs. Warren. "This nag's about dead already."

Mr. Warren laid on the whip good and hard, and I hurried along behind them. I was going to look back, but I remembered what Ma had taught me about someone doing that and turning into a pillar of salt. So I looked straight ahead and whistled a tune, considering myself lucky.

When we got to the Warrens' place, I saw it was gone to ruin, and those Warren boys, likewise. They were big, strapping boys, fifteen and seventeen. I could tell they hadn't had a single bath between them since spring. They took one look at Belinda and started planning a barbecue. "It's a milk cow, you imbeciles!" hollered Mrs. Warren, taking a swipe at Jonas, the younger one. "Get on, now, you loafers. Show Clem his bed, then get him started on the back field."

"It's plumb froze, Ma," whined Billy, but his ma paid him no mind, and I was sent out to my first labor for my benefactors. I caught a glimpse of Molly, standing at the hearth, stirring something in a great, black kettle. She turned and gave me a wan smile and a shrug that seemed to hold meaning. At least, it seemed so to me, and my heart was lighter as I set out to work that frozen field.

CHAPTER 2

I Acquire a Friend and Several Enemies and Am Evicted

Their horse was an old Clydesdale, swaybacked and over-worked, as was obvious by the beast's drooping eyelids and morose, incessant bobbing of its head. It must have been an imposing creature once, nut brown in color with a mask of white on its face, about nineteen hands high and deep chested. Now it was wasting away. Long years and hard labor were not the only causes of its misery. The horse was starving.

Albert, they called it, and I was to become its caretaker. "Hitch up old Albert" was a daily command. Albert hauled away timber and pulled heavy stones out of a field. He took the Warrens to town, and he was put to the plow at planting time.

I told Mr. Warren, "That horse needs some grain, oats, and hay. There's not enough pasture for it here."

"You tellin' me how to farm, boy?" snapped Mr. Warren. "It's a lazy beast, is all. Needs the lash applied now and again."

"We could get more work out of him," I argued, "if he wasn't starving."

"You telling me I starve my animals?" yelled Mr. Warren, and his wife put in, "Shame on you, boy, sassing your elders. What's this world coming to?"

I said nothing more but went out early each morning and last thing before dark to gather up what grasses I could. I found some apple trees half a mile up a hill and took the fallen apples to Albert. Sometimes I could bring him a carrot. The horse seemed to brighten, not only from the extra food, but from the attention. I'd stroke his head right between those wide-set eyes and rub the soft place between his nostrils. He had a keen sense of smell and would nuzzle my chest and neck, and it got so he knew I was coming, lifting his head and sniffing the air to catch my scent.

Molly sometimes came out with me. "I think Albert was lonesome before you came," she said, giving the horse a lump of sugar from her hand.

"Horses are sociable creatures," I said. "They like company."

"They're like people, I guess," said Molly, and she blushed. "I haven't had any company since I stopped going to school."

"When was that?" I asked. I felt fortunate having gone to the town school, and having parents to teach me at home.

"Last year," she said brusquely, turning away.

I didn't ask why. For school a person needed shoes and a coat, especially in winter, and money for books and teacher's pay. It didn't seem like the Warrens had any extra. They survived on game and wild greens and some potatoes that mercifully grew all over the hillside behind their house.

Molly had no shoes but for a pair of tattered old boots that must once have belonged to her brother. Mostly she went barefoot. Sometimes we sat down on a pile of hay, just talking. It was so easy to talk to Molly about anything at all—like how people were all so different, some puttin' on airs and others just folks, and about animals and their ways, and later, about books we read together. Molly remembered every tune she ever heard, and she sang to herself while she worked. As it turned out, I could teach her a tune or two, and she loved that. We had ourselves some fine times, me singing, her twirling One day I grabbed both her hands and whirled her round and round. She laughed so hard, calling out, "Stop! Oh stop, Clem, I'm all dizzy."

Then she sat down on a pile of hay and rubbed her bare feet in her hands. It was a habit she'd gotten from being so cold, though she didn't realize she was doing it until once I remarked on it, saying, "Your poor feet, Molly! They must be about froze."

Molly started and blushed. "No, I'm used to it. I like to go barefoot, like this here mule."

"But it sure would pleasure me to get you into some fine leather shoes. I've seen them with buttons all the way high up the leg."

Molly blushed the more, and I was astounded at my own boldness, mentioning such body parts as were always tucked beneath a skirt. I went on. "When I get some money and go to town, I'll buy you a pair, and then we can dance good and proper."

Molly seemed to be holding her breath. "I'd like that," she whispered.

"Could be a barn raising in the spring," I went on, heady with plans. "We'll dance and show 'em how. There'll likely be a barbecue."

"You ever been to a barbecue, Clem?"

"Once," I said. "But it was a long time ago, and there weren't any pretty girls I'd want to dance with anyhow." I was amazed to find myself sweet talking her like that. Such notions had never occurred to me before. Maybe the barn had a bewitching effect, I thought, for I took to spending a great deal of time there with Molly. We curried and groomed old Albert until he shone. Molly even slicked his hooves with boot black once, and then she plastered some of it on my face, and I did likewise to her, and the two of us laughed so hard we were bent down double.

One Sunday, when the Warrens had gone to church, I was out in the barn with my book, *Oliver Twist*. The smell of the horses, the hay, and the warmth of it all mingled with those words of Mr. Dickens and took me clear away from myself. I'd been reading for about an hour when I heard a creaking and a rustle. To my surprise, there stood Molly with a bucket in her hand, though it was too early yet for milking.

She started, then said, "My ma was wanting for a bit of milk. You think Belinda might be willing?"

"Cows seem to have clocks built right into their bellies," I said. "If you could wait a while, I think she'll oblige."

Molly nodded and seemed about to go, then she turned. "You're reading," she said.

"Looks that way," I said.

"Anything good to hear?"

"The best," I said warmly. "Dickens, all about a poor orphan boy, gets himself in a heap of trouble through no fault of his and some no-account thieves he falls in with."

She smiled. "It sounds good," she said.

"Well, it is," I said. "Do you like to read?"

"We don't have any books."

"Well, you could read with me."

"Maybe I wouldn't know all the words."

"You could sit next to me, if you want, and look over my shoulder while I read the words out loud," I suggested.

Molly said nothing at all for a long moment. Then quickly she settled herself down in the hay, her back against the wall, and I sat down beside her with the book propped up on my knees.

"Guess I should start from the beginning."

Molly nodded, already entranced by the sight of all those pages of print and the promise of a good tale.

I had never shared a book with anyone before, except when I was doing lessons at school or with my pa. Then, there were always interruptions, corrections, or explanations. Now, with Molly beside me, I could let my thoughts rove over the story, my voice taking on the tone of Oliver, then the magistrate, the coffin maker, and all the others bound up in greed or cruelty or want. Somehow, reading out loud brought me closer to their deeds and their feelings. When at last the shadows crept over us, sending a smoky haze over the pages, and Belinda's clock extracted from her a long, loud "moo," both Molly and I shook ourselves back into the real world, standing up, stretching, smiling shyly, as if we had just been somewhere far away together.

After that, Molly and I read every Sunday. Sometimes Molly even stayed back from church, claiming a headache or other such, just to be reading with me. As for me, church never held much interest. After Ma passed on there wasn't anyone to make me go, and the Warrens cared little about my soul. I figured, as long as I took care of the body, the rest would follow. And my body would rather go fishing or picking apples or reading stories than be sitting in church. I realized that a friend is someone who wants to do the same things you do, and never has to be argued into it.

I'd never really had a friend before. The boys were wild and the parents were mean, but Molly made up for all of it. Somehow it didn't matter that they worked me like a dog or that the table was so skimpy my stomach started rumbling half an hour after meals. I figured that if a person could laugh, it made up for a lot of deprivation. And then, I also had my pictures.

I had put up a shelf in my dug-out cellar, using an old board and some nails I found.

Sometimes at night I'd sit there and draw, something I had done ever since I could remember. When I could just barely walk, I'd take pieces of coal from the stove and make marks on paper or on flat rocks outside our door. Soon my father took to bringing me paper and graphite from town, taking pride in my drawings. I drew trees and hills and houses. As I practiced, I was able to draw the animals and birds. I drew my ma sitting in her rocker at night, stitching, and I drew baby Joy May. I had the notion, then, that if I could keep them on paper they'd be with me forever, but of course, that was foolish.

After Ma died, nobody ever saw my drawings until the day Molly happened into my cellar room to call me for supper. I had brought my drawings to the Warrens' house in my sack, along with some books, a blanket, Ma's pewter pitcher, and a photograph of my parents on their wedding day. These were my secret treasures, until one day Molly poked her head in, yelling, "Clem Fontayne! Where are you?" I hobbled to my feet, pained by a sore on my big toe due to the lack of proper boots.

"Dinnertime," Molly said. "Don't get excited. It's mustard greens and potatoes again."

"Sounds good to me," I replied, for I was hungry nearly all the time, and took to trying to trap things, even rattlesnake, for want of meat.

Molly eyed the shelf with my belongings. "My stars!" she exclaimed. "You've made this place right hospitable, Clem Fontayne. Look at all these books!" She edged closer, reading the titles out loud: "*Plays of William Shakespeare, McGuffey's Reader*, the Bible, *Oliver Twist,* and *The Oregon Trail* by Francis Parkman. You read all these here books?"

"Sure," I said. "I even read some others too."

Then she noticed my drawings. "Can I see these?"

"Sure." I stood there holding my breath as Molly looked through my drawings.

She leafed through several—some blossoming apple trees, wildflowers in a field, a mouse crouched in a corner by a heap of trash, all drawn with a graphite stick Pa had brought me from town one day long ago.

Molly gasped, seeing my initials, C.F. "Clem Fontayne, did you draw all this?"

"I'm guilty of it," I said soberly.

"Where did you learn it?" Molly demanded.

"It was always"— I paused—"just in me, I guess."

"What? The mouse was in you?" We both laughed at that, and next thing I knew, there was her brother Billy hunched over, scratching his chest, peering at us.

"What's goin' on here?" he grumbled. "Ma says to fetch ya. What's that?"

"Leave it alone!" I yelled.

In one swoop Billy grabbed my drawing, and he held it high and away, as if it might catch fire. "Ho! What a caution! This what you do in here? Scratching out pitchers, like a girl! They say yore pa was sorta queer, reading and all that truck. Hey, Jonas!" He ran out, yelling. "Lookit here, at what this sissy boy does!"

Before I knew it, the two of them had struck like a cyclone. They scooped up my papers, laughing and yelling, and trampled them into the mud. Fury pumped through my body, and I wished for a weapon, or at least a good foot with which to deliver some kicks. I hobbled toward them, but they made a game of it, dodging and balking, yelling with delight.

Molly's face had turned red. She grabbed a stone and threw it—wham! It caught Billy on the shin, and he howled. Now, being as I was so skinny and light, there was nothing to do but jump on Billy's back and hang on like a monkey, which I did, more to impress Molly with my courage than to imagine I could inflict any damage on that big ox. I pounded and scratched and kicked his sides. I felt Jonas's hands prying me off. Down I went, the wind knocked clean out of me, my mouth hitting dirt.

"Time to eat!" From the doorway the bell clanged, Ma Warren working it almost to death. If there's one thing those Warren boys loved more than a fight, it was food. They galloped to the door and sloshed the bucket over their heads to make do for washing. Billy turned back, glaring. I saw now that one of his eyes was bruised black, and there was a welt rising up on his lip.

"I'll get you for this," he threatened, growling low, like a wild-cat.

I washed up, wiping my hands on a rag already crusted and black with soil. Mrs. Warren didn't seem to notice anything unusual, seeing her boys filthy and bruised.

Mr. Warren eyed the strop he kept behind the door, and he grumbled, "Set down, all of you, and be quiet."

We sat.

Mrs. Warren pronounced grace upon the bowl of greens, which floated wetly in some kind of sauce I'd rather not try to determine.

After dinner, during which Mrs. Warren preached the virtues of hard work—meaning she had a heap more chores in mind for me that day—I hurried outside, letting them think I was headed for the outhouse. Of course, I looked for my pictures. All that was left were crumpled and curled strips of paper, precious paper, that was hard to come by.

I pushed the whole of it into a ball, stormed inside, and flung the mess into the kitchen stove.

Molly, bringing in water, caught me at it and cried out, "Your drawings! Why'd you do that, Clem Fontayne?"

"They were ruined," I said with a shrug, like I didn't care.

"Are any left at all?" she asked, her blue eyes wide.

"Just a few they didn't get their paws on," I said.

"Let me keep them for you, Clem Fontayne."

I set upon her, angry, confused. "Why do you always call me Clem Fontayne? What sort of a notion is that?"

Molly drew back, almost as if I'd struck her. Then, defiant, she lifted her chin, her nostrils flared. "Just a name that has a fine sound to it," she said. "If you don't like it, don't take it out on me!"

"Where would you keep the drawings?" I asked, wishing I wasn't so uncivilized.

"There's a wooden chest in my room, under the bed," Molly said. Her face turned pink again; I marveled at the workings of a girl, turning colors thataway.

"What's in that wooden chest, Molly Warren?" I asked, teasing just a little. I had heard about how girls keep hope chests, inventing their future.

"Just some stitching I do," she said. "A quilt and napkins and fancy things."

"Fancy that," I said, imitating a fine eastern gentleman adjusting his cape.

Molly giggled. Then, seriously, she said, "They don't dare come in my room. Pa will take the rifle out after 'em if they do."

"Are they for sure your blood brothers?" I asked. Maybe Molly was a foundling, like Oliver Twist we'd been reading about. She, too, was so different from her coarse surroundings.

"Surely they are," Molly replied. "There were others," she added. "Two girls, dead now for many years. It bore real hard on Ma. She never thought I'd live, either. But here I am!" Molly gave me a grin.

"Well, I'm glad, Molly Warren," I said boldly. "I'll get those pictures for you." I turned back. "If you like, I could make you one."

"Could you? Would you?"

"What do you like? I can do most any kind of critter or tree or . . ."

"Make me a mouse, just like the one Billy tore."

"A mouse, then."

"I'd like that, Clem Fontayne."

Later I found some scrap paper out in the shed, left over from packing up seed, and I scribbled a mouse for Molly. She tucked it into her hope chest, and I was mighty pleased.

I longed for a real notebook like I'd seen once in the general store, but I had no cash money at all. The Warrens paid me only food and a roof, and that was little enough for all the work I did, clearing rocks, trimming and chopping logs, digging for fence posts. I'm not saying I worked harder than anyone else, for Mr. Warren had in mind to clear the whole back field by spring, to put in some corn and wheat and beans. No doubt about it, the Warrens' luck was scarce, their land being full of rocks except where there were swamps and sinkholes. No wonder they were all so mean. They had only Albert and a mangy mule to do the hauling. That mule was as ornery as the rest of the family. Even I, who always had a way with animals, had suffered a kick and a bite from that critter.

It was the mule that got me expelled. Or maybe it was Belinda, my own cow, and the Warrens' lust for her milk. It happened early one morning, when I was out grooming Albert. Billy and Jonas ran up with their rifles to go hunting. They boasted as to how they'd bag a buck, but I knew they were too lazy for that. They'd be lucky to get a squirrel or a possum. Billy rushed ahead, bounding over the fence and off into the forest.

As Jonas passed the mule, he threw a rock at the critter, and the mule took offense. It began to snarl and kick, taking off after Jonas, who clambered up the fence with that wild-eyed mule following, bucking and squealing out its rage.

Jonas pulled himself up. He hung there. "Clem!" he yelled over the braying of the mule. "Clem, come loose me!" His pants were caught on a wire. "Come on, that devil mule's gonna tear the fence down!"

I was laughing so hard I could hardly stand, but I staggered over to unhook Jonas. No sooner did I get near, than the rifle went off with a blast that sent me reeling. A terrible shriek, almost unearthly, imposed itself on the blast, and then a scream from Jonas, "You shot old Albert! You done killed our horse!"

I was too dazed to make sense of it at first, then realized that Jonas himself had pressed the trigger, for the rifle was still in his hands. He dropped the rifle like a hot potato and began to scream, "Clem shot our horse! Pa! Pa! Clem done shot old Albert!"

Next thing I knew Mr. Warren came tearing out of the house, cursing. On the way toward me he grabbed an ax. I knew he wasn't about to chop down any trees. I felt his heavy arm pressed tight around my throat, and he was growling out threats. "You'll pay for this, you no-account scum. Who'd ever think you'd repay us this way?"

I broke away, dashing to grab up the rifle Jonas had dropped, for poor Albert lay on his side moaning and frothing, bathed in blood. I ran to him, my eyes blurred from tears. My shot rang clean, the bullet pierced his throat, and after a mighty twitch, the horse lay still, with blood drooling from his gaping mouth.

"He shot our horse!" screamed Jonas. Billy was back, speechless but looking meaner than ever.

"Yes, I did!" I shouted, and I ran for my cellar room to get my things.

But the three of them were upon me. From the far field I heard Belinda bellowing. Animals understand strife. I ran toward my cow, calling her name, and she followed me like a dog, head down and hind quarters swaying.

As I approached the cellar, I saw the flashing whites of Mrs. Warren's eyes. Her hand shot out, and she grabbed me by the arm, pinning me against her. That woman had the weight of a millstone. I twisted and squirmed. Some notion about ladies did not allow me to kick or bite, but I should have. She gripped my neck, as if I was a chicken due for the pot.

"You git," she spat out. "The cow stays."

I knew that Mrs. Warren loved Belinda's milk, especially the cream that floated to the top. Many a morning I saw her skimming some for herself before the others came to breakfast.

"It's my cow!" I shouted.

"It's ours now. In exchange for the horse you killed."

"I didn't!"

"Tell the sheriff."

By now Mr. Warren and his sons had caught up with me. They grabbed me and pinned me down. I felt the butt of that rifle come down hard against my shoulder as the Warren men decided to correct me of murdering horses. "You git on off our property! After all we done. . . . It don't pay to show charity to some folks. Now, git!"

I thought of my precious things still down in the root cellar, and I almost made a dash for it. But I considered my neck was worth more than my property, and I ran.

It's strange how one evil makes you think of all the others in your life. As I distanced myself from the Warrens, all the other misfortunes came back at me. I saw myself standing at the two graves. I saw again how Pa took off, leaving me and Ma to fend for ourselves. Why hadn't he even written? Why hadn't he sent word to us? Had he meant to vanish from our lives?

I remembered him reading advertisements for hours. "California, land of gold! Relinquish fever and pestilence in a land free of mosquitoes, where oranges grow wild and the native people are friendly. See the imposing natural monuments, great rivers, and splendid peaks. The difficulty in getting there is imaginary!"

I heard Ma's voice again, arguing and pleading. "What if it's all lies, Pierre?"

No matter. He was determined. I recalled the day Pierre Fontayne mounted Mr. Abe and, with extravagant promises and poetic farewells, set his face westward and vanished from our lives.

Trembling with cold, sore from injustice I began thinking. Maybe I should head out west. Maybe I could find my pa.

CHAPTER 3

The Wicked City Makes Me a Laborer and a Cheat

I had gone quite a ways down the road, my steps lagging from my sore shoulder and the anger that now raged through me. The Warrens never wanted me, not even for my labor. They only wanted my cow. That cow, I realized, was more a friend to me than anyone in this world.

Someone called, "Clem Fontayne! Wait up!"

Molly's braids had about come loose, and her face was flushed. "You forgot your drawings," she cried out, gasping for breath. "And your other things. I didn't bring all the books—they were too heavy." She was dragging my sack behind her. In it were Ma's pewter pitcher, the wedding photograph, my drawings, and a blanket. I took out the blanket and Parkman's *The Oregon Trail*, and waved the rest aside.

"Thank you, Molly, but maybe you'd keep these things for me."

"Where are you going?" she asked, walking beside me now, our steps together like a well-matched team.

"I guess I'll head for Saint Joe," I said.

"Saint Joe? My stars, that's over twenty miles away. How can you walk it, with that toe of yours?"

"Maybe I'll hop, like a bird." I grinned.

"Saint Joe! Pa was there once. He told us about this big old hotel, all fancy work and tables galore with people eating every kind of roasted meat and venison and fowl. Enough to make your mouth water just to think of it."

"Well, things are booming in Saint Joe," I said, sounding very worldly-wise. "What with all those wagons going west, I'll find work in some livery stable or smithy. If I can save up some money," I said stoutly, "maybe I'll head out west myself. Maybe I'll go clear to California."

"Out west! California! Oh, Clem, I wish I could see the world, like in those books we read together."

I gazed at Molly, amazed that she had so much fire in her. I'd never known a female who wanted to go a-wandering.

"If you went away," I teased, "wouldn't you miss your ma?"

"I could stand it," Molly replied. "I'd see all new people, Injuns and squaws and even Chinamen. I'd love to go. Take me with you, Clem!"

I laughed. "Now, what would you do, walk to Saint Joe in that dress?" And indeed, Molly was shivering, with only a thin shawl over her head, and she was barefoot too. On her face was a look of such disappointment and pain that I swiftly changed my tone. "I'm not even sure I can make it myself, Molly. That talk about going west— it's just talk."

"You'll find a way, Clem Fontayne," Molly said, looking at me hard and long. "I'll never see you again."

"Well, you take my things on home with you," I said. "Someday I'll come back for them."

I could see by the look on her face that she didn't believe me. Actually, I didn't believe it myself. If you once take off, life sort of carries you along, like a fast-flowing river.

Molly stood silent for a moment, then said, "I saw all of it, you know. What you did for poor old Albert." She turned away, and by the set of her shoulders I knew she was crying. "He was a good horse. At least you didn't let him suffer. Wish you would of shot Jonas, whilst you were at it!"

"Now, Molly," I said, drawing near to her. "You don't mean that."

"I do! They're so hateful!"

"Now, look, you can't go around shooting everyone that's a skunk. Look at Oliver Twist, all the wrong done to him, and he never was mean to anyone."

"That's just a story," Molly said, sniffing.

"Well, stories are just like real things happening to real people. It's just that somebody wrote it all down and put it together in such a way as to make it powerful good, things happening so fast and excited like. Remember how they made Oliver steal? And remember how he got away, and then Nancy tricked him and took him back again?"

"Sure, I remember," Molly said. She faced me again, her gaze challenging me, her hand on her hip. "How can we ever finish the story now?"

"You can finish it while I'm gone," I said. "And when I get back, we can read it together all over again."

"You won't come back just for some old books," she said pouting.

"Yes I will. And to see you, Molly."

It was an awkward moment, drawn out, filled with feelings of ache and regret and confusion. I did not know how to say good-bye.

But Molly knew a way. She stood up on tiptoe, and before I knew what hit me, she'd touched her lips to mine, quick as a bird sipping water, and then she went running back down the road like the devil was on her heels.

———◆———

Some days get burned into your mind, so that you remember them exactly, in every detail. I would remember that first kiss forever, just like I remembered the day Pa left. I remembered him walking back and forth, drawing on that peculiar cigarette he always had in his mouth. Nobody else smoked cigarettes. Most everyone chewed tobacco, and some smoked a pipe. But when my father rolled up those little brown stubs, it made him an object of curiosity and scorn.

"You know I don't really belong here, Clem," he began, his eyes gazing off to some distant place. "There's places we can do better. There's still adventure to be had, Clem, and I mean to be part of it."

"Why can't we go with you?" I asked, starting to get that funny pain way deep in my stomach and chest.

"You will!" he exclaimed. "I'll get settled, first. Then I'll send for you and your mama. I'm going to find gold, Clem. I feel it!"

Even then the thought flashed through my mind: what if he doesn't come back? What if we never hear from him again?

Now, as I walked along the road to Saint Joe, my mind was strangely pulled between two realities. One was the thought of adventure, facing danger and finding newness at every turn. The other was Molly's mouth on mine, the moist, sweet touch, and the way her eyes locked onto mine when she asked me questions and listened to my answers, making me feel like a king. How does a king feel? I asked myself, shivering as a strong wind began to blow through my shirt, forcing a clinging cold down my back. A king feels—warm, I thought, laughing to myself, and strong and powerful.

I walked faster, feeling the power of having made a decision. I'm going west! My heart cried out the plan, my feet raced as if to meet the mighty mountains and cross the dashing, frothing rivers I'd read about. *The difficulty*, I quoted in my mind, *the difficulty in getting there is imaginary*. So had said the respected doctor, John Marsh, having settled in California back in the late thirties, even before I was born. His words were quoted in all the literature about the West. "The difficulty," I recited, matching my steps to the refrain, "the difficulty in getting there is imaginary."

Another voice, cantankerous and nasty, countered, *Then what happened to your pa? If he got to California, why did he not even send word? He doesn't want to be bothered with you, is why. Prob'ly he got himself another wife and another boy too.*

Shut up! You don't know anything! Pa loves me! He went looking for gold just to make a better life for me and Ma. He faced danger for us.

No, he didn't. He just got rich and stayed put. He didn't want you anymore.

So the dialogue kept me going until a hard wet coldness struck me in the face. Sleet. I felt bent and broken, my fingers and toes and nose burning, eyes stinging, mouth and lungs feeling the cut of every breath.

I had to find shelter. I passed a house, then another, afraid to knock. I'd heard of vagabonds being taken for thieves, struck on the head with a wooden board or blasted with a rifle shot. At the next house a monstrous dog stood chained to a tree, its eyes beaming at me like lanterns, breath white as it growled and yelped in warning. Was it true fear, or was it pride that kept me from going to the door to beg lodging?

At last I came to an abandoned chicken coop, still smelling from its inhabitants, sparsely feathered within. I crawled through the opening, crouching in the darkness underneath the scant tin roof, shivering in my soaked clothes and listening to the rain and sleet beating out their tunes above my head. Soon I felt the benefit of heat from my own body enveloping me, a moist, moldering kind of steam. I wrapped the damp blanket around me and, imagining myself in a featherbed, I slept.

I awakened to a bold, benevolent sunrise. Astonished, I stretched my arms in the confined coop, and my fingers lit upon an egg buried beneath a heap of feathers and dung. An egg! I felt tears of gratitude.

Carefully I cracked the egg on a small stone and, cradling it in my hand, sucked out the nourishment of each half before I ground the shell down to powder with my teeth and consumed it too.

Strengthened, I crawled out of my lodgings and set my face toward Saint Joe.

One egg does not last long. Soon I was famished. I peered into every field and onto every limb. All was bare. I envied the birds their worms and seeds. At a creek I stopped to drink, filling my stomach with water, as much as I could hold.

Night came, and at a distance I saw lights that seemed to heave and flutter as I walked on, my feet nearly frozen. Just so, I thought, nearly delirious with hunger, just so had Oliver Twist walked for three days, escaping his master, the coffin maker, headed for London. I thought of that wicked city so well described by Mr. Dickens and wondered whether Saint Joe could match it in reputation, and I didn't care. All I wanted was a bed and a biscuit; I'd sell my soul for these.

Thus, I was overjoyed at the sight and smell of a tavern at the city's edge. From the chimney smoke, I knew that inside a fire roared, and from the savory odors, I knew that meat sizzled on a fire, and maybe there was a kettle filled with soup.

As I neared the place, voices rang out, loud and boisterous, and I heard the tinkle of a piano and high laughter from a woman. An evil place, I knew, such as to make my ma turn over in her grave to see me making my way up the path, pushing open the door, and allowing the warmth of a huge fire to soothe my shivering frame.

Several men looked up as I entered. The bartender laughed. "Look what the cat drug in. What you want, boy?"

My body rebelled at the sudden warmth. I began to shake uncontrollably.

"He's got the fits," someone said. "Give him a gulp of whiskey."

"You think I'd waste whiskey on a boy like that, you're crazy!"

"Oh, c'mon, I'll stand him."

The whiskey was poured, handed to me, and five or six old-timers stood around grinning, waiting to see how I would handle the assault of that fiery liquid on my empty stomach. I stared at the glass only a moment before I upended it, the whiskey sending sparks of fire down my chest into my gut. I gasped out loud, doubled over, all to the roar of laughter. Someone clapped me on the back, hard. Like a sack of meal, I sank down on the floor, humiliated and stunned, but at least I was getting warm.

"You hungry, boy?"

"I sure am."

"You willing to work for your food?"

"I always have."

"You sassin' me, boy? What I don't need is a boy with a smart mouth."

"No, sir."

"That's better. You want to eat, you can work here. You any good with horses?"

"Yes, sir."

"You know how to read and figure?"

"My ma was a teacher back in Delaware. She taught me everything, including ciphering and some history."

"You do talk a heap much, don't you?"

"Yes, sir."

"You want to work, you learn to hold your tongue. You got that?"

"Yes, sir."

So I began working in the tavern for Drogan.

A week, two, three—I lost track of time, there being no Sundays or days off in that hard-drinking and gambling place. Men pushed their way through the door, always with a roar, ready to fight or to drink themselves senseless. Sometimes they'd stagger upstairs with Miz Bea holding their arm, her twittering and laughing, like they were the funniest old codgers alive. The place stank of stale liquor and unwashed bodies and moldy clothes. And the work was hard, from dawn to midnight, tending the patrons' horses, dishing out their grub, hauling water and huge cook kettles from place to place, sweeping out the floor, throwing lime into the outhouse, chopping wood and bringing it in for the stove. I slept in the tavern itself, under the stairs, on a padded mat that Drogan gave me, and I ate the scrapings from the pot and the leftovers on the plates, sloshing it down with a bit of whiskey that the old-timers enjoyed providing, for I'd soon get dizzy and staggering, and then they urged me to recite. "Tell us a poem, lad! Tell us a song!"

So I made a fool of myself, singing and swaying until I dropped down on my pallet for the night. Room and board was my pay, and a quarter a week, unless I broke something, which was usual. Then my wages went for reparations and I had nothing left. How could I ever get to California without a penny?

"Want to earn some extra money, lad?" Drogan approached me one morning, when I'd been at the tavern for about a month. It was getting onto spring. New buds appeared and birds cried out exuberantly from the branches. *T'rit! T'rit!*

"Yes, sir," I said, knowing Drogan's prejudice against too many words.

He explained the scheme carefully. "This is what you do," he said. "You stand behind the players where you can see their hand. If'n a man has an ace, you put one finger to your cheek, so. If'n he shows a king, you scratch your head, so. If'n he has a queen, you stretch up your neck. Got that?"

"Finger, scratch, neck," I repeated. "What about a straight?" I asked. "Or a flush? What about jacks?"

"You sassing me, boy?" He cuffed my ear lightly. "Listen! You can stand there and whittle. A flush, one stroke. A straight, two. For a full house, make it three. You know how to whittle?"

"Aye. What I need is a knife."

"You'll borrow my knife. Tell you what. You make me happy, and I'll let you keep the knife after three weeks' work."

"Done," I said. With the knife in my pocket, I began my career as a criminal.

I know I should have been thinking of my poor ma turning over in her grave, or of the wages of sin. But all I could think of was that now I had a profession, and maybe I'd start to eat more regular and soon be on my way west.

CHAPTER 4

A Public Celebration and Private Humiliation Launch Me on a New Career

I became right clever at my craft, spinning and sliding, inventing postures to distract a wary watcher from my signal. Did I feel guilty living as a cheat? Did I feel the foretaste of hellfire against my heels? Can't say that I did. I got a strange pleasure from watching how the men grimaced and stretched, groaned or laughed, drew deep on their pipes or spewed out their tobacco. You could say I was studying human nature while I scratched and stretched and whittled.

Drogan flew back and forth, serving ale and whiskey, stoking up the fire, tossing out jokes. The best part of it was, when Drogan's man won, there was a slice of meat for me, a hunk of crusty bread, and maybe an apple. Once a stranger took a large pot and tossed me a whole Yankee dollar, which I hid in a hole by my bed. Sometimes in the dead of night I did think on it—had I sold my soul for the sake of my belly? What sort of man was I to become?

I remembered my pa telling me, it seemed like years ago: "You're about as clever as a man already, and you just going on twelve. Well, you'll do fine. You've got your mama's brains and your pa's good looks." He had laughed as he rode off, and now I remembered that laugh and felt sick with resentment and anger.

But how could I be angry at a man who might be dead? A hundred scenes of disaster played through my mind in the night, while the rats gnawed at the timbers of the tavern and outside the wind howled like a person in pain. I'd take the lantern and read again from Parkman, about the hazards of river crossings, the slick, narrow trails and steep ravines where a horse could plunge down forty feet or more, leaving his rider broken on the rocks. How many skeletons littered the trail to the West? How many graves were dug there, and then undug by the coyotes and wolves that feasted on flesh?

I pushed aside thoughts of my father, gave him up for better or for worse, until a day early in April that changed my life, though I didn't know it then. The commotion began hours before, around noon, with people shouting, horses neighing, little children running wild. By midafternoon the tavern walls rang with sounds of jubilation. Outside, the streets were filled with people, a chaos of shoving, singing, even praying. Along the streets came the blasting horns of several brass bands playing patriot songs. I ran outside. Men were holding children on their shoulders to see the grand event.

"The Pony Express! The Pony Express!" The words were on everyone's lips. Bunting was stretched across buildings. The merchant emporium was decked out, and vendors' carts appeared as if by magic, doing a brisk business in pretzels and pies. A band played "Yankee Doodle" and "America! America!" They say some women fainted from the excitement. I wouldn't know, because Drogan called me inside, all in a huff because customers were bursting in the door, all of them thirsty, bragging and wagering, with money to burn.

"Ten days, they say. He'll make about twenty miles an hour."

"Ten days? I'll bet you it takes fifteen, at least."

"Impossible! His horse will drop dead from the strain."

"He'll change horses, you idiot. There are relay stations along the way."

"What about nighttime? What about stopping for food? Here's five that calls you wrong."

"I'll see your five and raise you another five! This rider won't need sleep. He's young and tough. I say, ten days, maybe eleven, no more."

"Who is it? What's the feller's name?"

A chorus rang out. "Frye, young Johnny Frye."

"No, no, it's Alex Carlysle, taking the first lap out of Saint Joe."

"You're both dead wrong. The rider is Bill Richardson, and he's riding a little bay mare. He had to bring it back to the stable, they say, 'cause folks are pulling out mane and tail hairs for souvenirs."

Their words clattered in my head, and I bolted outdoors, yelling something about feeding the livery horses, but needing to see for myself what the din was all about. And then, smack in the middle of it, I felt that thrill of action, my heart pumping and my mind racing on the possibilities. To California in just ten days! Why, it was almost like flying on a magic carpet, like straddling the wings of an eagle. My horse, Mr. Abe, could make good time when he was pumped up— but twenty miles an hour! And if I knew where my pa was, I could send him a letter and get one back in less than three weeks. If I only knew where he was—and my mind spun over the possibilities. What if I wrote and sent my missive addressed to Pierre Fontayne, "the gold fields," or picked a city like San Francisco or Sacramento. Surely there wasn't another man with his name. Surely someone might have heard of him and would deliver my letter, and then . . .

What would I say in the letter? I could imagine it: *Dear Pa, Mama and the baby are dead from fever, and I'm a gambler's swindler, working in a tavern for dregs of whiskey and leavings from other men's plates. . . .*

My father was always a bit of a dandy, with his cigarettes and his slicked-back hair. How he would groan to see me, turned into a no-account swindler, and then, to hear the awful news. And what if he had been overtaken by evil luck? Men sometimes lost a limb or suffered terrible sickness. What if he lay delirious and received such a letter from his only son?

My reverie was interrupted by thundering cheers and screams, and I was caught amid the surging crowd, pushed forward to the narrow strip of road where at last the rider appeared, hat cocked, back straight, grinning and waving and then, off like the wind. A cannon boomed, echoing, vibrating in my chest. Oh, the moment! The moment of glory! Tears came to my eyes, tears of pain and pride and longing. If only I were astride that little bay mare, I would be the hero, and nothing could ever shame me again. I strained to see everything, and I kept it sharp in my mind, so that later, by lantern light, I could sketch the little bay mare and the rider in his glory, with the crowd pressing 'round. And somehow the excitement of the day made me think of Molly. How I longed to tell her of these happenings! How she would smile and prance to hear of it.

A week later, the town was still seething with talk about the Pony Express, people laying odds on the post's arrival in Sacramento. I'd gotten a glimpse of the pouch bearing the mail; it was thick and swelled out with hundreds of letters, each wrapped in oiled paper, so people said. Now and then people talked about the incredible expense—five dollars a letter! Even if I'd known what to write and where to send it, I'd never be able to afford that kind of money. It made me gloomy to think that only the rich can ever benefit from progress; the rest of us stay down in our holes. I was depressed.

Maybe that was what made me careless. My mind wasn't on my work. I glanced, moved, whittled, scratched my cheek. A king, two kings, three fives. Full house. Slash went the knife, which by now was my prized possession. Slash. Slash.

Suddenly I felt someone grip my throat from behind; his knee in my back, and a knife blade behind my ear. "You young devil, think you can make a fool of me? I see through your game."

Viciously he tore the knife from my other hand. I felt the sting as the blade slashed across my thumb and wrist. A sudden spurt of blood poured from the wound, down my shirt, and onto the floor.

The man shook me, roaring into my face, "Cheater! Swindler! I'll teach you . . . !"

He flung me away. The side of my head struck the bar as I sank down, drawing my bleeding hand to my chest to try to stop the awful flow.

"What? You say the boy's cheating?" Drogan bent over me. I could see the hairs of his beard, the brown stains on his crooked teeth. "What are you doing to me? To my reputation? You scoundrel. You bum! Try to give a boy a break, see what happens. Out of the goodness of my heart, I take him in, I give him a bed, a job, and this is how he repays me. Who are you working for? You better tell me!"

"Don't worry," said the other, "I'll slice him up for you with pleasure."

"Get him out of here, he's bleeding all over the floor."

"Get out!"

I felt a boot against my backside. I clutched my arm to my chest and ran, unable to imagine where I might go.

Out in the stable, where the patrons' horses were kept, waited huge, hunkering Timothy, who hauled feed and mucked the stalls and oiled the leather. Unable to speak, Tim was called a half-wit and "dummy." I had accepted that description until one night when I stayed out watching the moon and stars. We sat together against bales of hay and Tim pointed out constellations of stars, and I saw how he tended to the horses, as if he spoke their language. I began to tell him things. His eyes told me that he understood everything.

"They call you 'dummy,'" I blurted, outraged on his behalf.

He shook his head and smiled slightly, then shrugged. He took a small, battered penny notebook from his back pocket and with a stub of pencil he wrote, "Don't care."

"But they treat you like . . ."

"They let me alone. I can think. Read." He went to the tack room and, after rummaging there for a few minutes, returned with several books, one about the stars, another on the care of horses, and the last a book of poetry. He opened the latter, its pages imprinted with finger marks, then pointed to a page, nodding vigorously to make me know he wanted me to read aloud.

Many nights after that, Tim brought me his book and I read him poetry. He loved Shakespeare and had his favorites, which I repeated over and over while he listened and nodded, as if the words were new:

> *"Blow, blow, thou winter wind,*
> *Thou art not so unkind*
> *As man's ingratitude:*
> *Thy tooth is not so keen,*
> *Because thou art not seen,*
> *Although thy breath be rude."*

That one always made him laugh. Strange, he could laugh and moan, though he never spoke a word. He seldom used his notebook to communicate, yet we understood each other.

He always had me end with the "Rime of the Ancient Mariner," tapping his hands together at the refrain:

> *"Water, water, everywhere,*
> *And all the boards did shrink;*
> *Water, water, everywhere,*
> *Nor any drop to drink."*

Now I crept out into the shadows, around the back of the shed, and into one of the empty stalls. Several horses turned to gaze at me, curious and a bit annoyed at my sudden intrusion into their slumber. Raider, a dray horse, curled his lip and snorted a loud complaint. It brought Timothy out from his lair, a pile of straw under the low end of the barn roof.

Suddenly too weak to speak, I watched him cradle the horse's head between his large, strong hands. He brought his lips down to that soft, moist place just above the nostrils, then he disappeared into the tack room and returned with an old blanket. Gently he covered the horse.

"Tim!" I called. "It's Clem. Here."

He sized me up at a glance, rushed for a bucket of water and a rag to bathe my wounded wrist and my eyes, which were puffed and swollen.

He raised my hand high to stop the bleeding, bound the wound, and finally laid me down, my head resting on a bundle of rags.

"Thank you," I murmured. His touch was astonishingly gentle for a man so large. He nodded.

"Drogan will be coming out after me," I said.

He sighed and gently took me by the arm, pointing outside behind the outhouse. Nobody would stop there to look for me. Timothy took the blanket from the horse, with a pat of apology, and hung it around my shoulders. With another nod and a slight push, he led me outside to the outhouse, where I waited, staring up at the cold, cold stars, thinking of the throbbing of my wrist and the pulsating pain in my head. After a time I became nauseated. Stink can be worse than pain, I thought, my mind running a competition between my assaulted nose and my festering hand.

Long after the sounds from the tavern had subsided, I saw Timothy venturing toward me, a black shape silhouetted against the deep purple horizon. He had crept into the tavern and retrieved my things, which he gave me now. I took the bundle with genuine excitement, as if it contained a vast treasure, for these few objects were the sum of my fortune.

Gratefully I returned to the stall, realizing that the residue of horse is not as offensive as that of man, something to consider. I wrapped myself in my blanket and curled up in the straw like a beast. For some reason, I remembered the nighttime prayer Ma taught me as a child, and I murmured it now for the first time in many months.

In the morning my hand felt swollen and raw. I could not move my fingers. But I had to leave. Even Timothy agreed, looking out as I slung my bundle over my back and, wordless, waved good-bye.

Where to go? How to find work?

Morning frost covered the ground. Horses blew out white breath, and women wound their shawls tightly around their heads. I walked as quickly as I could, both against the cold and the possibility that Drogan might come looking for me and whip my hide, just to prove his so-called innocence. I was sorely grieved, for my Yankee dollar was left in that hole in the floor. I should have told Timothy about it. We could have shared it. Should I go back? Risk my freedom for a dollar? Drogan might even call the sheriff and accuse me. Who would believe me against him? I'd end in jail. No, walk on. Walk on.

I'd had little chance, before, to go wandering around the city, since Drogan kept me busy. Now, as I walked I was astonished and alarmed at the crush of activity—animals and people, cargo and commerce filled the streets, setting up a constant din. At last I reached the river, a churning, muddy flow so wide that those on the other bank seemed like small figures on a shelf. The dock was full of activity, men loading the ferries, unloading ships, readying wagons, bartering for supplies. Everywhere animals clamored as they were being herded onto ferries, taken out for grass while they awaited passage. Conestoga wagons assembled at various points along the shore, their occupants shouting, arguing, packing for the long trek west. If only I could join them! But I had read enough advertisements and articles to know that funds were needed for the trip. Without a rifle of my own, I'd be of no use to anyone, only a burden.

My hand throbbed terribly, and my face was burning. Perhaps the wound had caused a fever. My throat was dry and parched. I had seen it in animals, a wound poisoning the body.

Had I been well, I might have talked my way into a job loading cargo or helping to drive a team or riding shotgun. But how could I hold a rifle? How could I lift any load?

I wandered on, without thinking, reeling and stumbling. I had crossed the city, all the way to the rails, where the locomotives stood, the terminus of the line from New York. I thought longingly of riding inside one of the cars. How wonderful it would be to go back to Delaware, maybe find my mother's people, be in their protection and embrace. I walked around and around, imagining just such a reunion. *What? Elizabeth's boy? How wonderful! We have this huge mansion and you are welcome to stay—didn't you know that Elizabeth's cousins are royalty from England? Yes, she was due to inherit a fortune, and now you are here, her heir!*

My imagination raced on, borrowing from Mr. Dickens's tale of

Oliver Twist, the beaten, penniless, and disgraced orphan discovering his true heritage and wealth.

I was ready to drop from fatigue when I realized I had circled back to the center of town and found myself standing before a building so magnificent that I blinked, thinking I had died and gone to heaven. The facade was brick and smooth cement, ornamented with beautiful carved window frames. I gazed up and counted four stories, and a small rounded tower topped by a lightning rod. A grand portico shielded the double doorway. Large windows looked out to the street, some canopied, some opening onto a veranda where ladies in finery might stand and fan themselves as they looked out upon the beggars.

Derelicts with ragged beards and soggy shoes lounged against the walls. Their gaze said that I was one of them. I bent my head under the disgrace of their brotherly glances. I'm not like you! I wanted to shout. I looked at myself in the pane, saw my bent frame, the shabby bundle across my back, and the rag around my wrist, and I was appalled.

I thought of Mr. Dickens and Oliver Twist, then determinedly I slipped in behind several gentlemen and beheld all the grandeur of the Patee Hotel.

Red carpets and a winding stair met my gaze. I heard a chorus of voices and peered into the saloon with its magnificent highly polished mahogany bar and brass rails. The men drinking here were no comparison to those at Drogan's. They laughed in a different pitch. They flung out their coins with a casual flip. I saw no pistols raised, nor fists. I longed to be among these gentlemen, but quickly I withdrew and made my way to a corridor, following a sign and an arrow: PONY EXPRESS HEADQUARTERS. I came upon a glass door and another sign, PONY EXPRESS. Through the glass I saw a stout man rifling through some papers, putting something into a strongbox. On the wall above him hung a poster:

> WANTED
> *Young skinny wiry fellows not over eighteen.*
> *Must be expert riders willing to risk death daily.*
> *Orphans preferred.*
> *WAGES $25 per week.*

Whatever it was, I would do it. Twenty-five dollars a week was a fortune, and I was absolutely qualified in every way. That sign was surely intended for me. I went inside.

Loudly I said, "You looking for workers? I'm your man." I turned to let him see me closely—wiry, skinny, obviously under eighteen.

"You want to work?" he asked. His eyebrows were thick as mustaches, and he was robust, his jowls jiggling when he spoke, belly hanging out over his trousers. "Come in!"

He led me to a chair and ordered me down with the force of his gaze. "You look a bit sickly," he said. "How old are you?"

"Fourteen," I answered. "Skinny, like you're looking for, but I'm strong." I flexed my fists, hoping my muscles would show.

"You been in a fight?" he asked, appraising my bandaged wrist and my swollen face.

I tried to grin. "You should see the other fellow. I doused him good."

The man laughed. "I like your attitude." He glanced over his shoulder. "You got family? You got folks looking for you?"

"No, sir," I lied. "Nobody. I'm an orphan. Like it says. Orphans preferred."

"Well now!" He seemed pleased, bringing forth a printed paper. I was going to have to sign my life away! I didn't care. For twenty-five dollars a week I'd go to Hades!

CHAPTER 5

I Determine to Journey Overland to Find Pa, and I Bid Farewell to Molly

"Name's Leader, Chester Leader," the man said, "like you can lead a horse to water, *ha-ha*, but you can't make him think."

Drink, I almost said, but I'm not one to spoil a man's story.

My eyes lit on the words: *Orphans preferred*. Why in the world did they want orphans? It sounded ominous. But then again came the astounding sum, twenty-five dollars a week. Nobody in the world could make or spend that much money! I'd never seen twenty-five dollars all at once in my entire life.

"So, you want to make some money." Chester Leader sat down and smiled at me. "You good with horses?"

"Yes, sir. I've broken wild ones, even. My pa says—"

"Your pa? Thought you told me you got no kin."

"While he was alive, sir, he did speak to me on occasion."

Chester Leader slapped his thigh and let out a laugh. "That's a good one! All right, then, you mind takin' the middle route? I've got the beginning and the end of the route pretty near covered. Middle's the long stretch, you know, pretty boring they say, except when the Injuns are havin' their scalping parties—*ha-ha*."

"Middle route? I thought I'd go clear through, sir, to California."

"Clear through?" Chester Leader started forward in his chair. "Straight through?" he repeated, aghast. "You pullin' my leg, boy, or are you ignorant? We run in relay teams, boy. We're not running a landferry here. Rider goes forty, fifty miles, takes a nap, turns around and starts over. Back and forth."

"Back and forth," I repeated, feeling faint.

"You're not the first boy I've seen itching to get to California, trying to use the Express for your own purposes." Abruptly he stood, pulled me by the shirt collar, and said, "You don't hornswoggle me! Now, git."

Outside again, I stood with the beggars, my heart pounding with hatred. I looked up at the gleaming windows of the hotel. My keenest desire was to hurl a rock and smash those windows!

A vagrant beside me muttered, "Got a penny or two, sonny?"

I gave him a scornful look, then saw how his eyes watered, and spit drooled slowly from his mouth devoid of teeth. A sour smell rose from him, a kind of inner decay. From the pallor of his flesh, I gleaned that he was dying.

"Sorry, old-timer," I said. Something about the sight of that man bore me up. I had my teeth! I had limb and heart and breath in my body! And I had something of value, after all. Belinda! That cow was mine, by right and by law. I had let the Warrens cheat me out of my property and run me off as if I were a common criminal. Jonas had lied. Why hadn't I defended myself? Because of the odds—I couldn't take on Jonas and Billy and Mr. Warren all at the same time. And if the sheriff came, why would he believe me, instead of an upright citizen who owned a farm, however poor?

Well, now I would be crafty. This was the end of whimpering and whining, running away, letting other folks determine my destiny. I'm going west! I vowed to myself, and I'll do it with cash in my pocket!

Somehow I'd manage to steal Belinda back and sell her for cash. With the cash I could buy a horse, to start me on my way to California.

I set my countenance out of town, back on the road to the Warrens' farm.

———◆———

When I got to the Warrens' place, I stopped, aghast. Always shabby, the hut now looked busted down, about as bad as my own homestead had been when the Warrens came to take me into servitude. I felt a sweet rush of revenge, followed immediately by guilt. My ma would have been ashamed of me. I couldn't see Belinda. Had they killed my cow, maybe eaten her? I stopped at the water bucket to wash the dust and grime from my hands and face.

As I walked up the path to the door, which hung loose on its hinges, I glanced about for those no-account brothers. How could people stand to be so ignorant? My ma had started teaching me from the time I could crawl. She'd draw letters in powdered sugar on the kitchen table. Pa talked to me in French; I never learned it, but I did learn that there was such a thing as other languages, and then, he read to me from his books.

I wondered whether Molly had finished *Oliver Twist*. I wondered what she had done with my drawings. I wondered how she'd look after these several months. And in the next moment, I knew.

She stood at the door, her hand shielding her eyes, and when she saw me she did a quick little leap, almost a dance, and she shouted out my name. "Clem Fontayne! Glory be! Is it you?"

I laughed. "None other. Howdy!"

She ran to meet me, then stopped short, and we faced each other awkwardly.

"Well, come on in. I'm just making up a batch of biscuits and gravy."

I went into the large room, which served for all purposes, except that a small corner was partitioned off with a limp bit of cloth for a curtain. It was quiet in the house, too quiet.

"Where is everybody?" I asked.

"Pa's working the back fields. Billy and Jonas are hired out. They come back on Sundays sometimes, and sometimes they bring us a bit of cash. Mostly, though, they drink it up." She said this with a shrug, without rancor. "We couldn't manage to buy any more seed," she said. "Don't know what's to happen, come next year, if this crop doesn't take."

I looked around the room. The smell of biscuits baking nearly made me swoon.

"Where's your ma?" I think I knew before Molly said it.

"Ma passed on a month ago." Molly gazed straight ahead, dry-eyed, but her voice took on a whispery quality. "Queer thing, she didn't seem to be ailing. Just laid down one night and . . ." Now the tears came, shaking her frame like a terrible wind.

I stood there, filled with grief, not only for Molly, but also for my own losses. She put her head down, sobbing, and I went to her and put my arms around her. We stood that way for a time, and I felt her tears against my neck, and I felt her body quivering.

I couldn't remember ever being that close to another person. My folks were not the kissing kind. Now I had an inkling of what it was like to need another body close by, for I hungered so that I couldn't think up nor down nor sideways.

Molly fed me biscuits and gravy, three separate helpings before I was full. She dipped into a tin of precious coffee. I could tell it was dear by the way she measured. Three cups of it she urged upon me, sitting opposite, watching me as I drank.

"Where are you off to, Clem?" she finally asked.

"California," I said. The word had the ring of a blacksmith's hammer sparking into the small room. "California," I repeated. "I'm going to look for a wagon train I can join."

Molly stared at me wide-eyed. "You going to go looking for your pa?"

"I reckon."

"What if you don't find him?"

"Well, at least I can see the world!" I said brashly.

"All alone? What are you going to use for money? Are you fixing to *walk* all the way to California?"

"I'll work my way along," I said. I was about to mention Belinda, but I couldn't. Molly was sorely in need. But Belinda was mine!

Molly went on arguing. "And out on the prairie, they say there's wild Injuns and bandits and wolves."

"Well, I've got nothing to steal," I said with a grin. "So thieves won't trouble me. Skinny as I am, no respectable wolf would bother to bite me. As for Injuns—I guess I can run fast enough to hide from savages."

Molly turned away. I saw her mouth fixed and tight, her cheeks red. "You have an answer for everything," she snapped.

"No, I don't. What I don't know is, why are you so mad?"

"Who said I was mad?"

"Your braids are standing straight up," I said, laughing. "That shows it."

She could not help herself from laughing too. Then she said soberly, "I guess you came back for your things." She went to the sideboard and pulled out my drawings, the books, and Ma's pewter pitcher, the wedding photograph, and some supplies she had found in my cellar chamber. I noticed that the cupboard was about empty, except for a few scraps of calico and an old tin cup.

I had forgotten about the pewter pitcher and the silver frame. I could sell them for a few coins, at least. If I took Belinda, I could trade her for an old horse. I desperately needed a horse, at least to get me started on the journey.

"Here," Molly said, handing me my things.

I gave her back the drawings. "Keep them for me while I'm gone," I said.

"What makes you think you'll be back?" Her voice was thin and high.

"I'll be back for the pictures," I said. "Maybe while I'm away, I'll make new ones. Wouldn't you like to see the face of an Injun squaw and her baby?"

"No."

"C'mon, Molly. Don't be so glum." My fingers itched to be drawing again. I plucked up my old penny notebook and pencils. I went on. "Out west there's trees so high—ravines and rock ledges, new kinds of berries and birds."

"Seems to me you know it all," sassed Molly. "Why bother going there, then?" She stepped away, looking down at her apron, poking her finger into a hole near the pocket.

"I wish I had a picture of you," I suddenly said.

"Ain't no photographer here," she said. "I've seen 'em, though, in town," she added proudly.

"If I had a picture of you, I'd look at it every day, twice." I could hardly believe I'd said those words.

"Draw me," Molly said, sitting down on a stool, her feet tucked under the rungs. "Make my picture, then you can see me twice every day."

I sat down on an old chair and began to sketch Molly, the oval of her face, the outline of her hair, then the shape of her shoulders and the bodice of her jumper, a faded checked calico, with a white blouse underneath.

While I sketched I thought of how I'd proceed now back to Saint Joe to sell my few possessions and prepare myself for the overland journey. Overland journey—the sound of it made my fingers fly over the paper, and soon the sketch was done.

"It's wonderful!" Molly exclaimed. "Is it really me?"

I had caught the pertness of her nose and, somehow, the sparkle in her eyes.

"How do you do it, Clem Fontayne?"

In truth, I don't know how; it simply happens. I only shrugged and said, "I'll keep you with me, Molly, every place I go."

"Oh, how grand it will be in California!" she cried. "Away from here, with mosquitoes eating us alive in summer, and winter freezing us to death—they say in California it never rains, except just a heavy dew to make the oranges grow. Those orange blossoms smell so sweet! Can you imagine it? I read about it, Clem," she said, breathing hard, "how there's free horses running wild, and game all over the place, deer meat and buffalo, nobody hungry, and gold in the streams—why, you just dip in a cup and there's a nugget in it!"

"It sure does sound like paradise," I agreed. "But it's no place for a girl."

Molly bristled. "Who said anything about girls?"

"It will be a rough ride."

"And what will you be riding?" She stood there, hands on her hips, challenging me.

"Well, I . . . I don't know." I frowned, seeing the bare shelves, the sagging boards.

Molly turned to the old stove, where a large black pot was sizzling with kitchen grease. She tossed in another large scoop of yellow fat and leapt back as it sputtered. When she looked up, her eyes were red from the smoke.

"You can stay the night if you want," Molly said. "I guess Pa won't mind too much."

"I guess I would mind, though," I said. "Last time I met up with your pa, he about broke my shoulder."

"All about that old cow," Molly said.

"How is Belinda?" I asked. My heart began to thump.

"She's out back. I guess you want to see her," Molly said. We went outside, and Molly strode to the gravel yard where the ash hopper stood. Black ash clung to the upper compartment. Below, the lye had formed, thick and odorous. I reached out to help, but Molly shook her head. "Stand back."

"That looks mighty heavy."

"I don't need anyone to carry my load."

I shrugged and stood aside. From over by the fence, Belinda bellowed and moved toward us in the way that cows do, head low, eyes focused upon us.

"Belinda!" I called. "Hey, Belinda!"

Molly strained to lift the heavy trough. She poured the lye slowly into a basin. "You planning on taking the cow?"

I took a deep breath. I swallowed, hard, feeling dizzy from the agony of having to make this decision. "Of course not," I said. "What would I do with a cow on the trail?" How desperately I wanted a mount of my own! But then there was Molly, afraid to look me in the eye. Molly bit her lip, then looked away, silent and subdued.

"You fixing to make that soap right now?" I asked.

She nodded.

"You might need some more wood, then." I gathered up a good armful and followed Molly back to the kitchen.

I recalled the last time my ma had made soap, how the sweat poured from her face and soaked her dress, how the lye stung when a spot of it spilled on my arm, and the acrid smell filled my throat and made me choke.

Soon I had a good fire going in the stove. Molly and I tipped the basin to pour the lye into the fat. Steam rose and with it, that sharp, greasy smell. We took turns stirring the mixture with a paddle, and I thought of all the chores in the world, so ugly, so tiresome, suddenly becoming new and friendly when there was somebody to share them. Somebody with blue eyes and shining braids and a strange sweet scent about her that even penetrated the caustic smell of lye.

It would take hours for the soap to come. I sighed, weary and eager to be outdoors. As if in summons, Belinda bellowed. I started.

Molly gave me a contemptuous look. "Go and court your cow."

"Thank you, I will," I said as I stepped out the door.

Outside, Belinda ambled toward me. I reached out to touch her bony head. "Belinda," I murmured, "I'm fixing to leave you here. Be a good girl, give plenty of milk, and don't wander."

Suddenly Molly was beside me, laughing softly.

"She likes her head rubbed," I said. "Right there on that white mark between her ears."

Molly nodded. "I know."

"Belinda, I'll be back someday," I said. I wished I'd had words for Molly. But what could I tell her? I dared not speak my thoughts.

They stared at me skeptically, both cow and girl. The cow bellowed, *Liar!* But the girl was silent. I left them there, feeling a combination of lightheartedness and dread, wondering how a person can ever really get free.

CHAPTER 6

I Acquire Some Old Possessions and a New Occupation from Chester Leader

My thoughts, as I made the long, long walk back to Saint Joe, hung on money. My britches were threadbare, my shoes flapping around my feet for want of proper stitching. How would I ever get to California without any provisions?

The sack across my back contained Ma's pewter pitcher, my parents' wedding photograph, several sticks of wood pencil, my notebook, Shakespeare, Dickens, the Bible, and Parkman's *The Oregon Trail*. I did not want to part with any of these. But when I came into the city, first thing, I stopped at a general store, the scene of intense bartering. People stood crowded against the walls, peering into bins, counting out goods, complaining loudly.

"What? You say you want *what* for a sack of nails? And seven dollars for rubberized sheets? Thirty dollars for a canvas top, not even waterproof?"

The shopkeeper leaned toward the harried farmer, smacked his hand down on the counter. "Take it or leave it. I've got other customers waiting."

The farmer reached into his overalls. He drew out some bills and put them onto the counter, along with a carefully written list, pencil on grocery paper. "Here. This is what I'll need."

I glanced at the list and saw the words: "Flour, sixty pounds. Bacon, five good slabs. Forty pounds sugar. Four big sacks beans. Pickles." Beside the word *coffee* was a question mark—obviously a luxury.

"You'll be wantin' some lantern oil," said another traveler, whose wife held a bolt of blue cloth under her arm and a camp kettle in her other hand. She looked pale.

"Much obliged," muttered the buyer, "but my wife laid in a good store of candles."

"You heading out soon?" asked the woman hopefully. "We're with the Watson party from Iowa, leaving in the morning, but not many women in the group."

The other shrugged. "We won't be ready for another week or so. Have to reinforce the wagon bed first."

"Ma!" Three boys and a girl came running, squealing. "Can we get some candy, can we?"

The mother brushed back the girl's hair. "Where's your bonnet? My stars, you'll be black as a field hand by the time we get there, if you don't keep that hat on your head!"

"Can we have some candy, Ma?"

She gave a quick glance toward her husband, then said, "No money for candy, child. Hush, now."

"Will there be children? Playmates?"

"I don't know. I hope so." The mother smiled at me. I smiled back. I bent down and spoke to the little girl.

"Hey, my name's Clem," I said. "What's yours?"

"Alice," she whispered, looking down.

"Pretty name," I said. "You like horses?"

"We have two oxes," she said.

"Oxen," corrected her ma.

"Maybe," I said, "your pa will need help to drive them. Maybe he needs someone good with critters, and strong. Someone who don't hardly sleep at all."

The mother turned to me, smiling widely. "Are you offering your services, young man?"

"I'd be proud to come along and help," I said.

The woman turned to her husband. "Hannibal, this lad is offering to come with us and help drive. Seems to me we could use . . ."

The farmer appraised me up and down, shaking his head. "No," he said.

"But Hannibal, we could . . ."

"We don't have the means to feed another mouth, Constance, and you know it. I don't want to hear any more about it. You take the children outside. They're bothering everyone. Go on. Outside."

"I saw this here cloth, Hannibal, for shirts and dresses . . ."

"Won't need new clothes on the trail, Constance. What are you thinking of? You think this is a church outing? Naw—we'll get it. Yes, I say—we'll get the cloth—don't cry. Glory be," he said, seeking a witness to his plight. "What causes a woman's tears! Never mind, go outside. Take those young'uns!" He turned to the other traveler. "They say we'll need some cash for toll ferries."

The other nodded morosely. "They charge whatever they will. Well, soon we'll have our own farms, eh? If you put in a pole, they say, it'll sprout leaves, the soil's that rich out west."

Finally it was my turn to stand at the counter. I spread out my wares, the pewter pitcher, the books, and the picture of my parents in the silver frame. The shopkeeper looked at me quizzically. "What's all this?"

"I thought I'd sell these."

"Git out! This ain't no pawnshop. Are you plumb out of your mind?"

I felt as if I'd been slapped. Around me, men muttered, women glanced away.

I stuffed everything back into my pack.

"Down the end of the street," someone offered as I neared the door, "is a secondhand shop. Don't think they pay much, though."

"I'm obliged," I said, nodding, keeping my head high.

The streets were filled with people, new arrivals, others waiting to pull out. A sense of urgency propelled their movements. I heard conversations, shouts. *"Who's gonna lead this train? Bennet? How do we know he's the best among us? Could be he just wants to lord it over us."* *"Who would make the rules? Out in the wilderness, without law and order, what's to keep one man from murdering another, taking his wife, his supplies?"* *"Listen, I'd rather go it alone than be beholden to strangers. I've got kin coming along from Kentucky. Thanks, but we'll go it alone."*

Along the river, women had set up posts for their last "civilized" efforts at washing, making soap, stitching garments, and drying meat or fish for the journey. "Wili, you get on over here and eat properly!" a mother yelled, pulling her son over to a makeshift little table. "You'll do no such thing as eat with your fingers—just because we go amongst the savages is no cause to forget your manners!"

Several women sat together talking, sewing the hard, tough canvas for wagon covers. Their mouths were set in determination. If spirit could make a mountain move, it was here.

As I entered the secondhand shop, a bell tinkled; the air was dense. The place was stuffed with goods from ceiling to floor and hanging from the rafters. My heart sank as I saw six or seven shelves filled with dusty pewter goods. Everything lay about in abundance—old mirrors, utensils, watch fobs and jewelry, china teacups, plates, paintings, chests of drawers, satin vests and feather shawls and felt hats. Every item had been brought along and abandoned as the realities of the journey dawned on the pioneers.

The storekeeper, a woman wearing a maroon flowered shawl, finally turned to me. "Well? You've come to sell or to buy?"

"Sell," I said, showing her my goods.

She thumbed through the books. She glanced at the pewter pitcher. "These are not in great demand," she said with a wave toward her bursting shelves. I saw now that several dozen similar volumes were eating dust on that shelf.

"People are looking for rope and camp stoves, chains and rifles."

"If I had those," I said brashly, "I wouldn't need to be here."

"You heading out west?"

I nodded.

She shook her head, glanced at the photograph in its frame. "I can give you seventy-five cents," she said.

"For what?"

"The frame."

I felt as if I'd been struck in the chest. "That's all?"

"The rest of it is useless to me, but I'll take it off your hands. You don't need this ballast on the trail. Seventy-five cents for the lot."

"The frame is silver!" I objected, aghast.

"Seventy-five cents. Take it or leave it."

"I'll take it."

I felt sick. In the corner I saw numerous pairs of boots and several implements and blankets.

I picked over the boots, at last finding a pair not too damaged, an old horse blanket, and a long bowie knife with a cracked blade. Resolutely I gathered these up and brought them to the proprietor.

"I'll take these in exchange for the frame," I said firmly.

"Wait a minute, I haven't set you any prices. You must be—"

"Take it or leave it," I said, meeting her gaze for a long moment.

She clenched her teeth. She inhaled deeply. "Done," she said.

"You won't need the photograph, will you?" I said.

Wordless, she dissected the thing and handed me the picture of my parents, smiling and young.

With my new possessions, I set out to find a company that needed a hand, and soon found that a boy without provisions or a rifle or a horse is considered of less use on the trail than a woman. A woman, at least, will cook and wash clothes. Was I able to do this? Men mocked me; some laughed outright, others ignored me completely, swatting me aside as if I were an insect.

I stood on the street again, starving. Oh, the times I had only to go down to the cellar for preserves, or to our small smokehouse for a hunk of salt pork. We had potatoes, then, lying there in friendly heaps. We had jars of applesauce and wild cherries and corn. Looking back, I realized that all this had been made possible not by my father's toil, but by the laborers my ma hired with the cash she earned from teaching and sewing and nursing people's sick infants.

No wonder she sickened. I remembered late nights, awakening to shouts and cries from around the table. Now I remembered those night fights, the measured coldness by day. As I walked, my thoughts were dark and despairing.

I hurried; the day was getting late. Purposefully I reached the Patee Hotel, flung open the heavy door, and strode along the red carpet to the Pony Express office.

Chester Leader sat with both feet on his desk, hastily comporting himself as I entered.

"What? It's you, back again, you young whelp! What did I tell you?"

"I need work, sir," I said quickly. "I will ride for the Pony Express, sir, anywhere you put me. I will promise to remain for a year at my post. I swear it!" My voice broke; I cursed myself for the tears that bunched up in my throat. My legs buckled.

Chester Leader came around the desk and grasped my arm. "Now, set down here," he said. "When's the last time you et?"

"I don't rightly remember."

"You'll do any kind of work?"

"Yes, sir."

"You good with animals?"

"Yes, sir."

"Well, speak up, tell me your experience. Don't just give me a mumble and a jumble *yes sir*!"

"I broke a horse for my pa. It was part mustang; some man found it out on the prairie and traded my pa for it. Nobody could put a bit in that horse's mouth. I worked him and got his confidence and had him saddled in less than a month. I used to care for our pigs when we had some, and the cow, of course. I know what to do when their udders swell. I can spot worms in a horse and flush 'em out, and tend to their feet and bring in a foal. . . ."

"That's enough," said Leader, wiping his forehead with a large handkerchief.

"I'm not scared of any critters," I added hastily. "Not even them on two feet."

Chester Leader's eyes widened, then creased as he let out a laugh. "Ho, that's a good one. Yup, mankind's the worst of the critters, it's true. You're not stupid, lad, that's plain to see. Tell you what. There's a job open for assistant stock tender. Stationmaster in Nebraska needs a hand. Last man got scared off by some bandits come to rob the place. I don't tell you lies, boy, and inducements, like some would. Those prairie dogs like to do a little mischief now and then, *ha-ha*. But you look like you can handle it."

"What's a stock tender do?" I asked.

"Tends stock, boy. You pullin' my leg?"

"What about the pay?"

"Twenty-five dollars a month."

I made a quick calculation. It was a whole lot less than riding for the Pony Express, but still, twenty-five dollars a month was a fortune. I could hardly believe my ears.

"You want the job?" he demanded, leaning toward me with a truculent air.

"Yes, sir. I do."

"You'll leave in three days then, with the supply wagons heading out. Report to the ferry station early in the morning on Thursday. Tell them Chester Leader sent you. Like, you can lead a horse to water— *ha-ha*."

I rose, feeling the power of being a rich man, a person with a place to go, with duties to perform.

"Who will pay me, sir?" I asked.

"The stationmaster." Leader took me to the door. "You got any more questions, boy? You're not getting cold feet now, are you? There's a dozen boys ready and willing to take the job if you're going sour on me. . . ."

"No, sir! Not at all. Just, please, what is the name of the station where I'll be working?"

"Pumpkinseed."

I started. "You pullin' my leg?"

"Pumpkinseed Station," he roared back. "Go tell cook at the wharf to give you some grub. You look about ready to faint. Now, get on out of here."

I did.

CHAPTER 7

I Avoid Death by Drowning and Learn about Indian Terror

It was easy to find my party of bullwhackers. A sailor directed me with a jerk of his head and a grimace. "That dirty, cussin' lot over there's who you're looking for."

In truth, they were enough to make a skunk shudder, both by the foulness of smell and mouth. I heard their curses before I fully came upon them, with every other word starting blasphemous, enough to make a flower shrivel up and die. Of course, there were no flowers on the dock, only filthy piles of rope, cargo, stamping, neighing horses, and harried folks waiting to be let across.

Three things I'll always recollect about those first days with the bullwhackers: their cussin', their pure fearlessness, and their stories. Now that I think on it, there was one other thing to recall: I almost drowned in the Missouri River. It was not an easy crossing.

We were headed for Nebraska City, where the freight company had its offices, and where more wagons would be loaded up before heading west with supplies for trading posts and forts. Adam was the man in charge of our train, broad fisted and heavily bearded, he was a redhead with steely gray eyes and a temper that, when it broke loose, came sudden and quick as summer lightning.

We had about a dozen wagons loaded with goods—woolens from the eastern mills, bolts of calico, flour, sugar, coffee, hardware and tools and whiskey, such as the folks out west would give their teeth for. Whiskey was the medicine everyone wanted, a dose of optimism when the going got rough and the kind of coin you could barter for anything you needed. Indians traded pelts for whiskey. I heard about men trading ammunition and even rifles for a keg.

The river that day was the color of soot to which a froth of whipped molasses had been added. The total effect was that of whirling mud that, for all its spume and mist, looked as if it were steaming. Under all that foam you couldn't see the river, not the speed of it, or tell how it could grab a person and pull him down.

I had lodged with the freight handlers the night before, making certain not to be left behind when they lit out in the morning. They had promised to be under way at first light.

I stretched out on the dock with my blanket wrapped around me, falling asleep to the smashing of bottles and the roaring refrain of such songs as "Oh, Susanna," sung about fifty times. A small war developed. Men came out cursing and slugging. I heard the mighty crash as one of the sailors scooped up the drunken minstrel as if he were a rag doll, held him aloft for a minute, then dumped him in a convenient horse trough. "Shut up, shut up, you confounded Missouri puke!" he railed. "If I hear one more 'Susanna' I'll cut off your——and pickle your——." I had never heard such talk before and felt myself consumed between mirth and terror.

Apparently that "Missouri puke" was no worse for his dousing, for the next morning he stood right and ready, bringing the oxen to the river's edge and commencing to tamper with the wagons. He spotted me standing there, immersed in the sights of river traffic— paddleboats and steamers, ferries and barges, and crazy adventurers trying to make it across with ropes and pulleys.

"Boy! Over here. Give me a hand with these wagon wheels. Look smart, now!"

Adam thrust the yoke upon me, and I staggered and nearly collapsed. The thing must have weighed a ton, complete with rings and chains.

"What's wrong with you, boy? Look smart, now!"

"Yes, sir!"

"Hook that ring in first. Slide the bar over. No! Not that way! Ho!" He shouted at the oxen. "Stand still, you blasted, no-account varmints!" Adam smacked his bullwhip onto the hide of that ox with a powerful arm and a string of curses such as seemed to be the primary and total vocabulary of a bullwhacker.

Somehow we got the oxen settled, with the help of three yapping spotted dogs that hustled about and nipped sharply at the beasts' legs, taking their work seriously indeed.

We stood in line for the barge, having got all the wheels off the carts and our personal possessions packed in an oiled sack, for the crossings were always tricky. Wetness is part of being a river, I'm told, and to cross it takes guts and a prayer.

All along the river stood families with their bundles and their wagons, their young'uns and their beasts, their faces set with hope and with worry. Hope belonged to the men, worry to the women. The women were no doubt fretting over how they would keep house out on the trail, with wind and rain, mud, and the usual kinds of accidents and sickness and, yes, babies being born.

I thought of my ma and understood her desire to stay at home. Yet I also saw young women whose faces were glowing with delight. Molly would have that look. I peeped at the sketch I had made of her, then set it into my pocket.

The plan was to float the goods on that barge, and to swim the oxen across. A stout rope was stretched across the river to guide us, with several men waiting on the other side.

I saw a paddleboat go by. From it came sounds of laughter and music. I looked longingly at the passengers within. Two of our party had been chosen to go upriver by boat instead of by land. "We'll cast lots," Adam had roared out, "though I don't rightly favor such a means of travel. Those boats hold naught but gamblers and drunkards and bawdy women, and the food is terrible, I'm told. Any volunteers?"

All the men clamored to go with the gamblers, the drunkards, and the bawdy women, but most were needed to tend to the oxen. The prize was won by a thickset man with bushy dark eyebrows called Ruski, and a skinny, delicate fellow by the name of Raisin, maybe for the way he frowned and puckered up his face whenever he spoke. Raisin was a tailor by trade, a strange figure among the burly bullwhackers. Rumor was he had fled from a domineering wife. Compared to her evil tongue, the bullwhackers' language sounded like holy hymns.

Adam and his sidekick, Silas, led our oxen into the water. I was on the barge with the wagons, holding down the edge of a tarp to keep the wares dry, for the spume and the mud from the river would damage our precious goods.

Now, oxen in general are slow and stupid, some more high-strung than others. Our lot seemed pretty calm, as if they were entering a meadow. Their heads were low; their eyes probably glazed. I wouldn't know, for I was behind them, watching their rumps rise and fall, and it seemed all was fine and dandy, my perch on the barge like a cradle. I was just thinking that this was a pleasant and tame adventure, when something happened. Who can explain it? Suddenly that muddy river rose, the barge lurched like a bronco. I leaned over to grasp the tarp that was slipping from my fingers, when in the next instant I found myself smack down in the river, backside first and screaming as the water rose over my neck and shoulders. I was caught in the grip of a terrible giant, one who charged and raged, breaking down trees, tearing out roots, sending debris and boulders crashing into its sides. I saw a horse go by, shrieking wildly as it tried to swim. I clung to a piece of board. It slipped way. I felt myself somersaulting, flying in an arc that seemed to stretch forever, so was time altered in that awful moment of doom.

This, I thought, with more wonder than fear, is how I shall die.

Then I was submerged, thrust up again, with things rushing past me—bolts of cloth, a keg, a whole tree. I heard the incessant barking of a dog. The angry little creature was stranded on an island of mud and tree limbs, but only for a moment, as it was suddenly swept away. I flailed and kicked, trying to keep my head above the roiling water. Down again, my eyes were blinded and my mouth stopped with mud. I held my breath as the river pushed me ever onward.

"Catch it!" someone was shouting. "Catch it! Catch it!"

And then I saw the ingenious trap that several of the bullwhackers had set to catch me as I rode down river. From opposite sides of the river they had run downstream, stretching a stout rope as they ran.

"Catch it! Catch the rope, boy!"

I saw myself gliding down, and in my mind's eye I had rushed past the mark, but my hands and my arms and my chest, which took the impact, knew better. Somehow, I had caught the rope.

They reeled me in. They laid me down on the bank and pounded me until I coughed up half the Missouri River, and that cold, stinking mud mingled with my tears, but none of the men saw it, or at least they pretended not to know.

In a matter of minutes they set me on my feet and made me stand. With a hard thump to my back, Adam shouted, "Come on! Let's go. Next time we'll tie you on. Clumsy beggar! Why, any wind will blow him clean over."

I had not the breath to argue. *Any wind*? I'd just survived a crossing so treacherous that, as I learned later, three horses, two adults, and a child were drowned that very morning. One of the oxen drowned, having broken loose from the reins when the current caught him. We watched the lifeless body hurtling over and over like a stone. I felt sorry for that ox; it had done its best, and now it was dead. The men cut it up. That's the thing about oxen; when they can't work anymore, they become dinner.

The small dog that drowned was Adam's blue heeler, a spunky animal, all black except for a squared-off spot between the eyes and a single white paw, as if it had been dipped in cream. Its name was

Hatch. Adam returned to the shore a dozen times, yelling his lungs out for that dog. Later I saw Adam set up against a tree trunk, his face all screwed up, bawling like a baby.

I gathered my possessions, which miraculously had survived the assault of the river. Only Molly's picture, swimming in my pocket, was spoiled. I wadded it up into a ball and tossed it away. Later I saw one of the oxen pick it up and make of it a tasty cud. Well, at least some good came of it, I thought, wondering if ever another artist knew the feeling of seeing his work being eaten.

I was pondering my loss but feeling proud to be still alive after battling the mighty Missouri, when someone chucked a sizable pebble at my foot and drawled out, "Don't you know never to set on a barge without you being roped to the planks? Don't you know how to keep your seat in a raging river?"

I looked up and met the gaze of a tall, lanky fellow of about seventeen or eighteen, with eyes as wide and green as a cat's. His mouth, too, was wide, set in a crooked kind of smile that was part sneer. He stood leaning back slightly, appraising me, his fingers hooked through a leather belt with a sturdy silver buckle. "You don't know much about traveling, do you?"

"I know a bit more now," I replied, "than I did when I woke up this morning."

His mouth puckered, then he broke out in a grin and extended his hand. "Name's Hank."

I clasped his hand, which was large and rough. He squeezed my fingers something powerful. I returned it as best I could.

"Clem," I introduced myself. Proudly I added, "I work for the Pony Express."

Hank nodded, though he looked unimpressed. "Not yet, you don't. Not 'til you get to your station. Right now, you're just another bullwhacker, like the rest of us."

"I wasn't figuring to be a bullwhacker," I said ruefully.

"You stick with me," said Hank. "I'll show you how to keep your socks dry."

I doubted that, but I didn't want to offend Hank by arguing, so I only said, "Much obliged."

All the rest of the day Hank made sure I walked beside him, and as we walked he rattled on like a soul just out of purgatory, telling me tales. He had been everywhere, done everything, knew people of highest and lowest estate, it seemed. While he spoke, all of a sudden he'd shout a warning, pulling me back, thrusting me forward as I stumbled around prairied dog holes, ox platters, and great streams of yellow ox piss, wagon ruts, and wasp nests.

"Look out there! Are you blind or just stupid? Well, never mind, stick with me, and I'll show you how to keep your socks dry."

He was lanky but strong, as quick with the oxen as with his tongue. I wondered what had brought him out here driving oxen across the desolate plains, but he never spoke of himself, only of others and their life stories.

———◆———

That first day we traveled a mere eight miles. At this rate it would take forever and a day for me to get to Nebraska, forever and a month to make it to California. The bullwhackers cooked up an ox stew, with some roots and potatoes tossed in. Not bad. I lay down on my blanket that night. Hank and I had built a campfire of sorts. It smoked and burned, providing little heat but a spot for brewing coffee and for sitting around and jawing.

I couldn't sleep, for the wide openness of the meadow, the stinging nettles and bugs, and the constant howls of distant wolves. It was that distance that kept me awake, the dread of it growing smaller between me and the wolves. I thought of what Molly had said, and I wished I were as bold as my talk. Besides that, I suffered the discomfort of unrelief. Purple worms, Silas had told me, with sharp pinchers and jaws would attack the backsides of anyone who kept his pants down longer than a moment. I wasn't about to get bit back there, so I waited.

After a while Hank brought his pallet close to mine, and we started talking about things. I guess I was feeling sort of lonesome out there in that empty space, with the wolves howling from afar.

"You got family?" I asked. I don't know whether I sought the strange comfort of another orphan or the pleasure of hearing about someone else's kin.

"None to speak of," said Hank. "But I did leave a pretty girl in Independence, and I mean to go back and see her come winter."

"What's her name?" I asked.

"Henrietta. You got a sweetheart, Clem?"

"No," I said. Immediately I got a vision of Molly, her quick smile, the way she tossed her braids over her shoulder, and I felt disloyal and mean, as if I'd betrayed her. "Well, I know this girl, Molly," I said. "She's in Missouri, too, keeping my things whilst I'm gone."

"You fixing to return?" Hank asked, setting himself up on one elbow.

"Can't say for sure," I answered, puzzling over my choices. "I'm off to find Pa. He left for the gold fields two years ago, and we haven't heard a word."

Hank made a groan low in his throat. "Well, that's a caution."

"I don't know what might have happened to him," I offered, hoping Hank would say something optimistic, but he only hunched his shoulders. It didn't seem to look good for my pa. "Of course, there's all kinds of trouble along the way," I said, trying to sound wise. "Bandits and Indians."

"You said right about Indians, they're trouble for sure," said Hank, sitting up and stretching his neck toward me. "Fellow I knew back in Missouri has quite a tale to tell about Injuns, and it's all true too. Someone even wrote a book about it."

"Like *Oliver Twist*?" I exclaimed.

"Who's that?"

"A feller in a famous book," I replied.

"This is a true story, not something somebody just made up. It happened, and not too long ago. This fella, Abner, lived down the road from us, and he was stuck on this girl named Olive. She was only twelve or so, but he had his sights on her. Pretty little thing, is how he told it, until the Indians captured her and spoiled her. They killed all the rest of her family, except one brother who was left to tell the tale."

"How'd they spoil her?" I asked, shuddering.

"Well, you got to hear the whole story, to get the flavor of it. Thing is, Abner's life was plumb wrecked by what happened. See, the Oatmans were headed west with their seven young'uns, lookin' for a homestead and better times, like Uncle Sam had promised anyone with the guts to move on. Their oldest girl was eighteen, a blond beauty, then Lorenzo, who was fourteen, Olive, and little Mary Ann, and three younger children, one only a baby. By the time they got to the Gila River on the way to California, they'd gotten separated from their party and they were on their own. They must have been mighty scared, their animals exhausted, food running out, and no water. They were in Apache territory."

I looked around me at the shuffling, scuffling sounds of others coming closer now to listen. Someone threw a bit of wood onto the fire. It sizzled and flared. Hank raised his hands and his voice, acknowledging his audience.

"One night the father had a premonition. Usually he was a cheerful sort. That night he started to shake and shiver and he cried out, 'Oh, Mother! Mother! In the name of God, I know something dreadful is about to happen!'"

The listeners shifted, spat, groaned. I tensed to the tale, and I gathered my blanket close around my shoulders.

"Well, some Indians came skulking around the camp," Hank went on. "At first they seemed just curious, poking their noses into everything. They asked for tobacco. Mr. Oatman had none. They wanted food. Well, the Oatmans did not have much food, but finally they divided it with the Indians. Still they stayed, gawking at the girls and the horses, and Mr. Oatman told his children to stay calm and not show any fear. He himself was scared to death, a-shivering and pale."

Nobody moved. Hank's features were grim in the pale light from the fire.

"Suddenly there was a shout, a war whoop. The savages struck with their clubs. First the father went down. Blood burst from his head. Then the mother. Then the oldest girl. Lorenzo got beaten on the head with a club. Blood flowed into his eyes and mouth. He lay there, conscious, but he didn't move, and he heard the screams of his parents and brothers and sisters—'help us, oh, help us!'—but it was too late. They were all dying, but for little Mary Ann, who sat apart holding the rope tied to the oxen, and Olive. The savages had pushed her to one side to keep her for themselves."

Hank stopped and sighed deeply while the men nodded to themselves meaningfully without looking at one another.

"Lorenzo was left for dead," Hank continued. "They had pushed him over a cliff. Much later he revived and crawled back to the scene of the massacre. He counted the bodies and knew that two of his sisters had been captured."

Hank told us in detail how they marched those girls over two hundred miles in three days. He told how the girls begged for rest, how their feet bled. When they complained, the Indians whipped them. Finally they came to the Indians' camp, exhausted. There they were displayed at a huge campfire. "Everyone danced around them, screaming, spitting into their faces," Hank continued. "When Olive and Mary Ann cried, all those savages just laughed and laughed. See, the Apaches think that to show pain is a disgrace. You can pull out their fingernails, even, and they won't flinch."

All around me now, I heard low groans, and my own stomach heaved as I moaned out loud at the horror of it. "How'd Olive and Mary Ann get free?" I asked. Others joined in, "Yes, what happened?"

"Well, Mary Ann only lived barely two years. She starved to death with those Indians. They never gave her enough food to stay alive. Olive wasn't as frail. She managed to find roots and berries and such. Finally, after four years of being captive, someone caught sight of her, and the news spread to the white town, and Olive was ransomed back. Then she told everything. Of course, she met up with her brother, Lorenzo, and the two of them told about it together." Hank nodded and said grimly, "Just the two of them left from that whole family. There's not many people get captured by the Apaches and live to tell about it but," Hank said, "not without scars. No, siree. Olive came back to civilization tattooed just like an Injun squaw. She'll bear those marks on her chin until the day she dies. My friend Abner went and saw her when she was speaking to a group of folks at a schoolhouse one day. Abner took one look at his sweetheart and fainted dead away. Never saw her again, he said, couldn't bear the sight."

I felt sick, imagining how it would be to see Molly's face hideously tattooed, and to know that her mind was marked with worse things that she couldn't even describe. Had she been forced to marry an Indian? Did she have to do such things as . . . my mind balked. I felt queasy and heaving.

Now Silas and Adam and some of the other men took up the talk about Indian atrocities. That was the word they used, "atrocities," and it sounded awful. Silas spoke of a Cree raid back awhile, where some five hundred settlers were killed, either shot or butchered like cattle. "Every one of the bodies," he said, spitting out a long squirt of tobacco, "every one had a little round red circle atop of their heads, where the Injuns had cut out their scalps."

"I heard about that," said Adam. "Know what they did to the children? Infants? Held 'em up by the legs and smashed their heads against the fortress wall, so their brains flew out. Women were cut open, a long slice. If there were babies in their bellies, those were scooped out."

My companions were soon worn out from the talk. I began to hear their snores. But I sat up half the night, shivering, haunted by feelings of dread. My journey had just begun. All in a single day I'd courted death, seen disaster, heard of massacres. I had a fleeting thought of turning back, but where could I go, friendless and poor and without prospects?

I must have slept, for next thing I knew, there was Hank standing over me, and I lay in a puddle of water, for a sudden rain had doused me, and even my socks were soaking wet.

CHAPTER 8

My Education Continues by a Black Bullwhacker and Prankish Pawnee

---

By the time we reached Nebraska City, just five days later, we had experienced every kind of weather. Some mornings we woke up to a bed of mud underneath us, and clammy cold rain. A wailing, loathsome wind made a fire impossible. My fingers were numb from cold, my back aching. We ate cold biscuits and a handful of sour berries and jerky, listening to tales of starvation and cannibalism by such emigrants as the Donner party years ago. The bullwhackers knew the names of every disaster, and they loved to tell about them.

We ran into a storm that had all the signs of the Hades I'd read about—quaking thunder, zigzags of flame across the sky, the very ground heaving with it, enough to make a body repent. I hid under the wagon and was sorely accused for it later. Adam said I should have concerned myself about the oxen instead.

Some days the sun rose so hot that we blistered. The cattle bawled and groaned, and there was never enough water. Thirst drove me to drinking from creeks that leapt with living things.

Those first days I had many different feelings. One was a powerful lonesomeness. The other was awe for the hugeness of things, the pitched peaks and cliffs on our right, the vast prairie stretching out forever to the west, and at night, the great, dazzling sky. With sunrise came the feeling of freedom. Here, I could do anything—climb mountains, swim rivers, trap beaver, catch fish, and hunt the bison that roamed the prairies. I could breathe, with nobody as my master. Give a year or two, and I could stake a claim of my own. But then the lonesomeness would grab me. What good is it being free if there's nobody else to be it with?

We were traveling so slowly with our oxen that all the traffic on the trail passed by us, and we ate their dust all day. My lips were cracked from dust and dryness. My eyes felt grainy. I imagined what my ma might say if she looked into my hair or behind my ears, like she used to do. I felt things crawling there.

It was a queer thing coming upon a city after the desolation of wild country, forest, and plains. Suddenly there stood a gathering of buildings—long bunkhouses and cattle pens and yards and merchant shops. There were blacksmiths and tanners, coopers, ship builders and peddlers, everyone letting out the sounds of his trade. We met our companions, Ruski and Raisin, both looking glum and exhausted. Ruski had been fleeced by a gambler who swindled him out of two months' pay, and Raisin said the food on the boat had so poisoned him that he couldn't even hold down an egg.

We spent the night at a grimy station house, infested with fleas and lice, sleeping on a straw-littered dirt floor. For supper, the proprietor and his slovenly wife ladled out a moss-colored soup in which swam a few specks of salt pork. A leaden mass of dough and some dubious apples baked into a turnover qualified as dessert. One of the bullwhackers broke a tooth on it. All this, for twenty cents apiece, a blatant thievery. Adam kindly paid for my lodging and board. Later I learned that this hospitality would be deducted from my first month's pay, along with the fee for crossing the Missouri on a barge, which nearly killed me.

Well, we took on some more wagons and oxen, dogs and drivers, one of which was a Negro man. The colored man went straight to the back of the train, which is the hardest position, demanding the most of the beasts, as they must carry the greatest weight. I inquired about him, and Adam said shortly, "His name's Gabriel. Let him be."

Gabriel never whipped the oxen. Of course, he carried a whip, for it was part of his calling, like a minister has his Bible or a fiddler his bow. With that whip in his hand, Gabriel was like a dancing man. He never missed a step, keeping rhythm with the animals over stones and gullies, bending to the curve of the trail. Poised on his toes, Gabriel would point the whip just over the animals' heads, so that the tip pulled a faint shadow across their vision, and they responded, moving right, left, forward, or stopping dead in their tracks with nary a touch. All the while, low sounds came from Gabriel's throat, a kind of crooning.

I wondered about this black man. Was he free? Well, he must be, to be employed by this freight company. But didn't he ever speak? Where had he come from? Where was he going?

All day, as I walked, I gazed out at the waving prairie grass, now and again broken by clumps of boulders, imagining savages ready to spring out and take my scalp. One hot afternoon, as I walked along-side Adam's team, I found myself drifting. I'd seen men walking beside their oxen, even muttering curses, their heads sagging in deepest sleep. So I guess I'd been sleeping, for I found myself back at the end of the train, beside Gabriel and his team.

I awakened to a soft sound, like singing. "Umm, Buck, that-away, hmmm, ahh, mmm."

I walked in silence, hearing the shuffling feet of the oxen as they pressed on, and the sound of the wind hissing through the prairie grasses. I watched Gabriel from the corner of my eye, for I had never had the chance to observe a black man up close before. Nobody we knew could afford slaves, and there was no such thing as a free black person in Missouri.

Of course, I'd heard talk. Ma thought it was the Lord's plan for white folks to rule their black brethren, providing work for them and a roof over their heads. The pastor preached that whites were born to be masters and Negroes were meant to serve. If they got ungrateful and ran away from their masters, it was up to good citizens to catch them and bring them back. That was the law about fugitive slaves, as my ma used to tell it, sitting in her rocker. Pa didn't agree. It seemed like whenever there was talk of black and white, someone got angry.

Like the time my pa took me to town to buy supplies. We stood out on the wooden steps of the general store, the men chewing and spittin' and talking about an "underground railroad" and a "conductor" named Harriet Tubman. I wanted to go inside the store and buy a pickle, but Pa hung on to my arm and made me stay where I could hear it all.

"Them blacks is just out to murder the whites."

"They'd take over the state if we let 'em. You give 'em a break, and they'll turn on you, just like a wildcat."

A passing peddler drank down his sasparilla, belched, and declared, "They've only got half the brains of white people. You can tell by looking at their heads."

Now I studied Gabriel's head from the back and side and everywhich angle, but I couldn't tell anything about his brains.

"You from Nebraska?" I asked, trying to start a conversation.

Gabriel continued his humming, singing to the oxen.

"Hot day, isn't it."

Gabriel said nothing.

On the way home from the general store that night, I'd asked Pa what all the talk was about, and he told me that folks in Kansas were voting about whether to have slavery there or not. He talked so long I stopped listening, but I could tell he enjoyed it mightily, and it made me feel smart to have asked. He went on and on, using words I didn't know or care about. Except one word I did remember, because it had a queer sound, and I liked it and sang it to myself: "Pottawatamie." That was where this wild man, John Brown, went and killed some whites for trying to get slavery into Kansas. This man, Brown, became a hero, or a villain, depending what side you were on. After my pa had left for the gold fields, I heard his name again, making a raid on another place called Harpers Ferry and getting himself hanged for it. But that wasn't nearly as interesting to me as the sound of "Pottawatamie," that other place.

"You ever hear of John Brown?" I shot out, before I could reflect.

I saw Gabriel's eyebrow twitch. His lips were pursed. I knew he'd heard me.

I don't know what mischief got hold of me, but I couldn't stop. "Pottawatamie," I said. "You ever heard of Pottawatamie?"

Gabriel never said a word but kept dancing behind those dumb oxen. To tell the truth, I was sore about it. Here I went out of my way to talk to a black man, and he wouldn't even answer.

It was getting near dusk when we came upon a pretty big encampment. We heard the callings of women and children, smelled meat roasting and baked goods getting done in Dutch ovens. My mouth watered. The men all stared, trancelike.

"Let's stop for the night," said Ruski, already taking off his hat and looking around for water where he might bathe himself and appear less coarse.

"No," said Adam. "We'll move on." He pointed toward some mound of brush in the distance.

"The animals are tired," argued Ruski. "We've made our miles for the day. I'm going no farther."

"You'll go where I say." Adam strode toward Ruski, swinging a thick chain used for holding the oxen. Everyone tensed, moving to one side or the other. I wasn't looking forward to a fight—but then again, it would liven up a boring day.

"Why can't we stop?" Ruski demanded, fists balled up.

"Mormons," said Adam. "I can smell them."

"So what?" challenged Ruski.

"I don't like their kind. Queer folk. Look, they're staring at us, plotting."

The Mormons were observing us from a distance, hands shading their eyes. We must have looked like rogues, unkempt and filthy.

I saw the flash of a gingham sunbonnet, and I thought of Molly. What would it be like to have Molly here? I recalled her bright talk, the way she laughed and flipped a braid back over her shoulder, how she'd confront me and call me "Clem Fontayne."

"Well, I wouldn't mind some real cooked food, and I hear them Mormon women do know how to cook."

"They know more'n that," said Silas, leering.

"We'll move on," said Adam. "I'm not lookin' for trouble."

We moved a bit farther on, a compromise. We could still smell the fires from the Mormon camp.

"Go git something to burn," Adam called to me. I was part of his mess, which meant he provided the meal and I sang for my supper, any tune he called.

Someone had bagged an antelope a few days before. All the meat was gone, but the head remained. Raisin, who usually did the cooking for our mess, would boil the head for soup. We had some cornmeal to use for cakes, and occasionally we might get a handful of beans or prunes, but the stores we carried were for sale, not for us. Adam was sparse with anything that could bring cash.

I wanted Hank to come with me, but he was tending an ox that had a swollen shoulder. So I set out alone to find fuel, at the same time searching for wild onions and gooseberries to bolster up my meal. The gooseberries were everywhere, small greenish white things, and tart as sin, but if I could gather enough of them I could trade someone berries for sugar and we'd both be glad.

It felt pretty good to get away by myself, away from swearing and laboring and breathing dust off the trail. The cool of late afternoon beckoned me toward a clump of trees that seemed to be ever receding. I had taken off my shirt and filled it with berries; I tied the sleeves together to form a pouch and followed a small stream, searching for wild onions and greens to add to our antelope head soup.

Soon I realized that I no longer heard human sounds around me, no longer smelled the fires of other travelers. Darkness was approaching. Shadows turned quickly into dark holes. Quite alone, I felt a surge of panic as a series of terrible cries rang out.

For a moment I could not move but stood rooted, trying to make out the direction and meaning of this alarm.

A terror-filled shout came closer, high pitched, distraught. "Help! Help! Help!"

I whirled around and saw just beyond a young man, leaping up and down as if his feet were aflame, waving his arms and screaming. And he was stark naked.

"Injuns! Injuns!" he shouted, running toward me. He grasped my shoulders, clinging to me as to a rock. "Get out! Get out! They mean to kill us!"

"Come on." I pulled him with me as we ran, retracing my route with some difficulty, stopping on a ridge to look about us. He gasped, sputtered, told me how he'd been out hunting alone when Indians assaulted him.

"They stole my horse and my rifle. They stole my clothes!"

Indeed, they had taken everything but his boots, which were fine leather and hardly worn. I looked at the boots, then at him, standing there so petrified and pale and naked that I began to laugh. I laughed so hard that even he got caught up in it, and there we were, two fools roaring out laughter when we should have been dead sober and running.

Well, we got back to our camp, and the fellow started all over again, introducing himself as Matt Bryant, from Massachusetts, Thoreau country, he added meaningfully, proving himself to be a student just off on holiday with two of his friends. "We came to do some hunting and see the wilderness," Matt said. He had expected to bag an antelope or a bighorn sheep and impress his companions. All of us, gazing at Matt, shook our heads in doubt. He had neither the frame nor the courage to bag any beast, and in his present nonattire, he looked ridiculous.

"Young fool," snorted Adam. "Never leave your group out on the plains. Never go out alone. You should have known that."

"I was attacked," yelped Matt. "They surrounded me. They are headed this way, a war party."

"How do you know?" Ruski asked.

"They were painted. Fierce."

"How many?" Adam asked.

"A bunch! At least a dozen. With war paint and guns. They pulled off my clothes, they stole my rifle . . ."

"How did you escape?" asked Hank, scratching his head.

"I ran. "They're headed this way!" insisted Matt. "Oughtn't we to—to *do* something?"

"Who are they? What kind?"

A cloud of dust warned us of approaching riders. We looked at one another. Men reached for their revolvers. But in minutes we knew that these were Matt's companions, dressed in buckskin, one riding a fine sorrel, the other a thoroughbred, their saddlebags bulging with equipment.

"Ho! John, Andrew, wait 'til you hear what happened."

Matt went through it all again, and his friends were duly impressed. One asked, "What kind were they, Matt?"

"I don't know," Matt admitted. He suddenly seemed embarrassed and tried to cover himself. "Toss me a shirt and pants, Andy," he said, his voice cracking. He gazed all around, then said, "Paiute. Yes. Paiute. Those killers." He quickly struggled into his clothes.

"The same ones that did the massacre?" his friends cried.

"The same."

"What massacre?" Adam exclaimed. He approached the three boys sternly.

"Haven't you heard?"

"What massacre?"

"Last week we met a mountain man, and he told us. Paiute raided one of the Pony Express stations."

"What station?" Adam demanded, his eyes blazing.

"Williams Station, I think he said. Yes, Williams."

"My God! What happened to Williams? Is he . . ."

"Don't know. Killed five men. Don't know their names. Set the station on fire. Then they went and burned down seven more stations, drove off the horses."

Nobody spoke. I didn't know where to look. Each face bore that granitelike expression that men get when feelings threaten to burst out but still they bear up and master themselves.

"How many stations?" Hank had to hear it again. We all did.

"Seven stations."

"Must be the ones we supply."

"We supply all of them."

"Don't know what we'll find, who's still alive, who's dead."

"They are not Paiute."

Everyone turned to stare at Gabriel, who stood there with his lip thrust out, grumbling. "Paiute don't roam here."

"They were on the warpath!" cried Matt.

"If they were on the warpath," said Gabriel, "you'd be dead."

"They were vicious, I tell you. They stole—"

"Pawnee," said Gabriel, turning away. "Play pranks. That's their way. You are lucky they left you your hair."

We laughed, but it was a self-conscious laughter. Matt pulled himself up behind the one called Andy, and the college boys whipped their horses around and took off, deprived of their heroic tale.

Later, while we were eating our soup without onions or greens, for I had dropped everything when Matt appeared, I asked Adam how come Gabriel knew so much about Indians.

"He lived with the Pawnee for a year," Adam told me. He took up a piece of the boiled antelope skull and sucked out the eye. "He's a tough bird. Let him be."

It made me more determined than ever to get to know Gabriel better.

CHAPTER 9

We Encounter Civilized People at Fort Kearny and Witness an Uncivilized Murder

We made our way toward Fort Kearny, following the Platte, a lazy mud hole with low, yellow banks that concealed broad patches of quicksand. The bogs hid themselves even from the experienced drivers at times. Then our oxen strained and pulled like engines. They worked themselves to the point of death. Indeed, we saw ox skulls and bones all along the way. Poor old fellows! Yet the skeletons made interesting subjects for a sketch, and I composed many of them.

The Platte was a poor excuse for a river, its water thick as moving sand, mostly undrinkable and unlikely for washing, unless one desired sandpaper shirts. But it made a highway for us and for the emigrants who came with their wagons, mules, horses, and carts on both sides, north and south. We were traveling the south side.

Sometimes, walking, I'd turn to see a long train of wagons coming up behind us, or clouds of dust just ahead. Now animal life was so abundant that herds and throngs often roamed before us, darkening the grasses like a stain. At a distance, the buffalo spread far and wide. We could hear them bellow; soon we would come upon them.

There were large colonies of prairie dogs, leaving small mounds of earth as they tunneled under the grass. They stopped to peer at us, then scurried into their holes. The holes they left were a danger to people and beasts. A horse or a man could break a leg stepping into one of them.

Now and again as the grasses parted, I would see the brown head of an antelope, then two, three, a dozen more. The antelope cocked their heads and stared, and I had a fleeting thought of my Belinda. I made many sketches of the prairie animals, usually taking up my pencil after the noon meal while the others caught a brief nap.

When we came upon Fort Kearny, I understood what weeks of wandering can do to a person's mind. I had grown accustomed to our dogged pace, our rough beds, and the laziness that numbs one's thoughts when there is nothing ahead but prairie and sky. Suddenly we were once again civilized, with clean water and outhouses and bunks. The sight of a building, however crude, caused a terrible yearning in me. I was divided now, into two parts, and might be that way forever. The one wanted adventure, open fields, and independence. The other longed for a warm fire and orderly days, with food that did not need to be hunted down, and beds that carried their own blankets. And it was a grand thing to be able to buy pencils, notebooks, soap, and a comb.

The fort was filled with novelties, more goods than I had seen in months, more people of various types and kinds that I had ever known existed. There were several Negro women and children, soldiers in uniform, Spaniards with bright blankets slung over their heads, Indians wearing bangles, feathers, and beads. Others looked craven, nearly naked, with shaven heads or bristling combs of hair riding atop their scalps. The squaws appeared subdued and fearful. Most had papooses on their backs.

At the fort was one family from Iowa, a mother, father, and four little children, all pathetically thin, except for the young mother, who was again heavy with child.

Two little boys, five and six years old, latched on to me for some reason. Their names were Malcolm and Rusty, both redheaded fellows brimming with questions. "How long you been travelin'? You come with your folks? You know how to drive them oxen?"

And they told me tales. "Some naked Injuns came to our camp and stole all our sugar one night! Pa lit out after 'em, but Ma stopped him, saying she didn't want no dead husband to bury on the trail." They told about a child in their group who fell out of the wagon, and, "He got smashed up. We sent for the doctor in the next train, but he died anyway, and we buried him. Did you see the grave? His name was Thomas. Did you see it? We all said prayers and now he sits in heaven and we can see him at night, lookin' like a star. That's what my ma says."

"I have seen stars like that," I told them. "How come you left your group?" I asked, knowing it was unusual and dangerous for a family to travel alone.

"Ma's poorly," said Malcom.

"She's getting us a baby," said Rusty. "I think she's gonna buy it here at the fort."

"What a coot," sneered his brother. "That ain't how babies come, is it, Clem?"

Not wanting to get involved in such matters, I pulled them away with a game of mumblety-peg. Malcolm, the older, was proud to have his own knife, and I let Rusty take turns with mine, until he nicked his finger on the blade, and we went to play checkers instead. I'd seen an old board in the station house, with some battered disks to go with it. We used stones for the missing pieces, dark and light, and I taught them to play. Long ago my pa had taught me. I only beat him twice in my life, and those times he never minded; he said he was proud.

I drew sketches of the little boys. They were charmed and ran to their ma. "Lookit here what Clem's done!" they yelled, dancing up and down.

"Lovely," said their ma, smiling wanly. She looked exhausted, with a baby on her lap, close to her breast. "Run and play, boys. Soon enough you'll be cooped up in the wagon." She turned to me. "I can't trust them to run about. They take off to the hills, and one never knows." She glanced about. "Indians."

Before we left the fort, I came upon a surprise, unexpected as surprises always are. Outside the barracks were a dipper and basin, and above it a looking glass used by the soldiers to shave and trim their beards. As I passed the glass, I glanced up and beheld a stranger. My heart took a sudden leap when I realized the face was my own. It wasn't a bad face, either, half smiling, kind of cockey and not too stupid.

I did not see Malcolm and Rusty again before we set out the next day. But two days later something happened that sickened me, and even the memory of it still holds.

We were tramping along as usual, accustomed to seeing Indians. Sometimes they only stared at us, other times they begged or bartered. We had learned to tolerate them, occasionally to do business, as I had done for a pair of moccasins that I now prized. In exchange for a drawing of several antelope drinking at the river, a young brave gave me a handsome pair that were sturdy and also beautiful, with beads.

Well along the road a small party of Indians was encamped. The young braves must have gone off to hunt buffalo. Beside the ragged camp lounged an old man and four squaws, one ancient, the others in various degrees of motherhood, for all had papooses strapped to their backs, with a number of naked little children playing nearby. The Indian children were remarkably quiet in their play. As we approached them, they stared at us but spoke not at all, not even to beg.

Behind us came several riders on horseback and supply wagons following. They had brought along numerous sheep and two milch cows, and even chickens in a cage, to provide ample sustenance on their holiday. It seemed strange to see gentlemen of means taking pleasure where others barely survived. It made me think of Oliver Twist in the poorhouse, living on crusts while others feasted. Somehow I'd had the notion that in the wilderness there were no rich or poor, just folks moving on.

The travelers, gentlemen in their furs, sported large revolvers. One met my gaze and waved. I waved back. Then I saw him spur his horse as he spotted the forlorn group of Indians. His voice rang out, loud and exultant. "Look! Injuns! Look at the squaws. Good hunting!"

I had not a moment to ponder what he meant, for in the next instant he whirled his horse around in a savage motion, while he shouted, "Hurrah!" A shot rang out. I heard the report, the *ping* as it ricocheted from a rock. The squaw crumpled and fell, smashing the papoose on her back. The little one did not cry out. It was, like its mother, dead, for the bullet had pierced clean through the two of them.

I screamed out. "Oh, no! No!" I couldn't stop screaming, all the while running toward the limp and bloody bodies. I had waved back at the killers. Did that somehow put me in league with them? "No!" I screamed again, as Ruski and Raisin, Hank, and Gabriel came running too.

When we got to the spot, the other Indians had fled and hidden themselves completely. We searched and called, but they seemed to have melted into the landscape. Only the crumpled body of the squaw with her baby remained, and the stain of blood around them.

I knelt down, bawling, beating my fists against a stone until my knuckles were raw. No words came to my lips, only a single thought running circles in my mind as I gulped down tears of rage: Why? Why?

Strong arms surrounded me, pulling me away and carrying me back to our wagons. It was Gabriel who held me.

After some talk, Adam and Ruski rode back to the fort to report the outrage. I expected soldiers to come and investigate and to punish the guilty. But justice was not to be done. Our men returned with sullen faces and few words. The officers had shrugged at the incident and decided it was not worth their while to go in pursuit of a few vacationers who took for their hunting trophy a squaw and her baby.

I railed to Adam. "Not worth it? What in tarnation do they mean?"

"It is politics," responded Raisin, looking dour.

Adam pulled at his pipe. "You are too young to understand. Nobody wants to start a war or even a skirmish over this."

"It is wrong!" I shouted.

"You are young," they said. "You do not understand."

I had heard those words before, often. I despised them.

CHAPTER 10

A Prairie Becomes a Battleground as We Go Hunting Buffalo

We were coming to buffalo country. Under our feet lay their droppings, their hair, the shed of their horns. "You stick with me," Hank said, "when we get to the buffalo. No matter how much you think you know, you won't know what it's like till you're amongst 'em. You stick with me. I'll show you how to get yourself a buffalo robe."

"I don't have a gun," I said morosely. "How can I hunt buffalo?"

"Well, we'll just see about that," said Hank.

Hunting buffalo was a thrilling prospect. I lay down at night thinking about buffalo, wishing I had a rifle. One thought led to another, and of course it ended, as always, with my father. He had taken the Winchester with him and left us another, which Pa called an "Indian rifle," because of its long barrel and flimsy construction. In times past, Pa explained, the Spaniards had traded such guns to the Indians, knowing they would be broken and harmless soon enough. When the sight and trigger on my rifle broke I had nobody to fix it. So I'd left it at the old homestead, thinking to earn money for its repair, but when I had returned, it was gone.

While we were at Fort Kearny, I had inquired about my father. Had anyone seen Pierre Fontayne? Maybe they called him Frenchie. I described him: lean and tall, dark hair, merry eyes, good-looking. "He smokes cigarettes," I said, half embarrassed, half defiant.

"No. No. Of course, we do not take lists of travelers through here."

I could understand, now, how a man might vanish in the vastness of this country. What if I never saw Pa again? I burrowed through my memories like a miner looking for gold, striking a flake now and again, most often hitting mud. Yes, there were the times Pa took me to town and bought me pencils and notepads. He smiled at my drawings, ruffled my hair. But soon he was off in his own dreams, dreams too distant to share with a boy.

We never hunted together, or fished, or went tramping in the mountains the way fathers do with their sons. I always had the notion that Pa was waiting for me to grow up so we could start being friends. Well, I was getting older by the day. Maybe by the time Pa and I got together, I'd be up to his standard.

Meanwhile, I had friends among the men, not only Hank, as I soon discovered.

When we came upon the buffalo, I could see them from afar, like a brown stain on the green prairie. They grazed just below us near a creek bed. When the wind changed, we could smell them. It was a deep, rank smell. It made me lust for meat. Next thing I knew, there was Hank, wearing a grin and holding out a Springfield rifle.

"This here's for you to use," he said. "I got it from Blue. He's letting you use it in exchange for your kill, all but one. You can keep a whole one for yourself. You okay with that?"

I felt weighted down, breathless with excitement. "What about bullets?" My heart raced, my hands itched to hold that rifle and stroke the gleaming barrel, to know the feel of it.

Hank held out a pouch full of ammunition. "Here. Blue gets all but one, okay?"

I nodded and held out my hand. "Done."

I went to thank Blue, a stout fellow who played the fiddle. Night times by the campfire, his fingers hammered at the strings and his bow flew across them, tossing out tunes to make our feet tap, and we'd all sing, not sweet as a church choir, but with plenty of gusto. His favorite was "Blue Tail Fly," which earned him his name.

Blue was set against the side of a wagon, sewing up a hole in his boot with a thick needle and a piece of leather thong. He was handy mending bullwhips too.

I came up to him, suddenly shy. "Much obliged," I murmured, "for the rifle."

"Not for keeps," Blue said quickly. "It's a loan."

"Of course, of course! I know that, and I thank you kindly," I added, summoning my best manners.

"Don't waste your thanks," said Blue with a wave of his hand. "It's an investment I'm making. I aim to get myself a dozen or more of the beasts and sell the hides for robes." He stopped stitching and peered at me closely. "Listen to me. You don't get rich driving oxen. Got to keep your eyes open for advantages along the way. You understand me, boy?"

"Yes, I do," I replied, though I had only a dim notion of what he was talking about.

"Buffalo robes can bring a hundred dollars. Sell 'em to Chinamen for their kings. Sell 'em east to ladies for their carriage rides in the snow. Nothing warms like buffalo hide and, listen to me! If you've never tasted buffalo tongue, why, you don't know nothing about living."

"I surely aim to taste it, then," I declared, and Blue laughed heartily and praised me. "That's my boy!"

With his boot fixed, Blue jumped up, his rifle slung over his shoulder and a pistol thrust into his belt. It was one of those new Remington revolvers, and I wondered what he might do with it when it came to hunting buffalo, but I had no time to inquire. "Let's go! Let's go!" Blue hollered, and I saw the purple vein pulsing in his throat.

"Naw, we can wait until morning," said Silas, stretching, and Adam agreed. Perhaps they were teasing because Blue was so pumped up he seemed about to take off and fly.

"What'll you do with buffalo skins?" called Ruski. "You got an Indian squaw to dress them for you?"

"I can do it myself," said Blue. "Come on!"

"You gonna chew it?" Ruski laughed.

"Maybe I'll have to get me a squaw," retorted Blue. "Come on, boys!"

Gabriel smiled and shook his head. "They don't chew," he said. "They take the brains and rub them into the hide to soften it."

"You sure they don't take white man's brains?" asked Adam.

They all laughed and stood looking down at the buffalo who roamed back and forth, still ignorant of their fate. There was something sweet about that moment, seeing the huge beasts quietly grazing, with an occasional bird setting down on a buffalo's rump, pecking for mites. Hank came up beside me. He was breathing heavily. "Come on," he said, his voice husky. "Stick with me. Stay away from the horses. Sometimes they bolt. Keep your head down."

"Come on!" Blue called, commandeering us with a wave of his arm, like a general. Everyone tensed, collecting shot and guns and knives. With Blue in the lead, we moved out at a trot.

Hank pulled me along. "Stick with me," he said in a husky voice. "I'll show you how to keep your socks dry.

I had not breath enough to answer. We followed Blue. Around us were the sounds of men and horses panting, trampling, rushing. I ran, keeping Blue's shape before my eyes as he loped and lunged across the field, down a ravine toward the creek bed. Blue's shirt was stained with sweat. My own shirt felt damp, and my face was steaming, but I didn't care. I had never felt so alive, so powerful, together with the men and the horses and the guns, surging down toward the buffalo. I thought, in my strange joy, this is what I was born for, this is what I always wanted, to be here now.

We came near enough to smell them, and Blue motioned for Hank and me to kneel down in the tall grass. My chest felt expanded, aching. There they were before us, awesome beasts, woolly, wild shapes, abuzz with flies. My eyes took in everything at once, the brightness of the sun, the fuzz on the tips of reeds, the thin, tasseled tails of the buffalo, the shadows of bramble bushes, the silver bolts of rifles, the streams of sweat on men's faces. In the stillness time seemed to stretch. I heard the droning of flies, the breathing of horses and men, the whirr of a bird's wing.

Blue stood up. He seemed larger than life, his chest thrust out, rifle at his shoulder. "Now!" Blue shouted, and he let go the shot. A volley of answering shots rang out, echoing, redoubling, cracking all around me, like thunder above my head. I froze, caught in that avalanche of sound, the way I'd been caught and dragged down the river, helpless, hurled, battered. I was battered by the noise of guns, the roaring of the buffalo, the pounding of their hooves, the screams of horses, shouts of men. I was in the middle of a storm unlike any I could imagine. And I loved it, the sheer force of noise, and I was at its center.

"Shoot!" screamed Hank. He hurled out curses. I felt him slamming against me, knocking me flat. "Get over, get over!" A buffalo came crashing down just beside me. I felt the vibration of earth, the tremor beneath me. I saw the flash of hooves. Blood gushed from the beast's mouth and from the holes in its side. Dirt and debris, fur and flesh flew around me.

I crouched down, stunned, watching. Still the shots came coursing all about, sinking into the hide of the buffalo. They did not die all at once but, wounded, staggered from side to side. Others, still intact, bolted and reared. One came, crazed and swaying like a bear, zigzagging toward a horse and rider. Two shots in quick succession struck the buffalo's head, knocked out an eye.

I kept my eyes on Blue, my hero, watched as he shot, as beasts crumpled and staggered and fell. Blue darted about, his face transformed. All the men gathered themselves like a human net around the buffalo. The men's face looked enlarged, with gaping mouths, distorted jaws and brows, slobber and blood and sweat all mixed together.

In my ear Hank screamed, "Shoot, damn you! Shoot!"

I shouldered the rifle. I squinted, steadied my trembling hand, hunched my shoulders, and pulled back the trigger, mustering all my resolve. *Bam! Bam! Bam!* Shots all around me confirmed that I was one of a team, an army. Men against beasts, wisdom against instinct. We were locked together in danger and in the joy of the hunt.

The buffalo bolted and panicked, aimless and stupid, until they reclaimed their leader and followed him, a roaring stampede. We moved as one into formation, taking those in the rear, the slow, the dull, sometimes a calf. I counted my trophies—one, two, three!

Something loosened in me. My fingers flew, my feet flew, my brain raced, my eyes focused on my targets, and I loaded, shot, loaded, ran, again and again and again. Only the moment mattered now, the kill and the craze of it, the shot, the mark, the howl, the final crashing fall, all hailed me. I was a warrior! I plunged in, heedless of anything else, utterly given to the kill.

It went on and on, for more than an hour, I suppose, because when it was over, dusk had fallen, and an eerie reddish haze lay over us all. I looked around, in my dulled mind thinking the haze was a reflection of all the blood that lay on the ground around us. But it was the sun's final call that day, nothing more.

I stood there speechless and awed at the sight of our slaughter. It was like a battlefield. Though I had never seen one, I knew. I felt the combined exhaustion and amazement of a conqueror. And I felt the horror. Over a hundred beasts lay spread out with mouths agape, eyes wide, limbs stiff. Everything was broken and wasted.

From a great distance, sound returned to the landscape. Birds called and a few stray cattle bellowed. Otherwise, I felt alone with my shame, for we had butchered wildly and carelessly, far more than we could possibly use.

The men began to slice into the hides, tugging and straining, spoiling many in their haste. They cursed as they ripped out the tongues and tore flesh from the humps, cursed the length of time it would take to cook these delicacies, when they were lusting after meat. One man took a heart and pressed it, dripping, against his mouth. Others hacked off tails and horns and hooves.

Raisin ran over to a felled calf, squatted, reaching into his boot for a knife.

"Get away!" It was a roar, accompanied by a click of a gun bolt being drawn back to position. "I mean it."

"What? What?" I heard the tremor in Raisin's voice, saw the twisted amazement of his brow.

"That's mine," Blue shouted. "The boy shot it with my rifle."

"But how—how can you know?"

Silas and Gabriel stopped to listen; the others were intent on their own business, stripping, cutting, starting fires.

"I know. Look at that hole." Blue waved the revolver. His eyes narrowed. "Get away, Raisin, or I swear, I'll shoot you in the leg."

Raisin, his head down, slipped away, walking backwards.

I felt a sickness spreading through me, but I said nothing. Blue's face was stern, his bearing like iron as he went from one carcass to the next, stripping, cutting, tearing.

Blue was crude with his knife, random in his movements. Later, I learned how it is really done, the careful slit, the pulling of intestines, severing of head, leaving the rest intact. But Blue ripped and hacked, often tearing the hide, rendering it useless. We skinned seven of the beasts. My hands were slick from it, my shirt covered with blood. My limbs ached so that I could hardly lift my arms later, to bring the roasted meat to my mouth.

As I ate, I almost forgot the slaughter. Buffalo tongue and hump steak are the most delicious fare on earth. I ate to bursting, then took the buffalo hide Blue had promised me, and for a trophy, a tail. The hide was stiff and sticky, laden with hair on one side and flesh on the other. I would work for weeks to soften it with my knife, rubbing it faithfully with buffalo brains, as the Indians do.

The tail needed no working. It stiffened into a fine flyswatter. But I could never look at it without recalling the slaughter, and soon I abandoned it and let the flies light where they would.

CHAPTER 11

I Get Some Heart, Hear of a Strange Romance, and Take Part in a Funeral

---

As we traveled toward my destination at Pumpkinseed Station, I wondered how I would feel to be among strangers again. The bullwhackers were an odd assortment, sparse with talk or tenderness. Still, I was used to their ways.

After the incident of the squaw, when Gabriel carried me, I thought we might be friends. But Gabriel kept his distance. He did not hunt with us, nor did he sit with us. After supper he rolled himself up in his blanket and vanished into his own world of sleep. In the morning he was always the first one up, setting the fire for coffee.

One morning, when I awoke, there he was dragging a huge portion of buffalo, already skinned and quartered. Apparently he had been up for hours doing his hunting in private.

The other men commented lightly, "Got yourself a fine cow there, Gabriel."

"Good job with that hide—nary a scratch on it."

"How'd you hit it, Gabriel? Musta been clean through the breast and forehead."

To all their comments Gabriel grunted and nodded, setting himself to the task of stripping the meat for jerky. But I saw the trace of a smile at the corners of his mouth. He was pleased with himself.

I ambled over to him and said, "How will you fix the meat up to dry?"

Gabriel grunted. He drew a long cord taut along the side of his wagon, fastened it down, and hung the slivered meat, doubled over, upon it.

"How long will it hang there to dry?"

"Long enough," replied Gabriel, continuing with his task. I saw that he had saved the heart and liver, putting them inside the pouch that was the stomach lining.

"Will you eat those?"

Gabriel nodded. He gave me a long look. "I guess you could use some heart."

I nodded. "Much obliged," I said. So, I had found a way to reach him. He would make a ceremony of eating these parts, Indian fashion. Had he taken on Indian ways? Was that why he resisted getting close to white folks?

I wondered what gods he might serve, for I had heard that the Indians prayed to many spirits. Ma would take a fit if she knew I was about to eat with a pagan. How long, I wondered, would the voices of my absent parents continue to haunt me?

That night Gabriel gave me a taste from the stew he had prepared, all boiled together in the pouch. He handed me a portion in an old tin plate. I nodded my thanks, looking up at him as he squatted by the fire, sampling his stew. It was savory, spiced with herbs he had found. I waited for him to speak.

He drew back and said, "I see you lookin' at me. You think you know about me. You know nothing."

"I—I'm sorry."

"Just quit lookin' at me, you hear?"

"I hear. And I thank you for the victuals."

"Try to give you some heart, is all. You gonna need it."

He gave me a long, hard look that made me shiver. I wished I had never spoken to him.

———◆◆◆———

As we traveled from one station to the next, all along the river, we left supplies. When a wagon was emptied, Adam left it for the return trip, to be filled with hides and dried fish and Indian works to sell in the East.

At the stations we took on water, occasional garden tomatoes, onions, or corn. Fresh vegetables were the greatest treat, and I recalled my childhood, when Ma made me eat them. Now I craved them powerful bad.

Sometimes we'd catch glimpses of the Pony Express rider as he whipped past us on the road, hair flying, horse and rider looking like ghosts in the night, swift as wind. Once the rider waved back to me. Usually they just pressed on. How I envied them! What I wouldn't give for a sturdy pony and a bag of mail to deliver, along with whoops of admiration and cheers even from such as the bullwhackers.

We had pulled into Platte station one late afternoon, when I saw Ruski sitting under a tree, patting and pulling the thick orange beard that hung down to his chest. He was swaying back and forth, eyes closed, lips moving silently. In his hand was a letter. I saw the stamp. Five dollars was the price. I wondered what news could possibly require such extravagance.

If the others noticed Ruski's trance, none spoke about it. A man's private business is private. Women are different; they will stuff your head with words. I felt proud to be silent among the men, bridling my curiosity.

But Ruski sat there for over an hour, caressing his letter, and at last I could stand it no longer. I let myself down beside him, as if that particular tree trunk were the only backrest around. Like him, I stared and swayed and nodded to myself. Finally I had to speak. "You got a letter?"

"Yup."

"How'd they know where to send it?"

"I arranged it beforehand. Knew we'd stop here."

"I guess a body would have to plan it, then, knowing their kin was passing by."

"Yup."

"And it costs dear."

"Yup."

I ventured the question. "Is it good news or bad?"

He looked up at me, eyes wide. Then he gave a shy smile. "A bride," he said in a low voice. "I'm getting me a bride."

I was astonished. "By letter?" I whispered back.

"Yup. Wanna see her picture?"

"Sure do." He brought forth the picture, tucked into the envelope, and held it out for me to see. The woman was surely plain, round faced and doughy, hair all tucked under, and she frowned even while she tried to smile.

"Fine-looking woman," I lied.

Ruski nodded with pleasure. "Tall, she is. Five foot eight. A good, strong woman. Look at her hands."

Indeed, her hands, folded across her lap, were as large as a man's and gnarled from toil.

"She'll make a fine wife," I said.

"Aye. She will. We're to live in Virginia City. I found me a spread out there some miles past town. We'll grow cattle and sheep. I'm tired of wandering. You'll see. A man needs a woman to keep him sane."

I went into the station, a dismal hovel infested with vermin, smelling horribly of rot and filth. I thought about Ruski and his bride. I had only been to one wedding in my life, that of a farmer's girl nearby. Who would I ever talk to about such matters as marriage, unless I found my pa? My only real friend was Hank, and soon we would part. There were things I wanted to ask, but I didn't dare.

I never knew Hank had a harmonica until that night. We sat out under the stars, and the moon beamed down like a large, round face. A spell of loneliness came over me. It must have infected Hank, likewise, for he brought out that harmonica and began pulling chords out of it, sad and melancholy, like a coyote baying for its mate. I asked him, "What'll you do after this trek's over, Hank?"

"Told you," he said brusquely. "I'm going to see that girl of mine."

"You going to marry her?" I asked.

"Naw. Some men ain't the marryin' kind."

"How does a man know a thing like that?"

"Well, my pa married himself five different women."

"Five! How can that be?" I exclaimed.

"Two died, two run off, and the last one's so sharp nobody can stand it. I guess Pa's got his just deserts, beating up on everyone, and now getting beat up by that woman with her broom and her tongue. No, I don't aim to marry anyone. Glad I got out of the house when I did."

"When did you leave home, Hank?"

"Oh, I was a bit younger than you. Thirteen. That woman took her tongue to me one time too often, and I lit out."

"Don't you miss your pa?"

"My pa's a drunk, and a mean one at that. Don't nobody miss a mean drunk."

Well, I was lucky, wasn't I? My pa never drank. But now I wondered, was he the marrying kind? Surely he had loved my mother. Didn't they have that picture of their wedding, all done up so fine?

But then I remembered hearing sharp voices and cries in the night. I recalled Ma's face the day he left, how it tightened, and her smile was never quite the same after that. Oh, they used to be merry sometimes, even dancing 'round the cabin, Ma whirling, Pa singing. But that was so very long ago it seemed like mere dreams and shadows. What would Pa say when I told him she was dead? Would he sob and grieve? Oh, of course he would, sob and grieve something terrible, pained that he had left her, left us. Oh, poor Pa, how it would tear at him. I felt so sorry for him now.

"What about you?" Hank asked. "You and Molly?"

I was startled to hear her name spoken out loud, here in the lonely night. I felt my face flush. "Well, Molly's different from other girls," I began, "not squeamish or scared. Why, she'll stand right up to anyone. She ain't afraid of horses or hard work or her mean old brothers."

"I guess you'd say she's brave," Hank murmured. I thought I heard a queer little smile in his tone.

"Well, I guess so!" I said stoutly. "She even wanted to come out west, with no fear of Indians or storms or bandits. Said she wouldn't even miss her ma."

"Not if you were with her," said Hank in that same silly tone. "I guess Molly's sweet on you, Clem."

Now my face burned, and I started up with a jolt, quick to deny it. "What? How can you say such a thing, Hank? You don't know her at all." And then my voice got sort of husky, and I asked him, "How do you know when a girl is sweet on a fellow? How can you tell?"

Hank laughed and laughed, then drew out his harmonica and started to play a jig, enough to make anyone laugh. I did laugh right out loud, so glad, but why, I couldn't say, except that those words kept tumbling through my head . . . *"I guess Molly is sweet on you, Clem!"*

<hr/>

It made me glad, the next day at nooning, to see the familiar faces of my friends from the fort, the two little boys, Malcolm and Rusty. I knew them even from a distance by their red hair. They stood beside their wagon, Malcolm holding the baby over his shoulder, and Rusty sitting down with his younger sister, a child of three. The four small figures looked lost amid the wide expanse of prairie, with the road spread behind them and before them, like forever.

We came near, with myself in the lead. I stopped short when I saw the father, a lean redheaded man, with threadbare clothes, bent over a hole. His cheeks were feverishly red and moist, his face contorted, so that his eyes were all but concealed. He did not cease his shoveling even as we approached.

"Need some help there, brother?" asked Adam.

"No, thanks."

"It's powerful hard digging alone, brother," said Adam. Never had I heard him call another man "brother." What was this fellow to him? And then I saw the two bundles, one tiny, the other large, both wrapped in sheeting.

"Your wife?"

"Died birthing the baby. It's dead too."

"You alone here?"

The man nodded, still digging. He struggled to master the tears that poured freely down his face.

I turned to look at the children. Their faces were blank, their backs to the soft prairie wind, eyes straight ahead. What had they to look forward to now? Who would care for the baby?

As if to answer my sorrowful thoughts, Malcolm and Rusty came toward me, with baby and little sister in tow. "Ma and the baby are gone," Malcolm told me solemnly. "It's my job to look after these young'uns now, while Pa does the driving. This here's Phoebe. I can't let her run off."

"Well, that's fine," I managed to say. "You'll do a good job."

"Got a bed for the baby in the wagon," he went on. "Want to see? We got wrapping for her to wear, and a blanket. Want to see?"

I nodded and let the boys show me their wagon. With Malcolm's prompting, I opened the flap and peered inside. There stood an upholstered chair, bright blue material in a design of small squares of a deeper shade. The chair belonged in a parlor, alongside the spinning wheel that was wedged in between several pots and barrels, an open trunk containing dishes and silverware. Along the sides of the wagon, tucked into the staves that held the canvas top, were several dresses, an apron, and some boys' shirts.

I stared at the dresses. One day soon the little boys would feel sick at the sight of them. Now, they were still numb. I knew the feeling. I wished I could take those dresses away for them, but I must not meddle.

Adam, Ruski, and Gabriel had gone back to our wagons for their shovels. Now they stood with the father, digging, throwing the hard dirt into mounds. A string of covered wagons rolled past. A few of the emigrants stared as they went by. Most kept their eyes peeled straight ahead, and I heard a man call to his children, "Run on ahead, boys! Get along, now."

At last the digging was done.

We gathered around.

"Wisht I had wood for a coffin," gasped the father. He seemed to lack breath; his whole body sagged. "Is it deep enough? They say that wolves will come and dig up . . ."

"No, no. We will put stones on top." It was Gabriel, his voice low and reassuring. "Nothing will disturb them. Look, see that rock. We will bring it over. It will make a fine marker. We can write on it."

I was astonished at Gabriel's control, while the other men only stood with their hands clasped, heads hanging down.

Gabriel led us to the rock. Together, with the help of a single plank, we managed to move the boulder that, while of middling size, seemed to weigh tons. I was glad for the ache and the agony of lifting. I was glad to lend a hand.

The father and Adam laid the woman down, still wrapped in sheeting. "I kin hardly spare the cloth," gulped the husband, "but nor can I leave her without . . ."

"It is the right thing to do," said Gabriel.

The husband nodded. He picked up the baby, held it close to his chest.

"It—we did not name her yet. She lived only a few minutes."

"Let me baptize her." Gabriel took the tiny bundle into his arms. He turned to Adam and murmured, "Water."

Adam handed him the leather flask he always wore slung around his shoulder.

Gabriel shook several drops of water onto his large, dark hand. He touched the drops to the baby's forehead. "I baptize thee," he said, "in the name of the Father, the Son, and the Holy Ghost." He turned to the father. "What is her name?"

"Martha. We had thought—Martha."

"Martha," echoed Gabriel.

"Amen," we all said.

The father took the baby and placed it in the mother's arms. I dared not look at his face, yet I could not look away. The struggle raging within showed only in the trembling of his hands and lips; otherwise, he was staunch.

He put a hand on a shoulder of each of his boys. "You go along now," he commanded. "Lay the baby in her bed, and the three of you go and gather fuel. Go along now, and no lollygagging."

The children went to do as they were told. Then the men filled in the grave. Finally, straining with every ounce of our combined strength, we moved the boulder on top of the raw earth. The father knelt, one knee on the ground, brushing away some stray dry grass.

"Would you carve in their names?" he asked.

"The boy can do it," said Gabriel, nodding at me.

I reached for my knife, cursing the knot in my throat, the pain in my chest. "What was the lady's name?" I asked, trying to bring my voice up to normal.

"Agnes. Agnes and Martha. Last name's Mills. And put the date."

"Yes, sir. I'll be proud to."

Somehow I realized that the father could neither read nor write. It made me more determined to do this proper. I set my mind and my hand to it, bearing down hard.

It took a long time to form the letters and etch them into the stone. I didn't care. If it took forever, I would inscribe those names, Agnes and Martha Mills, and the date, July 1860.

We walked back—Gabriel, Adam, Ruski, and I. Our shadows stretched before us. Mine was half the size of theirs, but I felt as tall as the rest of them. Now I had seen the elephant, as they say, but I was still going ahead.

I dared to ask Gabriel. "Are you a preacher, then?"

He did not reply.

"Anyone can baptize," said Ruski. "It does not need a preacher."

"Well," said Adam. "Well."

We went on, each thinking our own thoughts. I was glad to be among men. There was nothing to say, nothing that would explain or change anything.

After that day I began to notice the number of graves set along the trail.

CHAPTER 12

We Tell Our Tales on the Lonesome Trail, I Sing for Molly, and Gabriel Charges Me with a Task

At the small settlement of Plum Creek we stopped to deliver supplies and to bathe in a deep, quiet pool screened by a row of cottonwood trees. Plum Creek had the usual station house, blacksmith shop, and dry goods emporium, meaning a wooden stall with sundry barrels of dried beans, pickles, sugar, and flour, some broken wagon wheels, and an enormous, abandoned bedstead. There was not a mite of cloth to be had, nor rubberized sheets or any decent tools. Nails cost twenty-five cents for a handful. A woolen blanket, rare to find, was twelve dollars. I wished for a tin pot of my own but hadn't the nickel to spare. I was glad that my creature cravings were few, as I had little in coin to satisfy them.

What I craved, however, at the sight of the homesteads tucked into low hills, with wild rabbits and turkeys running strong—what I craved was woodsmoke and hearth, real dishes, and a quilt. In short, I missed home.

Plum Creek struck all the men similarly. Perhaps it was the homestead we passed that afternoon, where a young farmer and his children worked together, clearing their own land. They looked happy as they worked their vegetable garden and split logs for their home. From a separate corral came a bellow. There lounged a bull, grandiose with widespread horns. The bull eyed our laboring oxen with disdain. They had some dogs, too, one old and moth-eaten but still wagging its tail and whimpering a welcome.

That night Hank brought out his harmonica, playing a doleful melody, "My Dog Tray." We sang the words:

> *"The morn of life is past,*
> *And evening comes at last;*
> *It brings me a dream of a once happy day*
> *Of merry forms I've seen*
> *Upon the village green,*
> *Sporting with my old dog Tray."*

The men got to talking about old times, their youth, and their plans. None but Ruski had his future mapped out. The bullwhackers lived from season to season until death or old age made their decision for them.

Now, for the first time, Ruski confessed his intentions to the group. The men clapped him on the back, exclaiming, "Oh, you're a gone sucker now!" They launched into a round of exuberant cussing, called him "Old Coot" and "Old Puke," they were that glad to see him happy. They passed around the picture of the ugly bride and drank to her health, praising and lamenting the marital state all in the same breath.

"Maybe next time we see you you'll have a young'un by your side," said Hank. "You gonna let him be a bullwhacker?"

Ruski shook his head, bewildered by all the attention. "Can't tell. It could be up to his ma."

"You never know what shapes a young'un," Adam said, with a solemn nod and a groan. "I always wanted to go to sea."

"Why didn't you?"

"Never got to the coast, is why. My pa caught me trying to run off and whipped me good. Got me a job tending stock. Pa was a bull-whacker. So's my uncle. Guess I have them critters in my blood."

"Well, what'd you want to do on the coast?"

"Wanted to go to sea. Smell the salt air and feel the rolling ocean under my feet. Always wanted it, ever since I could remember, a puny boy of three or four. Don't know how I heard about the sea, but I wanted it. Still do."

That launched Silas into his tale.

I have not mentioned his physique before, but Silas was a thickset, burly man who walked with a decided limp, one leg being remarkably shorter than the other. Running, Silas looked like a wounded bear. Now, Silas told of his childhood in Tennessee. "I was raised by my grandfather. My folks both died of the cholera the year I was born. That left me and Sister, who was only five at the time. Grandfather took us in."

"Wasn't there a woman too? Didn't he have a wife?" asked Raisin, frowning.

"Oh, he had, but Grandma was teched in the head and never left the house. She did bake biscuits. Yep, every day, that's what she did. Never want to see another biscuit as long as I live."

"So what made you want to be a bullwhacker?" asked Blue. He tossed a small stick into the fire.

"Not sure I ever really decided. Guess it was a matter of getting even, or proving something. I was four years old," said Silas, squinting against the firelight. "Grandfather had a bull. It was a mean-tempered critter, if ever I saw one. It pawed down a whole tree, stomped up chunks of earth. I swear, that bull snorted fire."

"You were rightly afraid of it," commented Adam.

"Dang right! Well, I was all of four years old, out there alone with my grandfather. One day Grandfather caught me and set me up on the fence, then put me down in that bull pen at the way far end, where the bull was standing under a tree, just waiting for trouble."

"He put you in with the bull?" I exclaimed.

"Yeah."

"Then what'd he do?"

"Told me to run."

We all gaped at Silas.

"I ran," said Silas. "Dang it, I ran like crazy, with that bull snorting at my heels. I could feel his breath. Slid underneath the rail fence. My grandfather was laughing so hard I thought his sides would bust."

"But the bull didn't get you," I said.

"Nope. I ran fast. Even with my bum leg."

There was silence, as nobody had ever made mention of Silas's limp. I wondered whether the grandfather was responsible for that too.

Silas sighed, then said, "Maybe he was making me run to show me I could do it, even with this bum leg of mine. Maybe it was a kindness after all."

I sat there pondering the difference between kindness and cruelty, and how you might tell one from the other. The talk went on, about bulls and steers and oxen, and you'd be surprised how many stories were just waiting to pour out, once the ice was broken.

Hank had a tale about Brigham Young, the Mormon leader. At the word "Mormon," Adam recoiled, but it was late, and everyone in the mood for talk, so Hank went on. Seems that at the start of his ministry, Brigham Young came upon a bunch of Norwegian fellows beating their oxen.

"The wagons were heavily loaded and stuck fast in the mud, blocking up the road," related Hank. "Some of the men were whipping the oxen and cursing them in their language, which seemed to scare the oxen, but they couldn't get the wagons moving. So Brigham Young jumps out of his coach, steps up and takes the whip out of the hands of this Norwegian fellow, and tells everyone to stand back."

We all waited, turned toward Hank, and I knew I would sorely miss such nights as this when they left me off at Pumpkinseed Station.

"Well, Brigham Young spoke to those oxen in a tongue that nobody understood, neither Norwegians nor Americans. But those oxen went to work and pulled the wagon right out of the mud, quick and smooth as a wink. Just talked to them. Hard to believe, but there you are."

Silas slapped his thigh and turned to Gabriel. "Is that why you don't use the whip, Gabriel? You a Mormon?"

"No," said Gabriel. "I just don't like whipping anything alive."

"Well, if you was to meet a Mormon face-to-face," said Adam, frowning darkly, "likely you'd want to whip him."

Gabriel turned his face away, hunkering down under his blanket, as if he refused to hear any more.

"You ever hear of the Mountain Meadows Massacre?" Adam persisted. "Those Mormons tricked a bunch of emigrants passing through their land, told them they'd protect them from the local Indians, then turned on them and killed them. Slaughtered all but a few babies, which they kept for themselves. It happened just outside of Salt Lake City. Man, I'd never set foot in that place. I always take the northern route. Can't pay me to go through Salt Lake, it's a devastation."

"They got themselves their own empire," said Ruski, breathing heavy and pulling at his beard. "They are rebels, if you ask me. Needs our cavalry to teach 'em a lesson! You know they take all sorts of wives. They say Brigham Young has two hundred of 'em, all young girls."

"Adultery," said Raisin. "That's what it is. Adultery, clear and simple."

"Oughtn't to allow it in the United States," said Blue. "It's against the law."

I'd heard about adultery in church, but I hadn't a clear notion about it, and neither did I care. It did interest me that a man could sweet-talk an ox out of a ditch, however, and I was determined to try it sometime.

Well, the talk had gone 'round, and Adam said to me, "You'll be leaving us soon, Clem. Next day or two we'll be setting you off at your station. How about a story to leave us with?"

I allowed as I had no stories, but they prodded and insisted, so I thought again. Sure, I had a story. I told them about poor old Oliver Twist and how he was abandoned and ill-treated, and how my own life was like that after Ma and Joy May died. I launched into my days at the tavern with old Drogan, how I was cut up, and I showed them the scar, which they viewed with interest. I told how I'd wanted to sign up for the Pony Express and how, I was setting out on my new job as assistant stock tender, and that I planned to go to California before too long to find my pa.

"Clem, how do you think you'll get to California?" asked Silas.

"I don't know," I admitted. "I guess I'll earn some money and then take the stagecoach."

"How're you gonna find your pa when you ge there?" asked Raisin, looking troubled, chewing a straw.

"Won't be any trouble at all to find him!" I cried, suddenly agitated. "He's a Frenchman, and so personable, everyone would know him."

This was met with silence, men twisting their mouths, pulling on their pipes.

"They'll be ways!" I insisted. "I'll go hunt him up in the gold fields, and if he ain't there, I'll go to the city. Maybe—maybe I'll check out the cemetery." It felt like a stone had landed on my chest. I had finally spoken the thought that was on every man's mind: Pa was probably dead. Why else wouldn't we have heard from him all this time?

"Sure, you'll find him," Hank said. "Likely he'll have struck gold and got so busy tending his money he didn't have time to write. Likely he's a big man in the West, with a place of his own, just waiting for you to come and work it with him."

"He'll be right glad to see you," Ruski said.

I still felt glum. What did they know about Pa? Nothing!

"Tell 'em about Molly," Hank said, and I could tell he was trying to cheer me up.

"There's nothing to tell." I grumbled.

The men all started grinning and slapping their thighs.

Hank took up his harmonica and commenced to playing "Molly! Do You Love Me?" Blue caught up the tune with his fiddle. Those burly bullwhackers actually got on their feet and started dancing. Silas and Adam pretended they were a couple, then they pulled Ruski and Raisin up to join them.

"Molly, do you love me?" they chorused.

I'd never heard the song before, but now I learned it well, for it was burned into my mind the way my face burned at the teasing. Just then, sitting by the fire so late at night, I swear I could smell the scent of Molly's hair and see the blue of her eyes, as if she were here with me. And I sang along in my heart:

> *"Molly! Do you love me?*
> *Tell me, tell me true!*
> *Molly! Do you love me,*
> *Love as I love you?"*

Two days later we crossed over the Platte, for Adam had it in mind to visit a band of Indians he knew lodged in the vicinity. I saw their tepees from a distance, those pointed cones rising up starkly against the blue sky. I sat down and made a heap of sketches of those tepees.

Adam made all the rest of us stay with the wagons while he disappeared on horseback, taking only Silas along. The two returned at nightfall, laden with buffalo skins, beaver, and muskrat. With them came eight or ten braves, decked out in feathers and amulets, drawing a wooden cart between two horses, in the manner of Roman chariots I had heard mentioned in the Bible. Well, they loaded their chariot with three kegs of whiskey and were soon gone.

I noticed Gabriel sucking in his lip disapprovingly.

He and I had not spoken, except the merest necessities. Therefore I was surprised when he awakened me very early in the morning, shaking my shoulder and pushing a small, battered photograph into my face.

I looked up, startled.

"You'll be leaving us today," he said. "I want to show you this picture, just in case you get to California to find your pa. If you see this lady, tell her where I am."

"Where are you?" I asked, shaking my head in that confusion of semisleep.

"On the trail. Whackin' bulls. She can get a message to me at Fort Kearny."

"What's her name?"

"Sara."

"Is that all?"

"Sara Taylor. Same as mine. She's my wife."

Now I sat up in earnest, itching to know more. Gabriel went to start a fire for coffee. I followed. I had the feeling that now was the moment, now or never. I made myself wait, though patience has never been my virtue, and sure enough, while the water boiled, he told me his story.

CHAPTER 13

Gabriel Tells His Story of Slaves and Crocodiles, and I Make a Picture of Sara

G abriel waved over to several rocks and indicated we would sit down. Then he began. "You think by the color of my skin, you know me. Are all black men alike? Or white men? Are you like your neighbor or even like your own father?"

I was stunned and silent. What he said was true. I had assumed much about Gabriel, but I had not the courage to admit it.

"You see me as a slave. I can't blame you for it. Sometimes, when I look in the glass, I see myself that way too. That is what has been done to us. We cannot see each other the way we really are, inside."

I nodded, confounded by Gabriel's words and his look. He might have been a preacher, I thought, fierce and passionate.

Gabriel went on. "A man's history begins with his birth, don't you agree?"

I nodded.

"I was born in Ohio. I was born free. You ask me how that came to be?"

"How?" I breathed. I had never known of any black man who wasn't a slave.

"Glad you asked, so I will tell you. My father's grandfather, Thomas, was a slave in Virginia, on the plantation of General George Washington. Have you ever heard of Mount Vernon?"

"Sure. Home of George Washington, our first president. "

"Do you know how many slaves he had?"

"No."

"Hundreds. Washington was a very rich man. He owned over thirty thousand acres. He had his own mill for making his wheat into flour, and his own distillery, where whiskey was produced from the rye that grew in his fields. He had one hundred acres in peas alone. Corn, flax, vegetables—pigs, chickens, cattle, sheep. Think on it!"

I reflected on our tiny homestead and garden. George Washington was a wealthy man.

"It was all tended by slaves," said Gabriel. "Black men and women and children. They lived in crude huts, slept on the ground. If they were lucky there might be straw. For food they got one gallon of corn a week and twenty herrings a month. They received one pair of breeches every year, and a jacket. Many of the children ran naked altogether. No holidays, no Sundays; they worked every day of the year. General Washington treated his slaves better than most. He had them whipped only when the occasion demanded it. Others gave their blacks only bread and water and beatings regular."

I felt ill, with Gabriel's eyes fastened on my face. I could see the stark whites, the small red veins, the intense darkness of his pupils. The eyes seemed to jump and quiver, at the same time holding fast to mine, sorrowful, angry, and accusing.

"My great-grandfather, Thomas, worked in the wheat fields. Family lore has it that he could read, even when he was a slave. Don't know how he learned it, as it was forbidden to teach colored people reading. He must have been smart." I saw the slight lift of Gabriel's chin. "When the war came, Thomas volunteered to fight in the general's army."

"What war?" I breathed.

"Revolution, freedom from England," said Gabriel. "Freedom, of course, for the white man. Except that"—and here Gabriel sucked in his breath, hard—"if a black man would fight for a whole year in the army, he could win his freedom. That is what my great-grandfather did. That is why I was born free."

Gabriel shifted his weight, looked away. I wanted to cry out that I had nothing to do with slavery! Had I captured anyone? Had I forced them to work, starved and beaten them? All those words lay in my mouth like lead; I felt guilty, somehow, ashamed of my color.

"So, my father moved up north after he was grown, and he married my mother, who was also free and worked as a seamstress. My father was a cabinetmaker. He made bureaus and bedsteads and rocking chairs. Beautiful work. Every piece fit together with pegs and glue. No nails."

"How did he learn it?" I inquired.

"He apprenticed himself to master craftsmen. He didn't get paid, but he learned. But up north, he wasn't allowed to open his own shop. Oh, he could work for a white man, running and fetching and so on. But put his own name to his work? No. Never, not even in the wonderful North," he said, with smooth sarcasm, "where they *love* the black folks and *rail* against slavery. Let me tell you, sometimes those that say they love you are worse than those who admit to the hate. Worse."

I trembled at Gabriel's passion, for he rose and spoke like that orator I'd heard in the schoolhouse, his fist raised, nostrils flared. I asked, "Why couldn't your father open his own shop?"

"Colored can't be in the union," Gabriel replied. "Without the union, you've got nothing, no license, no customers. Have to be in the union, that's all. Oh, he found work, but his only customers were colored folks, with little money to spend. How could he ever prosper?

"So I decided to make my living doing something nobody can stop me from. I learned blacksmithing, piano playing, bullwhacking, and I read the law."

"You read the law? Like Mr. Lincoln!" I exclaimed, happy to have some knowledge to interject.

Gabriel sighed. "The more I learned about the law, the worse I felt," he said. He got the coffee and poured it into two tin cups. I could smell the essence of it. That coffee poured thick as mud into the cups, just the way I'd grown to like it, with a bitter, chalky taste.

Gabriel sat back down and continued. "It is the law that black men can be slaves to white. It is the law that they can be sold, like cattle. Some people think it is what God intended. Mr. Stephen Douglas said so in his debate with Abraham Lincoln."

"Maybe some folks do believe it," I said, thinking with shame of my ma. How could I stand against her, whom I loved? How could I not trust the terrible feeling in my heart, that slavery was wrong, dead wrong?

A muscle twitched in Gabriel's cheek; his breath was quick and hot. "This same Stephen Douglas told exactly where he stands. He said, 'When the struggle is between a white man and the Negro, I am for the white man. When it is between the Negro and the crocodile, I am for the Negro.'"

I was aghast. "A man is not a crocodile," I exclaimed.

"This Mr. Douglas wants to be president."

"What happens if he wins?" I asked.

Gabriel didn't answer.

"Tell me more of the law," I said.

Gabriel clasped his hands around his cup, and between swallows of coffee he went on. "Well, the law says a black man is not a citizen, so he cannot go to court if he has a problem. A black man cannot move from one state to the other, without being caught and sent down south, accused of being a runaway slave, even if he isn't."

"That's the law?"

"That's the law. Slave hunters from the South can come up north to catch a black man and bring him back to their plantation. Trouble is, sometimes they make a mistake." Gabriel's breath hissed between his teeth. "They can't tell one black from another."

I sat there silent, though disbelief must have shown on my face.

"You want proof?" Without waiting for an answer Gabriel stood up and pulled off his shirt. I saw his massive chest, muscled and wide. He turned. I gagged.

"Look at it!"

I looked again. Across Gabriel's back lay thick welts, where flesh had been cut apart and grown together numerous times, in a tree-limb pattern of twisted black lines that intersected and blistered.

I could not speak. My hands trembled. Gabriel reached over and took the cup from my hands, set it down on a stone. Slowly he put his shirt back on, sat down, his hands swinging between his outspread knees.

"I'm sorry," he said, breathing heavily. "It wasn't fair, I guess."

"Who did it to you?" I asked, blinking back tears.

"A black man. He was in charge of the slaves, you see, overseer of all of them, told when to punish, when to kill. He did exactly as he was told. This was eighteen lashes. I counted every one of them. Then I blacked out."

"They thought you had run away? How could they, if you were born free?"

"I was in Ohio, minding my business. One night, while I was walking home, three men came up behind me, and they threw a net over my head and a rope around my arms, and they took me south."

"They kidnapped you!" I cried, leaping up, indignant.

"Good word, kidnapping," said Gabriel, with a nod and a rueful smile. "Only *they* called it *recapturing*. They were sure I was a fugitive, runaway slave from Georgia. What was a black man doing, running around free? Maybe I looked like this runaway brother. Who knows? Next thing, I found myself tied up and transported in a cart, all the way to Georgia, dumped in front of this overseer, whose master gave him orders to teach me a lesson. The master looked at me. Maybe he knew the mistake, maybe not. Maybe one black man, to him, was as good as another. They put chains on my ankles. You can still see the mark." He showed me the place. "If I ran away again, he said, they'd cut the tendons in my heels. That keeps 'em on the plantation, all right!"

"But you did escape. You got away."

"Oh, yes. I did. After a year and a half. And I made it to Nebraska. I wandered all across this territory. I wasn't going to live among white men ever again. So I lived with the Indians for a time, and it was good. Very good."

"Then why didn't you stay?"

"Because, in my soul, I am not an Indian, either. I fall between two worlds, don't you see? The things I want are not the things the Indian wants. I want a home, a place to put down roots. I'm savin' for a piece of land, a little sod house. And there is my wife, Sara."

Now Gabriel brought out the ragged photograph of his wife. He stared at it. "Look at that—so pretty, so sweet. I met Sara at the plantation. See how that terrible thing turned out to have some good in it."

"That has never happened to me," I declared. "When my pa left us, and my ma and the baby died, I saw no good in it."

"Well, sometimes it takes a long time and a long distance to see it," he said. Then he laughed. "Sometimes it takes forever."

I shook that off and asked, "How come your wife went away without you?"

"She ran off. Had to. Master wanted her for himself, and she swore she'd kill herself rather than give in. We were already married. Oh, she was so good and pretty and smart. I taught her to read, and she picked it up quick! I was sweet on her the moment I saw her. Know what that's like? Well, you're young yet. You'll see. We were married there in the fields. Jumped the broom, we did. Oh, they all sang and clapped and made it a proper wedding, though we lacked a real preacher. I took the vow and so did she, so I expect the Almighty did allow it."

I was thinking that for a man who didn't like to talk much, Gabriel sure gushed out words once he got started. I didn't mind at all. I was curious.

He continued. "I had heard about the Underground Railroad, which isn't a railroad at all, but only some folks helping slaves on their way, once they've broken out. I told Sara about it, how she could find folks to help hide her."

"How did you know those people?" I asked. "Were you in that railroad too?"

"Not then," said Gabriel, hanging his head. "Until I was captured,

I tell you the truth, I didn't lift a finger to help anyone else. Later, it was different. But that's another story. Sara had to go, and I told her, 'Go as far as you can. Go west, all the way to California, if you can.'"

"Did she go?"

Gabriel nodded. "She went in the night, during a terrible storm. The weather would gain her some time. She went across the wetlands, swamps. She was terrible scared of snakes, but more scared of the master."

"Why didn't you go with her?" I felt the fury of that storm, the wetness, the wind.

"I still had the chains and could not get them off. I would have slowed her down or been recognized, for sure. Later, when the master thought I was broken, they removed the chains. I fled that very night—ran like a hound! And I found some folks to help me across the river, up through Missouri until I came here. Of course, I asked about Sara. I found out she had made it all the way across Georgia and into Kentucky. I asked everywhere, but the trail ended. Maybe she went to Canada, but I don't think so. She hated the cold. I've searched this entire state, one end to the other. Now, I'm not leaving Nebraska anymore."

"You won't go on looking?" If it were somebody I loved, surely I wouldn't give up, but keep on hunting for them. Wasn't I on this road to find my pa?

"I—have done some things," Gabriel said, his voice low. "I can't leave here and cross the border. But I have this picture of her. Master had it taken when he bought her, that's how pretty she was. He gave her the picture. Now maybe it will help me find her."

"Maybe so," I echoed, looking hard at the photograph. She looked no different to me than a hundred other black women, with a nice, round face, wide-apart eyes, full mouth, and a bandana twisted around her head. "If I find her," I said, "I'll surely tell her to write to you at Fort Kearny."

Gabriel clapped his large, warm hand over mine. "I know you will," he said. "You've got heart." He grinned. "I ought to know! I'm the one that fed it to you."

An idea lit up his eyes. "Hey! I've seen you draw. You could copy this picture and take it with you, show it to folks and ask about her."

"I suppose I could try," I admitted. "At the same time, I could make a picture of you too."

"No!" he shouted. "There is to be no likeness of me. None!"

I had made a sketch of Gabriel, dancing with the oxen. Now I drew it out of my sack and showed it to him. In the picture I had caught Gabriel's back, head, and shoulders turned to the side, one leg swinging in a kind of dance. "It doesn't show your face," I said. "Can I keep it?"

"Yes. It is not a real likeness. Now, if you want to draw a picture of Sara, I will tell you something while you work."

And while I sketched, Gabriel began another tale.

As I worked on the drawing, looking closely, I realized that Sara had her own personal look. Her brow was wide and high, her hairline dipped like a heart. At the right corner of her mouth was a small fold. When she smiled it would deepen, and her large, almond-shaped eyes would crease with laughter. By the time I had finished the picture of Sara, I felt that I knew her. By then, too, I knew Gabriel, for he had finished this tale with its twists and turns of fate.

CHAPTER 14

John Brown's Raid Was a Close Call, and I Find Some Awful Needy Critters at Pumpkinseed Station

---

Blackbirds and hawks soared and dipped and rose again to the blue, blue sky. Beneath my feet crept the lizards and field mice and spiders. Black-faced prairie dogs and gray squirrels rushed about, searching for food.

As I worked on my drawing of Sara, my eyes moving from photograph to paper, Gabriel said, "Remember how you asked me about John Brown?"

"Yes, I remember," I said, glancing up.

"Well, I knew John Brown. I was nearly there with him and his group at Harpers Ferry. I would have been hanged for it. If I'd been there, I'd now be stiff and cold."

Gabriel's voice had taken on the tone of the storyteller. I did not interrupt for fear that he would become silent again.

"That John Brown! He was some kind of man," said Gabriel, with awe in his voice. "Fire sparked in his eyes, and when he spoke it felt like thunder from the skies. He could look right through you, raise you up so high you thought you could fly! Oh, the crowds he gathered, how they listened and hung on his words, and then when he called out in that great voice of his, arms raised to heaven, 'Who is with me? Who marches with me?' you wanted to shout and march and fight. Yes, you wanted to do anything, everything, for the cause."

I looked up, waiting, seeing the transformation in Gabriel's face. He gleamed.

"His father was a preacher, you know. John grew up with a fierce hatred of injustice, especially of slavery. He traveled everywhere—Ohio, Pennsylvania, Massachusetts, New York—with his family, preaching against slavery, *screaming* against slavery. And then there came the time that talk wasn't enough for John Brown. He had to act. He had to take the Lord's vengeance into his own hands. That was John Brown, saint, prophet, sinner, murderer—all depends on your view. I'd never met any man like him before, never will again, and when he called us to action, how could I hold back? Here was a white man willing to lay down his life for black slaves. How could I do anything less?"

I glanced up to see Gabriel's face. It was wet with sweat or with tears, I could not tell which, only that his brow was furrowed, his mouth tight and grim.

"I knew the law. I knew injustice in the law. That was what John Brown was talking about to the crowds, and most of them listened and went home to their wives and their beds and did nothing. While John was speaking, the noise was loud! But later, there was only silence. Except for a few of us, who felt his fire and were consumed with it. And that was the question, the torment. Do we kill for the sake of justice? Or is this only vengeance? Do we dare have blood on our hands, and call ourselves servants of the Lord?

"I don't know whether John Brown asked himself any of these questions. Maybe he, too, was tormented. But he was a man of action. So he went to Kansas with his army—yes! We were the army of the Lord, he said, fighting to keep Kansas free of slavery. There was no possible compromise, he said. Only cowards compromise. Men of principle must act now, act strong, act bravely. And there, at

Pottawatamie, five men were killed. Murdered. They were unarmed."

The silence then was so long that I thought Gabriel had turned to stone. His face was set, eyes staring, as if he saw retribution clearly in his future. He was a wanted and a haunted man.

He went on. "After that, I lost track of John Brown, and I looked for Sara and could not find her, and then, just last year, I heard him again, and it all started over, the hope and the anger. He had this plan. There was no progress against slavery, only speeches and new laws— terrible laws that divided the country in half, that allowed slavery and called the black man chattel and said he could be sold, his children sold away from him, hunted down like a fugitive. Nothing was changing! We were in the middle of a war, he said, a holy war, though we didn't know it yet. 'I would forfeit my life for the furtherance of the ends of justice,' he said. John Brown had spent most of his life begging the abolitionists in the North to give him money for guns to use against the South, to make war against slavery. He had a few arms, but not enough. So he made a plan to take the government weapons, the arsenal at Harpers Ferry, capture the guns and ammunition, and to go south and arm the slaves with these weapons."

I stopped drawing, compelled now by Gabriel's story. I could see it all, John Brown inflaming the people, determining to give his life for the cause, ending the evil once and for all!

I said, "You were going with him? To Harpers Ferry?"

"I was going to join his army. Yes. He talked to Frederick Douglass about his plan. The great abolitionist, Douglass, begged him not to do it, said he'd never succeed. It was federal property; the president would call out the whole army! But John Brown wouldn't back off. No, he went and rented a farm across the river from Harpers Ferry, and there his small army gathered. Twenty-two of us. Six black men, the rest white. We were going to raid the arsenal the next morning, capture some of the leading citizens of the town and get their slaves to join the cause, then march on to gather a bigger and bigger army."

"And?" I prompted, for again Gabriel hesitated. "What happened? You said you didn't go."

"In the night I took sick. Shivering, shaking, I was out of my mind, saw things, like ghosts. My face was on fire with fever; I couldn't stand up. They went without me, of course. Left a woman behind to tend me. She's the one that got me up and out of there, for we heard that Brown and his men had captured the arsenal and the rifle works and took their hostages, but no slaves would join them. *None at all.* The local militia surrounded Brown. One of Brown's sons was sent out to negotiate, carrying a white flag. The militia shot him dead. They sent word to Washington, and the president sent Colonel Robert E. Lee with an army to Harpers Ferry, but by then the local militia had already killed ten of the men and captured the rest, including John Brown himself. Meantime, that woman got me out of the farmhouse with the help of two men. I never saw them before or afterward, never knew who to give thanks for my life, but there you are. They carried me like a sack of grain, dumped me in a horse-drawn cart, and took me to a shanty, where I lay until I recovered and then lit out for Nebraska territory. Here, nobody knew me or John Brown or seemed to care. Bullwhackers and mountain men and Indians just want to be left alone. And that goes for me too. Except that I do want to find Sara and set up in a little sod house, and maybe even have a family."

I had finished the picture of Sara, and I handed it to Gabriel now. He looked at it for a long time. Then he said, "I'm not a brave man, Clem. I'm just looking for a little peace in this world, and maybe some happy times along the way."

I don't know whether I'd call him brave or not. But it occurred to me that my goal was about the same as Gabriel's. Both of us were looking for loved ones, both of us were running from our pasts. Maybe everybody has something they're ashamed of and something they desire. Maybe that's what keeps 'em going.

I was nervous as we approached my new home, having by now met all manner of uncivilized station keepers living in various degrees of degradation. Every station was different. Sometimes it would be a tiny hut built of wood and straw or stuck into a hillside, to save a wall. Some were but heaps of stone without mortar, others an old barn welded together with mud. Occasionally, to our huge delight, we would come upon a real clapboard house, and a woman in it to serve up proper meals at a table.

We'd bed down on a heap of straw tossed onto a dirt floor, or a wooden plank with a blanket that had to be shared by three sleepers. Rare was the station where soap and water held any value. Towels were only a memory.

I didn't mind about dirt or vermin or lack of beds. What concerned me as we approached Pumpkinseed Station was food. I was hungry nearly all the time.

If Ma had seen me she would have been aghast, for my shirt-sleeves rode up halfway to my elbows and my pants legs, likewise, had shrunk as I grew. Where might I ever find money to purchase new clothes?

In the heat of the day we arrived at Pumpkinseed Station, and maybe the blur of heat made it all seem so unreal, so quick, like a dream. The bullwhackers bade me farewell in their way, with a hasty nod and a shrug.

Hank stood before me, shifting from one foot to the other. "Well, so long," he said. "Good luck. Hope you find your pa."

"I'll surely try," I said.

Hank nodded. I did likewise, saying, "So long, Hank." I watched him walk away, his shoulders sort of hunched. "Good-bye!" I hollered after him. "And keep your socks dry!" He turned around and gave me a wave and a grin.

Adam showed me to my new master. "This here's Bud Westerly, your new boss. Now, you mind him and you'll do just fine."

I said my best "how do you do," polite and gentlemanly, except that I was covered in grime from the trail.

"Howdy," said Bud, including both me and Adam in the greeting. "Expected an older man," he said.

I wondered what man of experience would exile himself in this forsaken wilderness? A single shed, a ramshackle hut, and a large corral were all the marks of human habitation—except for the outhouse, from which a powerful stink drifted clear out to the road. I had no doubt that I was to become its deputy.

Westerly didn't seem to mind the dirt on me. His own appearance was far from pure. An old cap, encrusted with dirt, lay over his stringy, blond hair. His long fingernails hosted enough dirt to sprout radish seeds. I had a notion of the sort of critters that might live in his beard.

I watched my friends, the bullwhackers, move out. Determined not to care, I watched their dust and heard the bellowing of the beasts.

Then Adam turned back to me. "Here's your pay for helping with the animals." He placed some silver coins into my hand.

My heart leapt with gratitude. Instantly I recovered, realizing that there was nothing out here to purchase. I was a king without a throne, a rider without a horse.

There was no point in having regrets. As Gabriel had said, who knows what Providence holds? I was here at Pumpkinseed Station, ready to take my chances.

Then Bud Westerly said, "Well, c'mon and get started. I know you was supposed to be the assistant, but my stock tender run off on me last week, and I don't know when they'll send me another. Meanwhile, you're it."

"Stock tender?" I exclaimed. I wondered whether my pay would rise according to my new position. Somehow, I dared not ask.

"Supper's at sundown," said the boss. "Meanwhile, there's an ailing horse out there, an ox with a festering shoulder, and a mule about to give birth. The fence has a break in it, and the stalls need to be mucked out. Think you can handle it?"

"Sure," I said. Under my breath I added, "If there were six of me!" But I put on a determined look and went out to meet my new charges.

The place hung at the edge of destruction, with torn rails, gouged-out turf, mean water troughs filled with green scum, and food bins infested with weevils. How any creature had stayed alive in this hotbed of neglect was amazing to me.

I took stock and found strength in my anger. First I pumped fresh water for the troughs, filled them to the brim and stood back as my grateful charges drank. I spread out the feed to let the weevils run loose; I filled in several foul-smelling ditches, bending to the shovel with all my weight. If I had feared loneliness, it vanished now that there was work to do.

For the ox I made a poultice of mud and wild mint and clapped it onto the animal's shoulder, holding it with my trembling hand. Until now, I had only been apprenticed, and the tending was left to Adam and the others. Now I was grateful to my teachers, the bullwhackers, for however they cussed and fumed at their oxen, they never neglected their wounds or illnesses. In fact, when an ox died, it was cause for real mourning.

This animal seemed to understand my concern, for he bellowed sorrowfully, head low, eyes fixed upon mine. There is something wondrous about seeing eye to eye with a creature. "There, buck," I said, "there, there, we'll make it, boy, you'll be fine."

In the corral we had half a dozen horses, mustangs mostly, but there was one little gray mare that was my favorite. Bud didn't know her name, so I called her Priscilla, for no other reason than that the name appealed to me. And she was a lady. She had certain ways about her. She rested with one foot held daintily off the ground, like a lady avoiding a mud puddle, stepping carefully. A beautiful white blaze on her forehead gave her a thoughtful look, and she was a serious animal, taking her feed slowly, reserved with the other horses. But first thing in the morning, she sported with the eagerness of a young foal. She would leap to meet me, running sideways with her head turned over her shoulder, bidding me to come and caress her. She had a way of raising her lip that made her look as if she were laughing, and it made me laugh outright many a time.

So it went, my work lasted from dawn to nighttime, when I took out a lantern and finished my chores by starlight, or I visited with Priscilla and told her tales. I had found some old sheets of ledger paper tucked away on a shelf at the station. I used it to make sketches of the animals, and I remembered all the times Molly and I had tended Albert together. Without those memories I'd have gone crazy out here on the empty plains, with only Bud Westerly for company, and an occasional Express rider rushing by.

The main work of the station, of course, was to provide relief horses for the Pony Express riders. They raced in, leaped from their mounts, slung off their special mochila saddle and tossed it over the fresh horse that waited, ready to run. It was my job to have the new horse ready when the rider arrived with the mail.

When the Express rider arrived to change horses, Bud Westerly would stand in the doorway of the station house and toss out half a loaf of bread and an apple or a potato. Within two minutes the rider was on his way. So it was that we gave refreshment and relief to the riders. Most of them were boys about my age, energetic and full of spirit.

I longed for a moment to talk to these boys, but it was not to be. Off they went, like the wind, determined to make their time. Then I was alone once more with the wind and the critters and Bud Westerly.

He was a study, that man. Not only did he seldom speak, but he was most likely one of the laziest men on earth. After breakfast, which meant a mix of cornmeal and hot water, sometimes laced with syrup, Bud yawned with exhaustion from the effort of getting out of bed. He resumed his rest on a thick straw pallet on the sagging old porch. There he lay, worrying a long straw between his teeth, that filthy cap pulled half over his face, until someone or something prodded him back to life.

Then he rose slowly, shuffled to whatever had demanded his attention, gave it a poke or a promise, and laid himself back down to recover from this labor. Occasionally he bestirred himself at dusk, went out, and flung a fishing pole into the river or sighted a hapless squirrel. Then we ate fish or squirrel potpie. The rest of the time we subsisted on field greens, wild onions, and the usual salt pork, dried beans, and corn pone that were the staples of emigrants and pioneers. We were fortunate to have a few chickens scratching about, but no cow. I longed for Belinda.

One day, after I had been with Bud for over a week, he sent me on an errand.

"About four miles thataway," he said, squinting and pointing northwest, "there's a sod house, woman in it, Elizabeth Silver, trades us some baked goods for corn. Ride on over there and take this sack."

"What horse can I take?"

"Suit yourself."

Of course, I chose my lady, Priscilla, saddled her up, and was off, with the sack of corn slung over my back.

I rode in the direction Bud had pointed, on and on, for the first time finding myself all alone on horseback on this vast prairie. For an instant, as I contemplated the sudden sight of Indians, a feeling of panic seized me. Somehow it subsided, and I let myself lean into the movements of my horse and the rhythm of the day, becoming calm and soon exhilarated. I was free! Alone and free, with nobody to charge me with any demands, to point me right or left. Free! I had not ridden Priscilla before. I discovered that we understood each other. She responded to the slightest shift of my weight, the turn of my hand, the touch of my heel.

Soon I came in sight of the house, which was not entirely of sod. Apparently the builder had run out of lumber before the little house was finished. The walls were logs of cottonwood, chinked with mud and clay. One wall was comprised of large blocks of sod, each perhaps three feet long, a foot and a half wide, and several inches thick. The blocks had been stacked like bricks to form the wall, which bulged slightly from the effects of weather and vermin. The house leaned to one side. Its builder was obviously an amateur, but he meant well and had provided several windows and a nice, wide door. The sod roof was tipped slightly forward, with tufts of grass and straw and sundry weeds making it part of the prairie. The windows had no glass but shutters that hung open. Outside stood various barrels and tubs, a mule that was loosely tethered to a rail fence, an old buckboard, several horses, and a trough. I heard the glad mooing of a cow and the squeal of a calf.

There was an air of tidiness about the place, for the front yard was swept, the mud caked and hard from numerous such sweepings, and a few clothes hung on a line at the left side of the house. I saw a curtain, some pattern of red, blue, and yellow, and my heart leaped at the sight. From the chimney came a thin trail of woodsmoke, and as I rode near, I inhaled the tantalizing odor of fresh bread.

I urged Priscilla onward with a flick of my heels. Two small dogs came running out, followed by three children, two boys and a girl, from perhaps the ages of six to ten or eleven.

Then out came a woman dressed in faded blue cambric and a long apron, her brown hair done in a twisted coil on top of her head. She looked to be about the age of my ma, maybe younger, with clear blue-gray eyes and a mobile mouth, and I soon discovered that she never kept still for a moment. She was in every way the opposite of Bud Westerly—quick, talkative, bright, and energetic.

"Hello! Welcome! I suppose Bud sent you. How is he? I heard about you coming; thought it would be a much older man. Never mind, you look quite capable to me, and it's nice to have someone with youth and spirit come to visit. Come on in, please! Children, stop screaming. Nat, take his horse, get some apples from the tree. There you go. That's Nat. The little one is Joey. The girl's name is Grace. Come in! My name is Elizabeth. Call me Libby. And you are?"

"Clem Fontayne." I took a deep breath. Like summer, like fresh air after a storm, Elizabeth Silver gave me welcome. I followed her into the house, and at her urging, sat down at her table. Scarcely had I settled down, than she asked, "Fontayne? By any chance, do you have a relative by the name of Pierre?"

"Yes," I said, barely able to get out the word. "He is my father."

CHAPTER 15

My Father's Trail Leaves
Me Dissatisfied, and I Meet
a Horse Called Cannon

"Go to your chores," Libby told the children. "Nat, we need some more split logs. Joey and Grace, I want you to weed the bean patch and then bring in some water, enough to fill the *whole* basin." The children went without a murmur, and I was glad for the privacy. My knees were shaking. I wanted to hear everything at once, yet I wanted to draw it out, to savor details. My father had been here! Maybe he had sat in this very chair.

"It was two years and eight months ago," said Libby. She brushed her hand across her face, tucking back a wisp of hair from her forehead. "I remember exactly, because it was when my husband died."

I glanced around the room, with its cupboards and the fancy settee, obviously a family heirloom. Dishes and books and clothing were piled onto shelves and wooden chests. From the ceiling hung a print curtain to mark off the sleeping area. There was even a pipe and tobacco on the shelf, an ax at the ready. A rifle hung above the mantel. I could not imagine the plight of a woman alone out here in the wilderness.

"How did you meet my father?" I finally asked.

"At Fort Kearny," Libby said. "My husband, Leonard, took ill. At first I thought it was nothing much, just exhaustion, as we'd finished the harvesting and canning and all for winter. But he worsened. I tried everything. I gave him all the laudanum we had, and herb compresses. He had a terrible, high fever. I fed him mold—"

"Mold?" I interrupted.

"From old bread. It is said to stop infection. But it did nothing for Leonard. He grew weaker, hardly able to speak. I decided to go to Fort Kearny and buy some medicine or fetch a doctor. I left Nat, the oldest, here with his father, and I took the other two, because who would care for them out here?

"Nat was almost eight, old enough to take charge of himself and his ailing father. I drove hard. Still, it took me almost the whole day to get there, and when I arrived, there was a mess of emigrants and soldiers and mountain men, everything overcrowded and sold out. There was no medicine, except for Dr. Flint's Quaker Bitters, and it was a very dear seventy-five cents a bottle. Still, I purchased it." Libby glanced toward the shelf, and I followed her gaze. There stood the bottle, still corked and full.

"The only doctor at the fort was gone, headed back east to visit his kin. I finally learned that there was a doctor along with an emigrant train some two days' distant, but I had not the spirit to sit at the fort and wait, with Leonard and Nat all alone at home.

"I was sitting there in the courtyard on a bench, the two little ones on my lap, and I suppose I must have looked quite dispirited, for a man came up to me in a kindly way—Pierre Fontayne, your father. He asked what was the matter, and I told him everything. I was frantic! Should I go home to Leonard? Should I wait for the doctor? I might have left a message with the soldiers at the fort, but I could not be certain they would remember it, should they be called away suddenly for some Indian attack.

"Pierre—your father, said, 'Never mind. I shall be here at the fort for a few days. When that emigrant train comes in, I will ask for the doctor, and I will bring him to you.'

"I tried to imagine what such a thing might cost. I thought of what we had in the jar, then decided I would give this doctor anything he desired, be it my jewels, my pewter mugs, even my wedding ring.

"'That can be decided in due time,' said Pierre. 'Let the doctor come. Perhaps he will tend your husband for a small fee. Perhaps a home-cooked meal and some fresh bread will be all that he desires. Just do not worry about it.' I was much relieved then, thinking it might be true. Your father said, 'Go home with your babies to your husband. Rest assured, I will come to you, and I will do everything in my power to bring the doctor. My poor horse is exhausted,' he said, 'but if I can find another mount, I will ride back and urge the doctor to come ahead and tend to your husband.'"

I felt a rich, glowing feeling within. My father, so kind, so heroic! I could imagine him helping this poor woman in her distress. My ma had always believed in Providence, and spoken of it with warm familiarity. Perhaps it was Providence that sent my father on his journey to help this woman in her need.

Libby continued with her story. "I could not leave at night, so I had to sleep with the children in the buckboard, and I set out the next morning, still shivering from the damp and cold of the night, and with dreadful fear of how I might find Leonard upon my return."

Libby sighed heavily and looked down at the table, tracing its deep scratches with her forefinger. "He was delirious. Poor Nat was beside himself, running from the bed to tend his father with cold cloths, then to the door to watch for us. I sat up all night, praying the doctor might come, thinking perhaps his train had made good time, that perhaps Pierre rode back to fetch him and urged him on."

Suddenly Libby leaped up and pulled several pans from the oven and set them down on a wooden block to cool. The room was filled with the fragrance of fresh loaves. She returned and continued, "I sat up with Leonard all night. I listened to his breathing, harsh and broken. Then just before dawn, suddenly there was a gasp. I ran over and stood beside the bed, looking down at him. His eyes were wide open, and he said my name. Only that. His breathing was regular then, and I thought in that moment of wild hope that somehow he had taken a turn for the better. I counted the breaths—five, six, seven. And then they stopped. He was gone."

My throat felt tight. I knew the feeling of such a moment, and somehow, I think Libby understood that I knew, for she placed her hand upon the table, not touching mine, but close, and we sat that way for a minute or more without speaking.

She drew back her hand, turned her face away.

"Did my father come to you then?" I asked softly. "That day or the next?"

"No. He never came."

I was filled with disappointment and confusion. How could he have deserted Libby, when he had given his word? He might at least have helped to bury her husband. But how could I assume he had simply failed her? Perhaps my father, too, had met with harm.

I told her now about his leaving, Ma and the baby dying, and my brief encounters since then. "At least I know he got to Fort Kearny," I concluded. "I aim to go and find out what happened to him, be it good or bad news."

Libby nodded. "It's best to know," she agreed. "But he seemed like a very literate man, the way he spoke. A real gentleman, and educated too."

"That he is," I said.

"One would wonder why he did not write to you."

"I wondered. My mother said it was not correct of me to question his actions but only to show respect."

"What did he seek out west?"

"Gold, he said. He would make us rich in the gold fields."

"That is curious," said Libby. "To me he said he meant to go to San Francisco. He had heard it was a great city, and filled with interesting people."

"Maybe he meant to do both," I said.

"Yes, surely, that must be so," she replied.

I hesitated, then asked, "Did he speak about his family? Did he mention me?"

She started, scraped back her chair, and turned her attention to the cooling loaves of bread. "Oh, yes!" she cried out. "Of course he spoke about his son, his wonderful son. He said how he hoped to come back to you soon. Yes, yes, you were very much on his mind."

The lie lay between us, like a fog, a presence. I went to the door and watched the children. They had hitched two large turkeys to a small wagon filled with melons. They laughed and leaped as they drove the turkeys onward with small sticks, and the large birds squawked out their indignation.

I felt empty. The day would have been so fair if only I could have known that Pa had been here, seeing this very landscape. Now I had to wrestle with conflicting thoughts again. I wanted to get away from Libby, back to Bud Westerly and his dull silence.

"Well, I have brought you a sack of corn from our station," I said, suddenly businesslike.

"I'm sure Bud is happy to have you to help him," Libby said with a smile. "Bud Westerly enjoys his hammock more than most men."

"I saw no hammock," I said. "He lies on a pallet at the door."

"Oh! Then that hammock broke again, and Bud is too lazy to mend it!" Libby laughed, and it was a wonderful sound. She clapped her hands together, calling the children. "Bring those melons in here! We'll be having a heap of company for dinner, I expect."

"Where do you find company?" I asked.

Libby pointed to the distance, where a thin line of dust hovered on the horizon. "Wagons. Eight or ten of 'em, I'll wager from the size of that trail. Word of mouth brings me customers. They like my bread and stew. Sometimes they stay the night. They have to sleep in the barn. Don't know what I'll do in winter, though. I ought to have another room built on. If I could just sell one of the horses . . ." She frowned, then said, "You must know about handling horses."

"A little," I said modestly.

"Well, I've got this mustang, acting strange. After Leonard died, the horse got shy. Now, he refuses to leave the corral. Things frighten him—a twig blowing or a broken rail on a fence—and he'll bolt. And he won't leave the corral. I can't ride him or harness him. He refuses to *go*. I would sell him, but who'd buy a horse that won't *go*?"

"Only for horse meat," I said.

"Oh, I wouldn't want that. He's still young," said Libby. "Perhaps you will look at this one and give me your opinion," Libby said, "in exchange for a good meal and a haircut. I think you could use both."

I had not contemplated a haircut, but I surely longed for a good meal. "I'd be much obliged," I said, and so the rest of the day passed very pleasantly. Libby offered me a large piece of potpie. For dessert there was cream and wild berries.

Afterward Libby had me put a chair outdoors, and with the children gathered around, gawking and chattering, she cut my hair. I felt light and clean, with hair just past my ears, enough on top to run my hands through and to keep me from freezing, but neat and respectable, as Ma would have liked to see.

"I'm obliged," I said again, looking at myself in the small mirror she gave me. It was a satisfaction to be groomed. "Now, I'll go and look at your horse."

Nat led me out to the corral and introduced me to the stallion named Cannon. "What's he named for?" I asked Nat.

"Well, he is fast when he leaves the corral. Used to be fast, anyhow," Nat said with a shrug.

"Cannon!" I called to the horse, clucking my tongue. He gave me the merest glance, then turned away, with a sassy flick of his tail. He chose that very moment to relieve himself at some length. Nat and I stood there watching, neither of us saying the obvious: that horse had no intention of being bossed by anyone. Cannon tossed his head and trotted over to another horse, a black Morgan. The two spoke together in the way of horses, and Cannon bobbed his head up and down and snorted, as if he'd just heard a good joke.

"Is that his pal?" I asked.

"Yes," said Nat. "His name is Quentin. The two are always together."

"Will Cannon let you ride him if the other horse comes along?"

"Yes. How did you know?"

"He's just buddy sour," I said, and under my breath I added, "and spoiled. He needs some work."

Nat went to tell his mother, and she came out eagerly. "Will you work with him, then?"

"Yes," I said. "Maybe next time I come, we can start."

Grace and Joey ran over with the melons. "Can Clem stay for supper, Mama?" Grace asked.

"Certainly," Libby replied, giving the little girl a hug. "Will you stay, Clem?"

"I wish I could," I said sincerely, "but I have to get back to prepare for the Express rider. He's expected before dark."

"Then you'd best be off," said Libby. "But come back soon. And take these baked goods—four loaves and this cake," she said, bustling into the cabin to get them, packed in oiled paper and laid into a sturdy sack.

"Come back," Libby called after me. "Come back soon."

I rode back as swiftly as Priscilla would go, savoring the day with new friends, a full stomach, and a haircut. But I couldn't help also wondering and worrying about my pa. Had he traveled along this very road? Had he gotten lost or hurt or killed? Had Indians scalped him, leaving his flesh to rot on the prairie, finally to be consumed by the wolves?

Or had he so quickly forgotten his pledge to a woman in need, someone he would never see again, who could never blame him.

A knot of worry tugged at my stomach, twisting my thoughts. Pa had made a promise to Libby, just as he'd made a promise to Ma and me. And he had broken both. Hank talked about some men not being the marryng kind. Adam and Silas and Blue surely had the wanderlust. They'd never stay in one place, no matter who was left waiting. Was my father like that? As I made my way back to the station house, I turned it over and over in my mind. Pa had left France for America, searching—for what? After they married, he and Ma left Delaware for Illinois, then Missouri. Then he took off again, looking for gold, telling tales of wonder and wealth. Telling tales.

I shuddered, realizing that I did not know my father at all.

When I got back to the station, I hurried to saddle up a fresh horse for the Express rider. Bud had prepared a pot of peppered beans and rice, to which he had added several handfuls of dried buffalo meat. While we waited for the rider, we brought our bowls to the table and dug in, mopping up the beans and meat with hunks of Libby's wonderful bread.

"Quite a woman," mumbled Bud. "Wonderful baker. Fine figure."

I glanced up at him, and he quickly looked down at his plate, his cheeks flushed."Did you know her husband?"

"Sure did. Fine fellow. Very ambitious. Used to work for a bank. Came out here from Ohio to settle about six years ago. Figured he'd buy up land and have himself a big holding—said the railroad was going to come through, sure as shootin', and then he'd make a killing. Well, I ain't seen no railroad yet, and Leonard's dead and gone and his poor widow don't have two coins to rub together."

"She's running a roadhouse," I said, with my mouth full, relishing the meal.

"Is she now? Right handy woman. I've seen her repair a wagon wheel and yoke a team all by herself. Even wearin' pants."

"No!" I exclaimed, laughing and nearly choking on my beans.

"Yup. Wears her husband's pants for doin' chores, even his boots. I seen her plowing and wearing pants."

"Well, she was wearing a dress today," I said, teasing, "and she looked right pretty—for an old woman, that is."

I was certain Bud had expressed amorous intentions toward the lady and had been rejected.

We were interrupted by the wild whoops of the rider, then a banging on the cabin wall as he called, "Hey! Hey! Where's my relief?"

Bud ran out with a skin of water, a loaf of bread, and a handful of prunes. The rider flung his saddle over the fresh horse, then hoisted himself upon it. He would ride the night through, stopping before dawn to catch some sleep at the next station. I wondered what it might feel like to ride in the moonlight, swift as the wind, to rush past the dark trees alive with owls and other forest creatures, to leap over streams and, finally, to sleep out under the stars.

CHAPTER 16

I Tame a Horse, Burn a Rotten Cow, and Earn a New Shirt

For my work as stock tender, I received the astounding sum of twenty-five dollars a month. My pay came by banknote, which was carried by the Pony, of course, delivered to us in the mochila saddle that the riders used. I saved nearly all of it, using only a little to buy myself a new pair of pants and a hat at the fort. From a passing peddler, I purchased paper and pencils, a small cooking pot, and a water flask.

Bud raised his eyebrows at the pot. His expression inquired, You fixing to go out on the trail again? But he said nothing, and neither did I.

Ours was not a home station, but only a relief station for changing horses. The bigger stations housed the relief riders between trips back and forth on their route. The home stations had bunk beds, I was told, several stock tenders, and extra animals and equipment. We had only four or five horses in our corral, and if anyone should wish to spend the night, they had to pull up a bit of the floor or sleep outside on the ground.

The riders were sturdy fellows, a bit arrogant, for all the attention they got along the way, especially when they passed through the towns. It was the great event of the day to watch the Pony come by. Little children squealed and clapped. Their parents waved excitedly. Girls would stand at their windows, screaming with delight, tossing down cookies and fruit. "Give me a token! Any token!" they would beg, lunging out to catch the rider's scarf or his tie.

Usually the riders made four or even five stations in a day, depending on the terrain. Of course, the mail itself never faltered. One rider passed the mochila, bulging with letters and documents, to the next. Horses were changed every ten miles or so. I would catch them as they were ridden in to Pumpkinseed, usually mustangs or Thoroughbreds, strong and swift and light on their feet.

When the rider came in, he would leap from his horse, leaving the animal standing too exhausted to move, its chest thumping with every breath, body covered with white foamy sweat. Every hair of that horse would be wet and reeking. Of course, the horse had to be cooled down slowly. I would walk it around the corral, keeping it from the water trough, then give it a vigorous rub. Later I allowed water, a little at a time, to avoid bloating and cramps.

It was pleasant to see how these horses conducted themselves. Their stance and demeanor suggested pride in a job well done. They were tired but the next day eager to begin again. I believe the horses were fed better than the humans. I gave them mash and grain to supplement the grass they chewed continuously. When there were apples or potatoes or garden carrots, the horses consumed those too.

I soon came to understand Bud's particular brand of laziness. He was a nighttime prowler. Drowsy by day, at night Bud came alive. He'd brew himself a pot of bitter coffee and sip it in the darkness, only outlined by the glow of a lantern. I'd waken at some sound, to find him tottering about fixing a broken hoe, mending a harness, or cooking up a pot of beans for the next day. By night, he did tooling on leather and a bit of silversmithing too.

It startled me when I awoke one night to see him sitting in an old rocking chair reading a book. It was about Indians and captives, a popular kind of reading in the East, but I was surprised to find it here, where Indians were a daily threat.

Occasionally some Indians happened by, skulking quietly around the station house. They always seemed amazed and amused by our ways and our things. Bud would toss them some dough balls or jerky, and they would leave, satisfied. Of course, at the same time, Bud would be holding his rifle, casual but sober.

Bud's lips moved as he read, and he mumbled the words under his breath. The next day, when I rode off to see Libby Silver, Bud lay on his pallet reading instead of sleeping. He called out, "Bring me back some sheets."

"What do you mean?" I called back, already astride Priscilla.

"Ask her. She'll know," said Bud, returning to his reading.

I had been working with Cannon for several weeks now, sometimes elated by success, other times ready to scream in frustration. In animal training, I knew, one must never show anger or lose one's temper. When Cannon turned from me and peed a yellow river, tossing head and tail in defiance, I learned to count to ten, hold my breath, and walk away, slowly. I always had an apple or a carrot or a bit of old bread in my pocket. We would eye each other from a distance. I'd whistle a tune, the human equivalent of tail flipping and head tossing. He'd chomp on some grass, maybe flare his nostrils and whinny. And so the contest continued until eventually animal greed was stronger than animal cunning, and he would come to me, swinging his body back and forth, shaking his head as if to say, "I was only joking." Horses are herding animals, after all. They need companionship. I had moved his pal Quentin into the barn and tethered Cannon outside alone. There was nothing else to do; if Cannon wanted company, I was it.

I walked him in ever expanding circles, murmuring, patting his neck, singing softly. Soon I got him quite far away from the corral and barn and the other horses. Occasionally he still rolled his eyes back, or burst out in terror at a stray tumbleweed. But after six or eight sessions, things mellowed. I became Cannon's buddy. When I arrived, he ran to meet me; he nuzzled my shoulder, my hands. When something strange came his way, he turned to look at me, seeking my opinion.

One day, when at last he seemed ready, I rode him out on the prairie for over an hour. When I returned, there was Libby standing in her doorway, beaming and shouting, "Hurrah! Clem, you've done it!"

The next time I came, a week later, I was nearly overcome by a sudden stench that assaulted me violently as I rode into the yard. Even Priscilla rolled her eyes, lifted one foot, and almost reared.

"What on earth is that?" I exclaimed when Libby appeared.

"Flies!" shrieked Nat and Joey. "Flies killed our cow!"

I looked quizzically at Libby, who had pressed a handkerchief to her nose. "It's true," she said, leading me to the house. She closed the door after us, but the stink was still there.

"How can flies kill a cow?" I asked. "And how do you get rid of that smell?"

"They settle in droves on a cow that's ailing," Libby explained. "Hundreds, thousands of them. It's as if they have their own telegraph system. Pretty soon the poor sick cow is black with flies."

Libby got up and went to the mantel. She took down the pipe, and the tobacco pouch, clapped them into her mouth, and lit the tobacco with a long stick placed into the fire.

I watched, dumbfounded, as the lady puffed and blew, puffed and blew. The children seemed oblivious to this phenomenon. Apparently they didn't think it in the least odd that a lady should smoke tobacco, just like a man. Then I noticed for the first time that under her wide, flapping apron, she wore pants. They bagged a bit, but otherwise they fit her.

"The only thing to do," Libby went on sorrowfully, "is to burn it."

"The carcass?"

"Yes. I was getting ready to do it, but to tell the truth, it's a mean job." She puffed desperately on the pipe. "It is the most hateful thing," she cried, "that smell!"

"Let me help you," I said.

Libby looked as if I'd offered jewels; her face was lit like the moon.

"I'll go on out with the kids," I said. "We'll set up kindling all around. Have you got some kerchiefs?"

She did. I tied the kerchief over my mouth and nose, bandit style, which pleased the children immensely. They did the same, making a game of it. I had them gather all the wood they could and place it around the oozing, reeking corpse. Its flesh was so sorely consumed that the head lay half severed from the body, the cavity filled with green flies and white, writhing maggots.

Soon we had a great bonfire going. The smoke rose in a thick cloud. I smelled roasting meat and felt the itch of heat and smoke and sweat.

Afterward, Libby gave me a pail of water and showed me a place out back where I could bathe. She handed me a bar of soap laced with wild hickory and rosemary. I emerged, feeling fresh and smelling sweeter than ever in my life.

Seeing me, Libby smiled and gave me several loaves of bread and a raisin cake. Then she held out a red plaid shirt. "This belonged to my husband," she said. "I've cut back the sleeves for you and hemmed the bottom. It should fit fairly well."

In her eyes I saw the value of the gift, and I accepted it gratefully. "Thank you. I'll wear it next time I see you."

"That will be lovely," she said, her hand on Grace's shoulder, another on little Joey's shining hair.

"Oh, I nearly forgot. Bud wanted me to ask you for the sheets, whatever that is."

"Just a minute." Libby went into the house and returned with a handful of printed papers. "Newspapers," she explained. "I get them from Sacramento every month or so. It's hardly news anymore," she said, shrugging, "but at least I can know something about the rest of the world. You might want to look at them too."

She gazed out over the prairie, where four large blackbirds dipped and soared, like symbols of the vast land and its freedom. "I rode Cannon the other day," Libby said. "I think you cured him, Clem. You're a fine trainer.

"He'll make a fine Express pony," she said. "Would you take him to the station? Perhaps Bud will buy him from me."

"What are you asking?"

"What are they paying?"

"Fifty dollars. Maybe more."

"See what you can do for me, Clem," Libby said.

In that moment I imagined making my home in a sod house like this one. I pictured returning soon, wearing the red plaid shirt and holding a fine sum of money in my hand to give to Libby in exchange for the horse. I so wanted to make her happy!

With Cannon hitched to my saddle alongside Priscilla, I mounted and started back toward the station. I thought about my life. Why should I be in a hurry to leave Nebraska? Maybe I would stay here even after the winter, to live another season on the prairie. I would get myself a rifle with some of my money, hunt deer and antelope and buffalo. I could help Libby build on the extra room she wanted for lodgers. Maybe I'd paint a sign for her, with a picture on it, burned into the wood.

I was full of plans.

CHAPTER 17

I Take My Last and Terrible Ride on Cannon

The afternoon began ominously. I put Cannon into the corral to let him get acquainted with the other horses. I meant to introduce him to Bud right away, to show him off and get him enlisted as an Express pony. But Bud was out of sorts, having had to tend to things by himself. A taste of Libby's raisin cake refreshed him somewhat, but then he began to worry and complain; the Express rider was late. Bud roamed about the cabin, stomped outside, peered to the distance, conjecturing all manner of catastrophes.

I became impatient and annoyed. Why did Bud always imagine the worst? Bandits, Indians, accidents, disease—Bud did not talk much, but when he did, it was a litany of disaster, and I wanted nothing more than good cheer.

I went out and did my chores, feeding, mucking out a stall or two, checking hooves and hides. All manner of ailments can assail a horse, and we had to keep one or two ready to go at all times. Priscilla was tuckered out from the ride to Libby's, one of our ponies had a bruised foot, and the other had come back from a tough ride yesterday and was still tired. I checked the ox, whose shoulder had mended now, and I thought I might take him to Libby's one day to haul off some fallen timbers. I enjoyed helping Libby—she made me laugh, told good stories, and always had good things to eat.

It was dark by the time Bud and I got our supper of potatoes and a bit of boiled rabbit, for Bud had been out shooting the night before. While we ate, Bud groaned and grunted and kept his eye on the door. Afterward, we settled down somewhat, to the old newspapers I had brought from Libby.

As I read, it seemed that our small cabin was inhabited with ghosts and spirits, all mocking me for my ignorance. Why, the world had been churning with events of which I was completely ignorant and mindless. Great changes were taking place! I began to read eagerly, excitedly, my heart thumping. I rose only once, to light the lantern, and by its yellow light I read on and on.

In California, San Francisco had become a great city filled with bankers, traders, and gold miners suddenly grown wealthy. New streets were springing up every day, lined with large hotels and restaurants. Theaters flourished, and famous actresses, like Lola Montez, gave performances for hundreds of people. I wondered whether my pa had ever gotten there. I could imagine him in San Francisco, smoking his cigarettes, telling stories, and speaking to Frenchmen in their own language. Were there Frenchmen in San Francisco, I wondered?

I read that fifteen Bactrian camels had come to San Francisco by schooner all the way from Asia. I was astounded. Should there be a war between North and South, the article said, perhaps the camel would replace the horse as a cavalry beast.

The threat of war was woven throughout the editorials. Tempers were flaring. Slavery was the issue. Some writers urged for war: "How can we sanction that most evil of sins, the owning of one man by another, rending asunder the ties of nationality, family, marriage? How can we sanction that which only spawns misery, debauchery, greed, and lust . . . ?" I could not imagine war of any kind, much less a war where Americans killed one another. There were countless stories about the coming election between Lincoln and Douglas. If Douglas won, perhaps slavery would become the law of the land. Certainly the South would rest content, its plantation life secure. If Lincoln won, some southern states threatened to leave the union and set up their own land. I read about turmoil everywhere and was half glad and half sorry to be stuck out here in the middle of nowhere.

There were articles about an intended railway, arguments about a route, about the impossibility of laying track through the mountains, and about Indians. Most of the papers were full of stories about the "Indian Menace."

One item in particular caught my attention: MASSACRE IN CARSON VALLEY.

"Last night a horrid massacre was perpetrated by the Indians, reported by J. Williams, the murder of his two brothers and five other white men and the burning of the station house. After witnessing the shocking butchery, Williams called at two other station houses on the opposite side of the river. He found no signs of life. He supposes all are murdered, 12 or 13 men. The Indians number 500 strong and are all armed . . ."

I felt the shock of having known this before, from Matt Bryant, the naked adventurer. He had warned us about the Indians, told of the massacre, and here it was in print. Of course, I knew there was such a thing as newspapers, but this struck me as almost too real, too close. For the first time, I understood the real danger of our situation. We were isolated here, Bud and I, miles and miles away from any help. Should Indians attack us, by the time word got to the soldiers at Fort Kearny, Bud and I would be dead, the horses and supplies stolen, the station burned down.

I squirmed uneasily in my chair, tense to every sound. I glanced at Bud. He had fallen asleep with the book on his chest and was snoring lightly.

Another article spoke of another massacre. PERPETRATORS OF MOUNTAIN MEADOWS MASSACRE ELUDE JUSTICE said the title. I skimmed the article, seeing that this massacre had taken place three years ago, in September 1857. A band of emigrants from Missouri were bringing their wagons through Mormon territory in Utah when they were attacked and killed, all except for the children too young to tell the tale. It was said that Mormon men, on orders of their leader, Brigham Young, went out to meet the travelers to "inform them about the local Indians," of whom the emigrants were naturally frightened. The Mormons told the travelers to lay down their guns and accompany them for safe passage. When the emigrants were disarmed, the Mormons fell upon them and, aided by the local Indians, completed the massacre. "They stole everything of value—wagons, furniture, and some 600 head of choice livestock. And nobody has been brought to trial for this horrible crime!" said the article.

The item continued with complaints about Brigham Young, that he was setting up "his own kingdom" in the middle of the United States. A bitter editorial followed, condemning Brigham Young for his policy of plural wives, denouncing "his adulterous relationships, which he has the temerity to call 'marriage,' that holy institution reserved to the eternal and faithful union of *one* man and *one* woman, sanctioned by both Church and State and approved as the only possible union by men of conscience and decency."

I read until the lamp went out, and I found myself suddenly awakened by several loud thumps at the door. Bud and I leaped up together, nearly colliding. I flung open the door. In burst the rider, gasping, holding his shoulder.

"What? What?" I stammered.

Bud dragged him inside. His boots scraped the floor. A red stain streaked the cabin floor.

"He's hurt!" I cried. "Indians! Was it Indians?"

"Highway—robbers," gasped the boy.

"Let me see," said Bud. He pulled the rider's hand away. The bleeding had stopped, but I could see a small round hole, clean through.

Sour juices rose to my mouth. I doubled over.

"Bring water and soap," ordered Bud. "We have to clean this."

"The mail," gasped the boy.

"What?"

He pointed to the mochila, which had been flung down on the floor, halfway across the room. "Someone has to—to take it. To the next station. Hurry."

The story came clear in the next few moments as Bud reached for the rider's revolver, kept in his pocket. It had been fired. Apparently the boy had managed to frighten the robbers away, but they had shot him as they departed, out of anger and spite.

"They didn't get—the mail," he murmured. His lips were pale, almost white, and also his brow. I began to tremble. What if he died?

"They did not—get it. We have to—take the mail."

I ran to fetch water for Bud, and I helped him clean the wound, then we packed it with moss I had scooped up near the creek. Bud tied the rider's shoulder with a bandana, and I wiped his face with a cloth. He had fainted. He looked to be no more than seventeen or eighteen.

"I'll take the mail," I said.

Bud looked at me in surprise. "You?"

"Who else?" It was obvious that Bud, with his bulk and his slug- gishness, was not the most eligible candidate. Besides, any of our ponies would buckle under his weight.

"Then hurry," said Bud, leaping up and grabbing the saddle with its four bulging pockets. "Take his revolver. And the rifle!"

"I can't carry all that on horseback!" I objected.

"You must. It's what they all do. And a Bible—"

"I have no room for a Bible!" I screamed. "Let me go!"

"All the riders are supposed to carry a Bible," muttered Bud. "It's a requirement of Mr. Waddell. And you have to take an oath that you won't drink or swear while you're on Pony Express business, and be faithful—"

"Let me go!" I roared, taking the revolver and rifle, but not the Bible. It lay there on the chair, worn and faded. "I'll take the mail to the next station and wait for the relief rider there. If I have to go to two stations, I can do it."

"What horse?" Bud cried distractedly. We ran out together.

"Cannon. The new horse. It will be a good chance to test him."
Without waiting for Bud to shout another objection, I got Cannon,
saddled him up, and mounted.

Bud handed me the revolver and the rifle. I tucked the first into
my belt, slung the second over my shoulder, feeling tough and ready
for battle. The mochila hung at my side, its contents secure in the
locked pockets. In my shirt pocket was all the money I had earned,
as this was something that *never* parted company with me.
Otherwise, I was light and skinny, as the advertisement for Pony
Express riders required. In the new red plaid shirt, I felt dashing and
daring. I wished I might ride through a town, where girls would
come to cheer me on. Well, perhaps the relief rider would be
detained, and I'd be able to go farther than the first station.

Bud dashed inside and returned with several biscuits. "Take
these!" he shouted, and I laughed at him, catching two of the biscuits and stuffing them into my pocket. "Keep to the road. Ever
west."

"You're a mother hen!" I laughed, dug in my heels, and was off.

It was quite dark, but there was a bit of moon to light my way. I
was exhilarated with the adventure of streaking through the dew-wet
grass under that night sky. Owls hooted. Prairie dogs and mice scoot-
ed out before Cannon's dashing hooves. I wanted to shout my exul-
tation. I was riding the Pony Express!

I rode and rode, trying to calculate time and distance, but this was
impossible, as the road was strange, and the whole experience of that
night ride was a mystery to me. Cannon strove valiantly, eagerly.
Perhaps he was too eager. Maybe that's why we missed the station.
Because after what must have been several hours, I realized that midnight had come and gone. The station could be anywhere in four
directions. In a word, I was lost.

What happened next was a succession of occurrences so bizarre
and extreme as to be considered a mere invention, but it is the whole
truth. As often happens in summer on the plains, the sky suddenly
turned from bright to overcast. Simultaneously a slight breeze
became whipped up into a wind, playful at first, knocking my hat
from my head, and then more and more furious, hurling leaves, sand,

and small stones all about me. The wind took on a wildness of its own, like an animal suddenly set free. Then came the distant baying of a wolf. Cannon leaped forward. He turned his head for an instant, and I saw the wild flash of his eyes.

"Don't worry, Cannon," I called. I patted his neck, leaning into his gait. I felt the sweat on his hide and I smelled it deep in my nostrils. Soon we would have to stop and rest, or Cannon would drop from fatigue.

The wolf must have summoned others. A terrible chorus of baying and howling seemed to surround us. Cannon shot forward in accordance with his name. I tried to slow him, pulling back, but not too hard, or I would force him to bolt. He ran on and on, dashing madly from side to side, his hooves clattering on rocks, lurching as he stumbled into a depression. "Cannon! Cannon! *Woah*!" I shouted, but he was beyond command, frothing and steaming, wild and terrified. My legs felt leaden from gripping his sides, my hands weak. Then came the rain, first pattering, soon drenching, the large drops turning quickly to sleet and then hailstones that clattered all about and assaulted us from every direction.

Cannon was not ready for this, I thought, not ready for the trail at night, not ready for any of it. How had I possibly thought I could break him to the trail in a few short weeks? *Pride!* I recalled Ma's admonition. "Pride goeth before a fall." I clung to Cannon with all my might, my fingers laced into his mane, and though I screamed and screamed for him to stop, my voice was lost in the wind.

Still the wolves howled, a bloodcurdling song, and now lightning came in gigantic streaks across the sky, ripping the darkness apart like a fiery hand, and then the thunder. *Crack! Crack!* The crash came so near that I felt its vibration.

Cannon let out an unearthly roar, almost human in its terror. He reared. I was flung aloft like a catapult, high, soaring, then down. I hit something that knocked against my skull; I heard the sound, like a large nut being broken. I felt myself rolling down, down, over rocks and thorns, down and down while thunder pealed above me, and then I saw and heard nothing more.

CHAPTER 18

Alone in the Wilderness, I Endeavor to Stay Alive by Eating Insects and Other Delicacies

---

After a long, long darkness, light appeared. I saw fuzzy rings of light—double, triple rings of light. A terrible, black weariness came over me then.

Once again I saw a flickering and realized that I had opened my eyes. It was night, and the round face of the moon doubled and spread, then slid into focus. Now I felt something beneath my body, the hardness of granite, piercing of thorns, wetness and chill. I heard something—the moaning wind, the scratching of a rodent, movements above me. I lay motionless, moving only my eyelids. With effort I closed my eyes deliberately, opened them again, repeating this exercise several times. Alive, I thought with wonder. I am *alive*.

I tried to move my arm. I could not; it felt like a tree limb beside my body, cut off and unresponsive. My head throbbed and pulsed.

"Alive!" I tried the word out loud. It came out a whisper. "I'm alive. I was thrown from the horse." Painfully, I rolled partway onto my side. It caused a stabbing sensation in my left shoulder. I pulled myself up on my right arm, half raised, and I saw in the pale moonlight that I lay on a rock slab. The only growths nearby were thorny bushes, and these thorns had cut into me as I fell.

Something was digging into my ribs. The revolver. I nearly laughed out loud, but the slightest movement made me wince with pain. I had a gun, but there was nothing to shoot, and even if there were, I had no strength to pull the trigger. My muscles seemed to have softened into pudding. My bones did not exist.

How long have I lain here? I wondered. I slid my tongue over my lips. They were cracked and dry and caked with dirt. My teeth felt grainy. I felt incapable of movement. I would die here in the dark, alone.

I began to tremble with fear, imagining clearly the sight of a hungry wolf or wildcat above me, its mouth wide. I could almost feel its hot breath and smell the rank odor of the beast as it leered down at me. I lay there, my body bound into a tight ball, until the trembling at last subsided.

Breathe deeply, something told me, and as I pulled the fresh night air into my lungs, I became calmer. My ledge was at least safe, a shelter of sorts. I slept again, and the next thing I knew it was day.

How long have I been here? How many days—five, ten? No, I decided. If it had been that long I would not awaken, but would likely have starved to death or been eaten. Why had no animals attacked? I gazed about and saw that I had rolled down a huge, sheer cliff, stopping only when my body slammed into a large vertical rock, into which was gouged a kind of shelf where I now rested. Like a half cave, this depression with its rock roof had no doubt sheltered me from preying animals.

Slowly I pulled myself to a sitting position and felt a terrible throbbing in my head. Sour bile rose to my throat. I heaved. My empty stomach rebelled in spasms that shook me and then subsided.

I sat up, trying to clear my mind. *Alone. Alone.* The word echoed through my mind. Panic edged into my thoughts, made me tremble again, and then I shouted to myself, Stop it! I had heard of people marooned, sailors lost in boats, miners abandoned in old tunnels.

Some survived. Those who kept a cool head often did survive, and then they had a story to tell.

I imagined myself sitting by a fire, telling my story. *Yes, I took this horse; he was a bit wild, terrified of weather and wolves, and he threw me in the midst of a lightning storm, and I rolled down a steep canyon—might have broken every bone in my body, but I was lucky.*

The idea of a future, of having a story to tell, filled me with sudden vigor. I would not let myself die, not without a struggle. I needed a plan. First, take stock. Don't be hasty. Don't waste strength trying to do the impossible. Keep warm and dry. Find water. Find food. Sit back and think about where you are—the sun sets in the west. Go west, ever west.

I reached into my pocket and took out the revolver. Somehow, the sight of that hard, dark steel encouraged me. And I had a pocket full of bullets. Now my mind skipped over my resources. I had a gun. I had the shirt Libby had given me and another one underneath. Sturdy boots covered my feet, and a rope belt had kept my britches tight around me. In my pocket was my knife. Digging deeper, I found one of the biscuits Bud had tossed out when I left the station. It was hard as a rock, laced with blue mold. Slowly I ate the biscuit, mold and all, remembering Libby's words. Maybe I'd be lucky, and the mold might be medicine for my wounds.

I searched in my pocket again for my money. The bank notes were gone. Remarkably, the drawing of Sara was still inside my pocket. Where was my money? Had someone come upon me here, searched me, and stolen my money? No—then they would have taken the revolver, too. The money must have fallen out of my pocket when I rolled down the cliff.

I imagined telling it some night to my amazed, admiring listeners: *There I was, all alone without a morsel to eat, except one moldy biscuit, and a cliff so steep that not even a mountain goat could climb it. But I had a knife and a gun, and I . . .*

As I sat there pondering, I became aware of a trickling sound. Water was dripping down from the rocks. There must be a pool somewhere.

It took an hour or more for me to straighten up and walk the few steps to the water. My left arm was useless, swollen at the elbow and forearm. Any movement brought excruciating pain. Carefully I took off my shirt ripped out a sleeve, and fashioned a sling, binding the arm close to my chest. Even this action took an interminable time, for as I moved I became dizzy again, my vision blurred.

The thought of water urged me on. When at last I reached the small pool, I bathed my swollen arm in it, using my other hand to wipe my face and head. When I took my hand away, I saw the rust-colored residue of dried blood. I felt along my head. No cracks that I could determine, but there was a swelling above my right ear and another lump over my eye. I must look a fright, I thought, then felt that odd tickling laughter deep within, thinking, Who cares? There's nobody to see me, only the lizards and the flies.

A handful at a time I brought water to my mouth, then sat back, resting from the effort, congratulating myself. I had found water! I splashed the water onto my head and face. Now a fragile feeling flowed through my entire body. Bone met bone, muscle was woven onto bone, skin stretched tight. I felt as if I knew intimately every detail of my manufacture, and that it was all new. The sweet sound of water soothed me. I must have slept again, for next thing I knew, it was night.

Then it was day, and I sat up, again seized by panic as the cliff loomed high above me and the sun already beat down on rocks, surrounding me like an oven. What if another storm came? The heat of day and the chill at night would kill me. And there was nothing to eat, no berries or nuts, no plants that I recognized as food. I had spied a spattering of small mushrooms behind a rock in a carpet of moss. My choice was to die from starvation or poisoning. I gazed up at the enormity of that cliff and contemplated the sight of my own bones, eventually piled in a small heap here on the rocks. There was no way I would climb that cliff.

I went for water again and drank my fill. Near the water, I now noticed, grew reeds and cattails. I reached for one of the reeds. It slipped through my fingers, slicing into the flesh. I cursed, using the words I had learned from the bullwhackers. I cursed the cliff, the rocks, the horse, the storm, and my own weak, aching body.

I fretted and gnawed over my fate and my failures. Cannon was gone, probably dead from a fall. Maybe he broke a leg, in which case he would die of starvation. Or he had run off to the mountains to join the wild horses. In any case, he was forever gone, and it was my fault. The mochila saddle with the mail was also gone, impossible to find in this wilderness. And it was my fault. I had taken an untried horse on the trail. I had ridden past the station. I had been filled with pride and certainty, whereas I was ignorant and foolish and unprepared.

All the rest of that day I kept going over my choices. I drank water. With my knife I cut down one of the reeds, slit it open, and ate the soft, white inner part. It had a dry, sharp taste, and was stringy in my teeth. I sat back to wait for the possible poison to affect me. But nothing happened, except that I belched vehemently.

Maybe, I thought, I could eat reeds and cattails, drink water, and live in this half-cave, a hermit. But how long could I last this way? Maybe a few days. I needed real food. It was perfectly clear to me that I would have to move from here or perish.

The decision exhausted me, and again I slept, awakening once in the night to a dark sky. Faces appeared before me—Ma and little Joy May, my father, Libby, Molly. All the people I had ever known seemed to crowd into my half-sleeping stupor, looking down at me, wondering what I might do next. I opened my eyes into the darkness and the faces melted away. I decided right then that, come morning, I would move out.

At dawn I rose and saw things anew. Worn into the cliff were small footholds, wedges, where I might place my toes and fingers. Straight up was not the way to go. As I moved around that massive cliff, I saw that on one side the going was less steep, and the rock was pocked with depressions. Weeds grew in small patches of powdery soil, thrusting their way out from the granite. I could pull these out and find footing. It was risky, but I had no choice.

I was reluctant to leave the water, not knowing whether I would find another source at all, and I had nothing to carry it in. The pouch Bud gave me had vanished, along with the rifle. Some fortunate wanderer would find them and maybe my money too. He would be thankful. I took stock again. I had a revolver and some bullets and a knife. I had a shirt and boots. Before attempting any move from here, I needed food.

It was still early, with dew on the reeds. Peering closely I saw a grasshopper dozing on a cattail. With the utmost concentration, I made my move, grasped the insect, closed my palm around it, and held it thus until I felt all movement cease. I dropped my catch at my feet, barely a mouthful, about the size of a hickory nut. Well, it was a start, and I would have to hurry before the sun shone full, causing the insects to go into hiding.

After half an hour or so I had my catch, six grasshoppers and a large insect I could not name. The effort of my hunt left me shaken and weak. I dropped to my knees and, to my amazement, was met with a pair of fiery eyes and a hiss. I grasped the revolver, pulled back the pin, and shot. The bullet pinged off the rock. I shot again in my frenzy. The snake recoiled and disappeared, and I stood there trembling in anger and shock.

I lay back, ready to die from frustration and fury. And then I got up on all fours, wary, like any beast hunting for food. I peered into the rocks and crevices. I lifted one, another, another, until my fingers ached. There amid some dry grasses lay the snake, only half coiled. I lifted a rock and struck.

I had crushed its head, which I now sliced off in a clean stroke. Then I slit the belly, salivating over this task. My stomach ached and growled. I stripped off the skin and carefully cut myself a wedge of snake, put it into my mouth, and chewed. It was hard and horrible, and I spat in disgust.

Panic nearly gripped me. I forced myself to stop, think, take stock. I had a gun, a knife, a shirt . . . what I desperately needed was fire. I don't know what instinct or half forgotten tale told me that it was possible to make fire with my possessions, but I hurried now to the cattails and cut several of them, some green, some dry. With the tip of my knife I dug a hole in the earth where they grew. Next I gathered a few dried reeds and from my shirt I cut a swatch of cloth at the hem, murmuring apologies to Libby. I was sweating from this effort and from the knowledge that if this did not work, I was doomed.

Carefully I pulled at the cloth, stretching the threads apart, then I tucked the cloth into the pistol, adding a bit of fluff from the cattails. I filled the hole with bits of dried debris, thorns from the shrubs that grew all around, and a dry, waxy plant that looked as if it would burn. Then, holding my breath and murmuring a prayer, I pointed the pistol into the hole, leaned back, and fired.

Something smoldered. I stepped up and blew softly, reverently. The smoke died.

I began again, spreading out to find dried bits of grass, weeds, seeds, and this time I cut a piece of cloth from my undershirt and added it to the tinder. I loaded the pistol, stuffed in a bit of cloth and dry matter, and I fired.

It took. It burned and blazed! Joyfully I began to hack down the dried reeds, twigs from the thorny bushes, feeding them into my flame, urging the fire to burn. Burn! I whittled a point onto a green reed, to use for a skewer. Never have I known such gratitude for anything as that bit of snake meat, roasted over my own fire. I took the grasshoppers, pulled off their wings, heads, and legs, and placed them on a small reed mat I had hastily woven together. The reed mat smoked, and the insects were quickly cooked and surprisingly crisp and savory. I decided to smoke the rest of the snake meat in the same fashion and take it with me.

As I ate, my strength and my mood rose by the minute. It is truly miraculous, how a bit of food in the belly can change despair to actual happiness, and how, when the mood is right, even nature seems to cooperate.

Beyond the reeds I found a small bush with very hard branches. These I swiftly cut and trimmed, using first the thinnest, gradually increasing the size until I had several good, stout pieces of wood burning red and hot. I would let this burn into hot coals. I had to save this fire, for my bullets were few, and I could not rely on starting another.

I crept to where I had seen the moss grow. This I carefully scraped up with my blade, making a thick pouch, which I lined with large green leaves, fitting them into the hollow of my shirt. When I pulled off my shirt, I realized that my arm had improved. Apparently it was not broken, only sprained. I could move it and grasp with that hand.

With the meat from half the snake, and the hot coals saved for another fire, I took a last drink of water and set out, with the shirt-pouch tied at my waist and the revolver and knife securely in my pockets.

I made my way around to the right, finding several footholds. I crawled up, clinging to the rock surface, from foothold to foothold, seeking every slight depression, every narrow ledge. With one arm still injured, the strain was almost unbearable, but I pulled myself up, at last reaching a wedge where I could stand and regain my breath and balance. My throat was parched. My face felt steamy from the heat. I squatted down on the ledge to save my strength, planning to continue when the sun sank lower in the sky.

How long I remained on the ledge, I cannot say. But after a time the sun had reached its zenith and began descending. I ate what was left of the snake, chewing carefully to make it last. I stood with my back against the cliff, feeling the heat and the hardness of it. I had gone past agony, and it seems strange to say, but I felt purely peaceful atop that enormous structure. Birds soared above me. I felt like I was flying too. And I thought, if I should die this very moment, it will be well with me. I began to sing, softly at first, then louder.

> *"Oh, I went down south for to see my Sal,*
> *Sing poly wolly doodle all the day . . ."*

I imagined telling my future audience: *"I stood there on the ledge with all that empty world below me, and I sang to keep up my spirits . . ."*

As the day cooled, I continued up, inch by difficult inch. I developed a pattern of climbing—right hand, right foot, left hand, left foot, lift, pull, stretch. I climbed without stopping, and as twilight came, the air turned cool and crisp, and I felt relieved. But I had to rest. I had to find some small space where I might stop for the night. Above me rose a plateau that I had to reach, but how?

I studied the angle, the distance, and my nerve. At last I pulled the belt from around my waist. Next, I ripped the other sleeve off my shirt and tied it to the belt, then tossed it up to catch a protrusion above me. It slipped and fell back. I tried again. Seven, eight times—and finally I succeeded in snagging the protrusion and tying the rope securely, testing it with my weight before I hoisted myself up.

Some miraculous surge of energy held me at the side of that rock, enabled me to pull my own weight, encouraged me to look up and not down. I reached my goal and lay in a heap, exhausted, panting, and I fell into a deep, blissful sleep, awakening to bright starlight. My stomach growled and gnawed, but I had been hungry before and likely would be again. Thinking of food did no good. Breathe deep, I told myself. Sing. And as I sat there on that plateau with nothing but the wind and the stars for company, I sang out: *"Molly! Do you love me . . . ?"* I pictured Molly's pert face, I heard the way she laughed and hollered at me, "Clem Fontayne!" I finally slept with Molly in my dreams.

In the morning, when I looked down, I could see the deep gully into which I had fallen, and I marveled again that I was still alive. I climbed and climbed, and finally reached level ground, and realized that I had done it. I was out of the gully, back on the plains.

I suppose I should have been filled with exaltation at my success. But strangely, I was overcome with despair. There was no trail. There were no trees. No sign of water welcomed me, no habitation of any sort, nothing alive save the birds overhead, and these did not stop to notice me. If only there were trees, leaves, straw, anything with which to build a shelter. Why had nature suddenly become so stingy? How could fate have so fashioned it that I was to exert every ounce of my strength in climbing out of that ravine, only to die here on this awful, parched plain?

I could envision nothing but days and weeks of increasing

hunger, confusion, and finally death. Why not end it now? I still had a few bullets. One of them, fired through my skull, would end it all.

A small bird landed near my feet. It pecked inquisitively at the ground, then flew to a grayish shrub that grew out of the rock. From its perch the bird stared at me, cocked its head.

"Go away!" I shouted, my fist clenched on the handle of my gun. The bird chirped. It jabbered.

Would I ever again speak to another human being? Would I ever again laugh? All in a rush I remembered moments of talk and friendship—Libby, Bud, Hank, Adam, Ruski, Gabriel, Molly. Always, my vision landed on Molly, the way she tossed her braids over her shoulder, the quick touch of her lips on mine.

Did Bud and Libby talk about me? What did they think of me? Did they perhaps think I had stolen the mochila and taken off with it? Did Bud suspect that all I wanted was a horse and a gun, and I'd take off on my own?

Somehow, I had to survive, to go back and tell them the truth.

I lost track of the days—eight, nine, or ten. I walked, hid, slept, and looked for food. I saw nary a soul, neither white man nor Indian, and I could not decide which was worse, coming upon a killer or a thief, or enduring this loneliness.

Several times I found water, once from a spring, another time a small lake that popped up suddenly on the horizon. I lay by that lake all night, waiting for game to appear, hoping to shoot a deer or a wild sheep or even a wolf, but none came, or if they did, I had fallen asleep despite my vow to remain awake.

I ate insects and berries, the inside of a cactus, dandelions, and some wild leaves that looked like spinach. From a fallen log I scooped out a handful of wriggling grubs and ate them instantly. I found a few nuts and shot a rabbit and a crow. And then I was out of ammunition and took stock. My coals had gone out days ago. I still had my knife and my shirt, though it was filthy and scorched. My britches sagged around me. I was thinner than ever. I could see my own ribs.

I kept walking west, toward the sun. How long could I go on? I began to invent pictures for myself, of walking into a fine little sod house, sitting down to a meal of salt pork and biscuits and cherry pie. I imagined hearing talk and laughter, playing with Libby's children in the yard, riding back to the station where Bud would meet me and sit with me in silence. Oh, how I longed for that boring silence! To see another face, hear another person breathing!

And then, one afternoon, in the distance I saw a tepee. Its white skins glistened in the setting sun. From this distance it seemed like an illusion, but I thought I heard the whinny of a horse. I ran toward the tepee.

CHAPTER 19

I Reenter Civilization as an Object of Terror and Am Rescued by a Mormon Train

I ran toward the tepee, my heart overflowing with gratitude. People! A family! These were not wild marauders but people settled down to hunt. I heard the whinny of a horse, I saw dust and smoke. In my eagerness to hear a human voice and see a face, I ran on, heedless of possible danger.

A root or some configuration of the earth caught my foot. I fell flat. As I dusted myself off, I stared straight ahead and saw several naked Indian children outside the tepee, three women sitting there, the flap of the tepee open to reveal some furnishings, woven backrests, a low bench set with several gourds. How I longed to enter that dwelling, to sit by a fire, perhaps to smoke a pipe, as Indians are wont to do, and to eat of their food. I wished I had something to share.

Outside the tepee hung various implements and decorations—the skull of a buffalo, several spatula-shaped bones from a deer or antelope, a tomahawk. My scalp prickled. What if inside or nearby warriors waited to take this scalp of mine? They would use it to decorate their shields. They would steal my boots, my knife, and my revolver. Caution now directed me to move slowly and stealthily. Very softly I crept nearer and nearer until I could smell their fire and the roasting corn.

I saw no men. Probably they were off hunting buffalo. They would stay in this place for several days, butchering their kill, then move on. Perhaps they would be joined by other hunters. I hovered between longing and fear, thinking how I might show my friendly intentions—should I call out? Would they understand a smile?

The children, three boys and a girl, sat on the ground, playing some game with seeds or small stones. From inside I heard an old man calling. A young squaw rose quickly and went in to him. A small pile of buffalo chips, a gourd of water, and a rack on which buffalo meat was hung to dry—these comprised their transitory dwelling and their fortune.

I crept forward. My foot snapped on a twig. Instantly the children froze, and spotting me, they erupted into ear-splitting howls. They shouted words I could not understand, but the meaning was clear— they thought I had come to kill them! And I realized now that the revolver at my waist showed clearly. The boys leaped up, grasping their bows, which lay by their sides on the ground. In a moment they had put arrow to bow, and they let fly, still screaming and howling while the girl jumped up and down shrieking, throwing stones that swiftly found their mark. I was pelted, head, chest, and feet, with their weapons.

"Wait! I mean no harm!" I tried to tell them. My voice was lost in the frenzy of their screams of fear. The old man came out, leaning on a gnarled stick, clumsily holding a rifle. A shot blasted out over my head.

I ran, shaken by the thought that they saw *me* as the enemy, the killer of women and children.

I ran and ran, awestruck and ashamed. I ran until I was thoroughly exhausted, unaware until I came fully upon it that I had reached a river.

I drank gratefully, then scavenged for blueberries and gooseberries that grew in profusion, along with wild onions, all of which I consumed by the handfuls, then drank again. With the river, I would find life. I was certain of it now.

That night I found a lodge made of twigs and mud, fashioned by a badger or a pack rat or a beaver. Into it I crept, and not a moment too soon, for the sky had shown menace, and rain poured down in torrents all night long. In the morning I lay in a bed of mud, and I dunked myself in the river, emerging only slightly cleaner and very cold.

But as the day wore on, the sun dried my clothes and warmed me. I felt very tired, my eyes strained from searching the horizon and from the glare of the sun. Mirages shimmered before me, false expanses of water and greenery. I stumbled. I rose again. My body seemed distant from my mind, too numb to inform me of pain.

The dust seemed like another fantasy, swelling and rising, moving ever closer.

And the white canvases looked like large birds in the distance. I thought I heard the cries of eagles.

And the sound of men's voices shouting as whips cracked, and the bellowing of oxen—was any of it real?

I suppose I lost consciousness, for the next thing I knew I was surrounded by wagons, with people looking down at me, men and women, their faces creased in consternation. "Why, it's a boy."

"Is he dead?"

"I don't know. Ah, he breathes."

"He looks near starved, and wild!"

"Let us carry him."

"Sister, take his gun. One never knows . . ."

"He is harmless, so thin, and wounded."

I felt myself being lifted. I sank into someone's arms. They were the powerful arms of a man. I felt his beard brushing my face. "Take it easy," he said, a deep, mellow voice. "We'll take you to our wagon. You're going to be all right."

His name was Wade Ferguson, and I owe him my life. He brought me to his wagon and cared for me, keeping me cool during the sweltering days, with wet cloths on my head, keeping me warm at night with a blanket wrapped around me. His family slept outside, under the wagon or in a tent they had brought, and which Wade Ferguson and his sons folded up each morning and laced to the side of the large Conestoga.

Those first few days I knew little of my surroundings, only that two women, Ellen and Candace, who were sisters, took care of me. They brought broth and gruel and bits of buffalo meat, so that my empty stomach might be accustomed to food again without rebelling. There were many children, all ages, one holding a basin of water while another bathed my face and washed my feet. The children whispered and peered at me. Sometimes they sang softly. I felt as if I had stumbled onto a band of angels.

Gradually I discerned who they all were—four boys and five girls, from infancy to the oldest girl, Lucy, a young lady of perhaps eighteen. I only saw Lucy at a distance, for she was constantly occupied finding fuel, tending the fire, setting up and taking down the camp, and chasing after the younger children.

Eventually I learned to know each of them—the boys, Spencer, Amos, Jason, and baby Wilbur; the girls, Lucy, Kathryn, Agnes, Hattie, and Penny. Among them they were a constant babble of ideas, jokes, and, to their credit, few complaints. Of course, somebody was always taking sick with something or other. The women would make a bed for the ailing child at the front of the wagon, but the invalid would be pulled out upon any crossing of a river or stream. Too many children fell out and were trampled or cut by the wagon wheels.

Spencer Ferguson, the oldest boy, was the image of his father, with a sturdy build, broad face, and slick blond hair. I reckoned him to be about my age. He assisted his father in all things. It made me wonder how my life might have been if my father had kept me with him. Ferguson held a tight rein on his troop. They bedded down precisely at nine, rose at dawn, and had obvious respect for the strap that hung visibly at the entrance of the wagon. Wade Ferguson had brought three wagons, each laden with provisions—food, blankets, furniture, and other household goods. He also brought several cows to provide milk along the way for the children.

"Where are we going?" I asked Ellen, when I was finally fully awake and ready to communicate.

"We're bound for Utah territory, the new place. Salt Lake City."

"How far?"

"I don't know," replied Ellen. "We will ask Mr. Ferguson."

I had noticed that in the manner of many women, she always addressed her husband formally as "Mister," as did her younger sister, Candace.

The two women resembled each other in plainness, and in their way of constant toil. Their hands were never idle. Even in the night I'd awaken to hear Ellen or Candace occupied with one of the children, lighting a candle, finding ointment for a cut, fetching another coverlet.

Ellen was tall and thin, with red hair and freckles. Her dresses were dark, her petticoats gray, and she wore a silver brooch tucked under her chin. In her wagon was a spinning wheel, and she occupied herself with it at all times. While walking, she worked a hand spindle, pulling and gathering the thread as she went.

Candace was rounder of face and body, the folds of her puffy cheeks rising agreeably when she laughed. She was constantly looking for a place to do the wash and time to do it in. From a small camp stove she produced wondrous cobblers and cakes.

I'm not certain when I realized they were Mormons. It must have been the second or third night, when I was feeling stronger and got up from the pallet Wade Ferguson had prepared for me. I lifted the flap and saw that all the wagons had been set in a circle, the animals picketed inside. Everyone was gathered around, and they were singing. The songs were new to me, different from the usual church hymns.

"Come, come ye Saints, no toil nor labor fear,
But with joy wend your way

Though hard to you this journey may appear,
Grace shall be as your day.
'Tis better far for us to strive
Our useless cares from us to drive;
Do this, and joy your hearts will swell—
All is well! All is well!"

I knew they called themselves saints, Latter-Day Saints, and that they claimed their prophet, Joseph Smith, had heard God's voice telling him to found a new church. Everything else I knew about these Mormons came from slurs tossed out in the tavern or among the bullwhackers. I'd seen many a fellow spit on the floor at the mention of Mormons, calling out, "Saints indeed! I say they are the scum of the earth, with their pretensions to piety. Filled with unholy lust, they are!" The Mormons had been hounded out of Missouri, this I knew from remarks I overheard in town and at school. It was whispered in my own mother's parlor, by the good church ladies gathered there making quilts, that these so-called Saints were more likely akin to the devil.

I had not heard a service like the one these people held out there on the prairie, with joyful singing and testimonies of converts to the faith, and well-wishing from one to another as they called each other Brother and Sister.

Then came a sermon spoken by a man with a powerful voice, invoking God's protection and blessing on this undertaking. "May we all be gathered together into one place upon the face of this land, to prepare our hearts and be prepared in all things against the day when tribulation and desolation are sent forth upon the wicked. Let us, then, Saints, go to our valley, to our Zion, to live together in service to our Heavenly Father and in brotherly love and assistance to one another. . . ."

I did not know what to make of it. I had heard terrible things about these folk, yet in their midst I felt welcome and at peace. I got up and went out. Someone had dressed me in a shirt of blue cloth, which I now wrapped tightly around my body. The hem reached below my knees, and the sleeves had to be folded back several times.

As I approached, the speaker nodded toward me and smiled. "Ah, brother Clem is with us! He appears hearty and strong. We recognize the hand of our Heavenly Father in his healing, and we give thanks."

Murmurs of thanksgiving came from the circle, faces shining in the firelight. I felt a hand on my back. It was Wade Ferguson, surrounded by children. He nodded and smiled. "Welcome back," he said. "We were a trifle worried about you."

"Thank you," I said. "I hope I can repay your kindness."

Wade Ferguson laughed. "Have you any skill with animals?"

"I have driven oxen, sir, and broken horses, and worked as a stock tender."

"It is clear then that heaven has sent you," said Ferguson with a hearty laugh and a pat to my back. "Candace! Young Clem is an animal tender! He has driven oxen too!"

Candace rushed over, laughing happily. She took my arm. "Ah, you can relieve me, then, for I'm a poor ox driver, for truth, isn't it so, Mr. Ferguson?"

"You try, my dear. Oxen are notably stubborn beasts. And we city dwellers make poor frontiersmen, I'm afraid."

"You need do nothing at all until you feel strong again," Candace assured me.

Several of the children crowded around. Candace clapped her hands together, calling, "To bed, now! And remember your prayers, all of you."

"I shall come and tuck you in," said Ellen.

The children lined up in front of Wade Ferguson, each in turn receiving his attention, a pat on the head, a soft admonition, and for some, a kiss on the brow. The youngest, a baby still in its infant dress, he handed to the young woman I had seen gathering fuel. She smiled and nodded as she took the infant. "I'll keep him tonight," she murmured to Ellen. "You need your rest. I'll try a sugar teat if he needs feeding, before I wake you."

"Lucy! You have been so busy with the children, you have not met Clem."

She turned to me and nodded. "How do you do, Clem."

Lucy held out her hand. I took her hand in mine and looked into her lovely face. She had soft blond hair and clear blue eyes. There was an innocence in her face that made me think she was even younger than I had first thought, perhaps my own age, though her figure was womanly. She was dressed, like the others, in plain homespun, but her hair was held back with a thin lace ribbon that might once have been part of a dress or a petticoat. This small adornment made her look even prettier. Perhaps I blushed as I tried to conceal my interest.

"I am glad to see you well again, Clem," said Lucy. She rocked the baby as she spoke. "I must get him to sleep," she said. Then she turned to Wade Ferguson. "Will you take some tea, then, before you retire?"

"Not tonight, my dear," he said in a soft tone. "I'm a bit weary."

"Good night then, Mr. Ferguson," Lucy said, and she went toward the smallest of the wagons, stepped inside, and drew down the flap.

I was left to wonder about these people—why did the children address their father thus, as Mister? How did they manage so well to organize themselves, with every chore apportioned, and so many people living together without arguments? All the wagon trains we had encountered on our trek from Missouri to Nebraska had shown strife, most splitting off soon after departure for want of agreement on anything. This was different. Here was a sense of mission and accomplishment, of shared purpose.

The next morning I was up early with the others. Already the men and boys were harnessing the animals and rounding up strays. The women and girls had the fires going, cakes on the pans, and coffee brewing.

I bade everyone a good morning. Lucy had set out our breakfast of cold cakes, dried apple, and jerked buffalo. Beneath her eyes I saw fatigue—she had probably been up all night with Ellen's baby. How good she is, I thought, noticing that she fed all the children their breakfast, taking only a cup of coffee for herself.

"Eat, Clem," she said kindly. "You've a long day ahead."

"And you too," I replied.

She laughed a little and said, "I don't need much."

I took some flat cakes and a cup of hot coffee, then leaned back against the wagon, watching the flurry of packing and gathering. Tents had to be taken down and folded, bedding shaken and put away. The children doused the fires. Lucy scraped and cleaned the dishes and packed everything away, taking innumerable trips to the wagons. Then the three women gathered the children, taking them apart for their morning care. I saw only the backs of the three women as they made a shield of their bodies, their skirts a curtain against the prying eyes of boys or men. I went with Spencer and the other boys to a spot by the river, and I was given a spade and a place for privacy.

We moved out, all on command, like an army moving to battle. Horses neighed, oxen bellowed, and cattle moaned, as if each knew of the long day of heat and toil that lay ahead. We were about thirty wagons, along with a multitude of cattle, donkeys, and extra horses, all laden and kept in line by riders aft and to the rear. One could not fail to see that these wagons were better provisioned than most, and the animals on the whole were not so jaded as others I'd met on the trail.

I learned that relief trains had been sent from Salt Lake with provisions and fresh animals to guide these pioneers along the way. Our leader, Curtis Strong, had made the trek several times before. It was a wonder to me that anybody should make this crossing more than once in a lifetime.

The sight of the horses brought a pang of grief; I remembered Cannon and wondered what had happened to him. Someday, I thought, I would return to Nebraska, seek out Libby, and explain, perhaps repay her for the loss of her horse.

For now, I had but one chore, and that was to move westward and to earn my keep.

To my delight, I was able to show my experience with the oxen, bringing them round with a mere flick of the whip, a song, and never a harsh touch or a curse. The Mormons didn't take to cussing.

At nooning Wade Ferguson sought me out. "I'd be pleased to have you take my boy, Spencer, alongside you and teach him how to deal with the oxen. Spencer! I want you to pay attention to Clem, heed what he does. You do well to take a leaf from this young man's book. Clem has been looking after himself, asking nobody for anything. You heed him, Spencer!"

I felt swelled with pride to hear such things as this. That night, around the fire, Wade Ferguson bade me share my history, and I did, to rapt attention and murmurs of approval and sympathy. And as I told my adventures, I felt elevated in my own eyes, having escaped death many times and yet kept to my mission.

When I was done with my tale, Wade Ferguson rose, as did all the others. "Let us thank our Heavenly Father for the grace He has shed upon our friend Clem."

"Amen," said all of them, including me. I glowed with goodwill and reverence.

Then I saw an odd exchange. As usual, the children were summoned for their good-night blessing from Wade Ferguson, all standing soberly at attention, while the women looked on.

The infant was given to Ellen, who received him with outstretched arms and bound him close in her shawl. With a nod to Candace, Wade Ferguson walked toward Lucy, his hand outstretched. Lucy met his hand and his gaze. I saw her smile, then lower her eyes demurely as they went together to her wagon.

And I was thunderstruck. A fool! How could I have not known it at once? Wade Ferguson was the father of all the children, both Candace's and Ellen's. But Lucy was not his daughter. She was his third wife. Here was the evil I had heard about, right in front of my face, and I had not perceived it.

I slept out under Ellen's wagon, trying to fathom my own revulsion—was it because of their family life, or because I felt personally deceived? I felt a strange fury for Lucy, young Lucy, who was half the age of her husband and forced to share him with two other women. Surely, this was sinful and wrong. Throughout the night I lay sleepless, wrestling with these thoughts that I could not share with anyone.

CHAPTER 20

Lucy Rejects My Gift and Teaches Me a Lesson

They carved out a place for me as naturally as if I had been born in their midst. I was the duly respected animal tender. I became almost a member of the Ferguson family and was a part of the Mormon migration. I watered the stock, took charge of their ailments, and taught Spencer and his younger brother Amos everything I could.

As we worked together, I soon discovered that Amos had a better feel for the oxen than Spencer, who could be excitable and short-tempered. It was Amos who had the patience for yoking the team and unfastening the lines, each in proper turn. It was Amos who learned the soothing words to whisper to the beasts while we administered salves or poultices or urged them to give their utmost on a hard trail.

By now the ruts were deep in the trail, where others had gone before us. Everywhere, too, we saw signs of the pioneers' hardships. At one point we traveled for days on a road lined with crosses and cairns. Cholera had taken the lives of hundreds. Sometimes, we were told, a family started out healthy in the morning and by nightfall half or more of its members were dead. Now and then a pitiful sign was posted: YOU WHO PASS BY, PLEASE RESPECT THIS GRAVE. Bereaved parents had built a poor picket fence around the grave of a child, in hopes that wild animals would leave it undisturbed.

Whenever we passed such a place, Amos darted out and found a small stone to plant there, a token of devotion. Sometimes, when some of the children walked with us, Amos told them stories of the Saints, how they were persecuted, driven out of Missouri, their homes stolen and possessions divided among their enemies.

Things were revealed to me gradually. During nighttime campfires, various people spoke of their journey of conversion, and I learned about Ferguson and his family, how Wade and Ellen had learned of the doctrine.

I had assumed, of course, that Ellen was Amos's mother. Amos corrected me. "Ellen is Father's wife, but not our mother. Spencer and I are brothers, but our mum died when I was born. That was in London, you know. Then Papa married Ellen and gave us a mother."

"That was good of him," I said, thinking of poor Oliver Twist. At least I'd had a family once, and now I had memories of it. Besides, I might soon again be with my father.

"After Father and Ellen heard the Teaching, they agreed to come to America," Amos went on. "But there was Aunt Candace to worry about."

I'd heard Wade Ferguson's testimony, how missionaries came to London and talked about the new church founded in America. It had excited Wade and stirred in him a tremendous desire to join these people whose prophet, Joseph Smith, was just a poor farm boy with a message and a mission. "The Lord spoke to Joseph Smith," said Wade that night of his testimony, "just as He also spoke to me, saying, 'You must heed this call, for it brings you new life.'"

For over a year Wade Ferguson and Ellen had spent every spare minute reading and learning the principles of The Book of Mormon. "We became convinced," Wade said, "that everything Joseph Smith said was divinely given. My life now had a purpose."

I asked Amos about Candace, how Wade came to marry her.

"Papa was worried about leaving her in London," he said, "a widow with three children. How could she manage?"

"I suppose she might have stayed in England," said I, "and married someone else."

"But Ellen couldn't bear the thought of leaving her sister," said Amos. "So Father decided it was best to marry Candace. That way he could take care of her and the children."

"It was not an easy thing," Spencer put in. "Father prayed on it for a long time."

It was still difficult for me to understand and accept this large family of wives, children, sisters, and brothers, all tied together through one man and one faith.

What about Lucy? I wondered. I felt a strange sympathy for Lucy, and resentment at her constant servitude. Lucy seemed distant from the others, pale and solemn, always working and providing. I watched her out of the corner of my eye as I walked beside the oxen or when we made camp. Occasionally she would stop and stretch, hands against her back, face turned skyward. It was a look of weariness and ache. Then I wanted to approach her, but it seemed wrong, and I wondered how Spencer and Amos could be so casual about this girl so near their age, knowing she was the wife of their father.

The action of this family together made me think a good deal about Molly and what it was like to have someone close, someone to love. These thoughts brought a hot flush to my face and spread to my entire body, a flame of longing. If we were by the river I dunked myself in to cool down. One such time ended in catastrophe, for I awoke the next day with an unbearable itch.

I told Amos. "Are there any remedies in your wagons?"

"Where does it itch."

"Where it oughtn't to," I said, trying valiantly not to scratch.

Amos chuckled. "Lucy's the one has the medicines in her wagon. Try her."

At nooning I approached Lucy, who was busy tidying up from supper, wiping the plates and packing them in a box. She had several of the younger children with her, and the baby strapped to a seat in the shade of the wagon.

"So you've caught the poison plant," she said pleasantly. "It happened to me the first day out, stupid thing that I was, I actually picked it!"

"Well, you couldn't know. It probably doesn't grow in London."

"I am from Liverpool," Lucy said rather sharply, then busied herself looking through the medicines stowed in a tin box. She pored through various bottles and came up with a vial containing a white liquid. Lucy pulled out the stopper and sniffed the contents.

"What is it?"

"Calomel. Very good for lots of ailments. Basically, it's mercury."

"Sounds strong," I said, amazed at my own ignorance and Lucy's wisdom. I wanted to ask how she knew about such things, but her cool efficiency stopped me.

"Do I have to drink that?" I asked anxiously.

"You could," she said. "But I thought it better to rub it on the rash."

She took a bit of red flannel, poured on the liquid, and turned to me. "Well? Where is it?"

I froze, my breath caught in my throat. "P-p-private," I managed to croak. Lucy gave me the cloth, pointed inside the wagon and, last I saw, was bent over in a fit of laughter.

It was the first time I saw her laugh. Reflecting on it later, that awful itch was almost worth it.

* * *

It is a dreadful thing, and I am ashamed to say it, but life on the trail can bring out the worst in a person. There is a keen desire for excitement, any kind. The sheer monotony of camping, breaking camp, trudging all day long behind the bellowing, stinking animals, makes a body long for change. Then excitement calls all hands together—there is something to talk about. Part of me reveled in those happenings, the other part writhed in disgust.

We saw things. Three children left behind when both their parents died of measles. Their train had gone on, fearing infection. Our leader, Curtis Strong, held a quick meeting. Two families volunteered to take turns with the children until we reached Salt Lake City, where the elders would decide their future.

The wagons were a constant trial. Wheels flew off and had to be mended. Once, crossing a canyon, two wagons careened down and burst into pieces. Debris lay everywhere. A woman gave birth in the night. We heard her screams. In the morning we dug two graves, one very small.

Jason and Hattie and a boy from another family were missing one day. All the parents were frantic. Stolen by Indians! It had happened before. We set out in a wide circle to search for the children, calling and firing shots to attract attention.

At last someone found them hiding behind a wall of shrubbery, stalking rabbits.

Wade Ferguson used the strap that night.

One late afternoon Hattie and Jason and little Penny came screaming to the wagons, dragging us to a bush where we came upon a woman, stark naked and bound with a rope. Who or what had done this to her? Her ordeal must have lasted several days. Wade and some of the men covered her with a blanket and attempted to move her, but the pain was so great that she screamed for mercy. "Let me be! Let me die!"

She expired half an hour later. His mouth set grimly, our leader, Curtis Strong, lifted his powerful arms and commanded the train, "Move on! Move on! We've lost enough time, move out!"

Every day the devil was at our heels. We must not lose time. September was passing; winter might catch us at any moment. Other parties had perished from cold and starvation. The tragedy of the Donner party had proved how well-meaning, ordinary folk could even turn to cannibalism if things got too bad. "They 'et their own dead relatives," it was told in the taverns and outside the general store. Every schoolchild knew the name "Donner," and it would forever be linked with the eating of human flesh. I shuddered at the thought of winter.

But summer was still raging, with fierce thunderstorms and hoards of mosquitoes that sang in my ears and leaped into my mouth and eyes. Mosquitoes and flies and grubs fed well along the trail. Daily we came upon the skulls and bones of dead animals, picked clean. Beside them, looking like skeletons, too, were remains of furnishings—chairs, bedsteads, bureaus, and hope chests—flung out when the going got too difficult and the animals could no longer pull the heavy loads.

I saw a quilt one day, stitched with pink roses and blue stars. I gathered it up. Loving hands had made it. What had happened to its owner? I thought of Molly, how she wanted to come west with me.

I brought the quilt to Lucy, an offering of some kind. "Thank you for curing me," I said.

She looked startled. "What's this?"

"A quilt. I found it on the trail."

She shook her head. "Put it away," she said, "back on the trail."

I was hurt and angry. "Why? What could be wrong?"

"It is stupid to pick things up!" she cried. "Maybe someone with cholera lay in that quilt. I tell the children all the time to leave things alone. You are just like them."

I turned away, feeling foolish and stung. Then I realized that Lucy was sitting on a trunk, her leg up on a crate. "What happened?" I asked.

"Nothing."

"Nothing?" I glanced down. "Your ankle's all red and swollen. What happened?"

"Let me be!"

I grasped the ankle, she made a fist and beat me on the shoulder. "Leave go!"

I saw the red point and the inflammation near the instep. "You were bitten," I declared. "Why didn't you tell anyone?"

"Because of my own stupidity!" Lucy cried, biting her lip. "I stepped on it."

"A snake?"

"A spider of some sort. It was in my shoe. You can see it."

"You saved it?"

"Here." Lucy reached into the wagon and brought out a flask. Stuffed inside it was a straw-colored scorpion, curled and horrible, with many eyes still bulging.

"Those are poisonous!" I cried.

"I sucked it out."

"Good God, Lucy! Why wouldn't you call for help?"

"There's enough helping been done me. . . ."

"What are you talking about?" I burst out in a rage. "You do twice the work of anyone else. I see you fetching and carrying, cooking, washing, getting up with the babies—are you a servant among them? Is that what a third wife is supposed to be?"

She drew back her foot and looked at me with fire in her eyes. "What do you know about it?" she cried. "You come here judging us, always watching and looking . . ."

"I am not judging!" I shouted.

"You are! I see it. When Wade Ferguson looks at me—"

"You're half his age!" I cried. "It's disgusting, you could be his *child*. He abuses you, Lucy, he and the women have made you a slave."

She struck me with a force I had not imagined her capable of. My face felt fiery. We confronted each other like two furious warriors.

"Moooove out!" came the shout. "Wagons, moooove out!"

The wagons stood ready. Hastily Lucy tossed things into the back. I helped, grabbing baby Wilbur, who clung to me, drooling.

In the flurry of packing and moving out, Lucy and I held a shaky truce. Her wagon was drawn by four mules. Now she walked beside them, switch in hand, striking them so, that the switch whistled and whirred in the air.

"Leave off those poor beasts!" I finally cried. "It's me you're angry at. Why take it out on them?"

She dropped the switch, her face red and streaked with tears. "I hate you!" she said, her voice muffled and choked. "Why did you come here? You don't belong with us. You're a stranger, a Gentile, and you have no feelings for—"

"I have every feeling!" I objected. "I cared about your injury, I gave you a quilt, I see you struggle every day. . . ."

"You see what you want to see," she declared. She walked on, eyes straight ahead, and the mules plodded along on their own, with only my hand on the leader's flank and an occasional pat to guide them.

"I see that you are young. You are beautiful. You are wasting your life. . . ."

"No," she said softly. "You don't know how it was for me before Wade Ferguson came. He found me on the street, sick and desperate. I had heard the Teaching, and I went back again and again to hear more. It gave me hope. I prayed for help. And one night there was Wade Ferguson and Ellen, come to a meeting, and they saw me in a doorway, filthy and horrid."

I stared at Lucy, her soft blond hair and clear skin. How could she ever be horrid?

"They stopped and spoke to me. Wade saw that I was—not well."

"What was wrong?"

"I was—about to have a—a baby."

"A baby!"

She lashed out at me, furious. "You've heard of them, haven't you? Babies? You know anything about it?"

I bit my lip. I wished I'd done so long before. My troubles usually began when I opened my big mouth.

"They took me in their coach to their lodging. They watched over me and called a midwife, and when the baby came, Ellen held my hands and spoke to me so softly about wonderful things, filling my mind during the dreadful pain."

"And the baby?" I asked, looking at the infant she still carried now in a shawl wrapped around her shoulders.

"She died two days later. I had some poison in me, they said. It killed my baby. I don't know whether I shall ever . . ." She broke off, stopped the wagon. "This one's limping," she said, pointing to the forward mule.

I lifted its leg and saw a stone lodged there. We stopped long enough for me to pry out the stone with my blade. "You should ride in the wagon," I said, "with that leg of yours."

"The beasts cannot pull more weight," Lucy said.

"Then what about Ellen's wagon? I laid there when they found me."

"You were very ill," Lucy said. "It was necessary. Besides, I won't have them nurse me again. They have done enough. More than a mother and father might do."

"But you're a wife!" I exclaimed. "Why did he have to take you to wife?"

"You fool!" she charged me. "I wanted it! Wade Ferguson paid my passage to America. He asked nothing in return. I begged him to let me work for him and work off the funds. I did not want to accept this charity. Can you understand that?"

"Yes, yes," I murmured miserably. "But why marry?"

"I grew to love him! He is the kindest, most honest man I have ever known. And Ellen and Candace—they accepted me like a sister. And when we came here and went to prayer, the elders asked about me, was I a daughter? A sister and aunt? And they said it was not right for me to be without a husband. Wade said he would find a husband to care for me. I begged Wade Ferguson not to find me another mate. For I had come to love *him*! Do you find that shameful? Do you, Clem?"

I shook my head, afraid to speak.

"I wanted to be in this family more than anything I've ever wanted. How can you know what it is like for us? You're a stranger, a Gentile. This is where I belong. I have everything now—people who help me and love me, children, sisters, husband. When we get to Zion we will have a real home. Nobody need be lonely or afraid or cast out. You say I work too much? I owe them everything. My life."

I said nothing, but I stopped the team. I ran ahead to the next wagon, and I quickly explained the need. The driver stopped and waited while I ran to Lucy's wagon to unload a trunk and a barrel full of potatoes, which I hoisted onto the other wagon.

Lucy watched, speechless.

When I came back to her I said, "Now up. You will ride until that leg is no longer swollen. If not, I will tell Wade Ferguson and the others what a fool you are, taking a chance with your life because you do not trust them to help you."

"Let me ride on the mule, then," Lucy said, needing to have the last word. "I hate the closed feeling of the canvas."

I helped her mount one of the back mules, and we walked on. She had handed me the baby. I had never held an infant so long, until I knew every curve of its body and every murmur it made. It sucked on my shoulder. It gurgled. I patted and crooned, pretending it was an ox.

My reward was a soaked shirt and a foul smell that lingered the whole night long.

CHAPTER 21

We Cross the Terrible Mountains, the Mountain Meadows Massacre Returns, and We Reach the Saints

I started having strange dreams. I dreamed of the landmarks we had passed, Independence rock, Devil's Gate, and in each one my name was carved. I dreamed of Libby, and then Libby was Ma, giving me a haircut, telling me to prepare logs and build a house for her and for Molly. Pa was not in any of my dreams. When I awoke, I felt guilty and mean, having cut him out of my dreams. All these months of supposing—I had been wrong to imagine our meeting. It was better to leave off hoping or imagining anything at all. Until now, everything I thought and reasoned out had turned out different. And as we came to the Sierra Mountains, once again I saw that I had been a fool, thinking the worst was behind us.

Just as we tightened our belts for the last time and goaded the animals for one more mighty effort, we beheld those awful mountains in the distance. First we sank in marsh and mud up to the wagon beds. Everything stuck and stank. Insects multiplied in the dampness.

One night, very late, I heard terrible shrieking and, grabbing a lantern, rushed out to find Lucy and Ellen bent over a washtub. Four of the children, Hattie, Penny, Agnes, and Jason, were leaping about, screaming. "What is it?" I cried, astounded by the anguished cries and the women's grim faces.

"Lice," Ellen said, tight-lipped. She grabbed Agnes by the sleeve. "We have to douse their heads with kerosene."

"Kerosene!" I called out gleefully. "Why, that's wonderful! Can I have some? It makes the hair grow fine and strong. You've heard of Samson? It was kerosene that did it, made his hair grow all lustrous, strong as a rope, and gave him muscles too."

"You can not have it," said Lucy, playing along. "We haven't enough for everyone."

"Oh, please! And can I wear a rag around my head?"

"Not you, Clem. You're nearly grown. 'Tis only for the children."

The children eyed me suspiciously, but at least they were done sobbing. We tied their heads with cloth to keep the kerosene on, and the next day, as we were walking, we hunted for feathers to trim the headgear, so the children were content.

One day we reached a crest and the train stopped dead. A murmur spread from those in front until everyone gathered to look upon this new disaster. I saw Ellen drop to her knees. Lucy's face was rigid with shock.

"'Tis impossible," said Spencer. "Nobody can cross those mountains."

"Others have done it," said Amos, but he looked stricken.

Before us stood mountains and more mountains, so high they seemed to block out the sun, so vast that when one range was crossed, another would appear, harsh granite, craggy and steep. How could anyone do it?

"It can be done, Brothers!" cried our leader, Mr. Strong. "I promise you, it was done by Brigham Young and all the others. This is the last test. Come on, brave hearts, we move on!"

But how? How to traverse those huge precipices and steep ravines without being dashed over the edge?

But we began, lashing the wagon wheels to keep from sliding, letting them go if need be, throwing out objects, anything to lighten the load. Our food dwindled. Of the three cows Wade Ferguson had brought, only one remained, staggering and bony. It would soon die. On one of the dangerous descents Ellen's wagon broke loose and was hurled down a ravine, breaking into pieces. I saw the spinning wheel go flying, food barrels crashing on the rocks, everything torn to pieces.

Ellen's face paled. Her lips were dead white. A faint cry escaped from her lips, nothing more. In the night another horse gave out. We heard the shot as its owner relieved the animal's misery. Each mountain demanded more of us it seemed, consuming our last ounce of strength. But then there was another and another.

After the steep climb came the canyons. Our wagons lurched and strained, the canvas tops became shredded by thorns.

All the children were ailing. Deep, dark hollows showed under their eyes. Day and night they coughed and sniffed. Baby Wilbur whimpered for days, then grew quiet, and Ellen and Lucy took turns holding him as they walked.

As we trudged over these awful mountains, Spencer and Amos told the children tales of Mormon heroism. "Those Saints in Navoo," Spencer said, "just left their homes and moved out to find Zion. What they couldn't sell, they left standing, often with the doors wide open for others to take. They didn't care! They were going to a better place, a place the Lord would show them."

"Well, why do they hate us?" asked Jason, and Hattie, who was riding a mule, glowered and said, "They killed our prophet. Ma told me. They tarred him and feathered him first." She turned to me. "Does it hurt to be tarred, Clem?"

"I don't know," said I, "never having had it done."

"We could do it to you if you want," Hattie suggested. "We've got buckets of tar for the wagons, you know."

"Thank you kindly, Hattie," I said. "It is a punishment, not a pleasure."

"Why do they punish us?" persisted Jason.

"Because we are different," said Amos.

"I'm not different from anyone," said Hattie.

"Oh, yes, you are," insisted Spencer. "You are a Saint."

"I don't want to be a Saint!" Hattie screamed. "Saints get killed!"

"They do not," shouted Jason. "We're tough. We got those Missouri wildcats, didn't we? We have our own militia. Pa told me. We can kill anybody if they bother us. Just like we killed those Missouri wildcats."

"Shut up!" shouted Spencer. "We don't talk like that."

"Butchered 'em!" Jason cried gleefully, running his finger across his throat.

"Stop it," said Amos, giving the boy a shake. "Those were innocent women and children."

"How dare you say such things!" Spencer grasped Amos by the collar, pulling him forward. "Anything the Saints did was for the glory of God, and by order of Brother Young."

"It was a massacre!" shouted Amos.

"Silence!" Wade Ferguson stood there, his thick arms crossed over his chest. "What sort of talk is this for decent children? I will not have it."

That night Wade called me to him after the others had gone to bed. "I don't want you thinking badly of us, Clem," he said softly. "This massacre thing . . . I know that people talk about it. The Gentiles use it as another reason to hate us."

"I don't hate you, sir," I told him. "It is true, I have heard about it before."

"What had you heard?" he asked me, leaning forward, intent on my answer.

"That the Mormons and the local Indians made an alliance, stopped a large wagon train passing through Utah, and killed everyone except the youngest children. That they took all the possessions, the cattle, the furniture. . . ."

"Do you know where those folks were from?" Wade asked.

"Missouri, I think."

"And that we were at the start of a war, a battle for our very existence?"

"No, sir. I had not heard about that."

"President Buchanan was determined to replace our leader, Governor Young, with his own man, someone 'more acceptable.' This, after we had built our own community here under Brigham Young's guidance. The president was planning an invasion, sending an armed battalion here to evict Governor Young and force us to give up our own rule over Zion. When that wagon train came in from Missouri, rumor had it that they were the same wild rebels who had killed Joseph Smith and participated in the Haun's Mill Massacre years ago. Did you ever hear of Haun's Mill?"

"No, sir."

"You see, there are two sides to every story," said Wade, shaking his head. "Usually folks only tell you one side. At Haun's Mill some of our people had gone for refuge. The local militia came in with rifles and, despite the fact that our people were unarmed and ready to surrender, killed about seventeen, including women and children. One boy of nine was found hiding under the bellows in a blacksmith shop. They shot him in the head, though he was but a child. 'Nits make lice,' they said. That is how they talked about us and showed no mercy, even to a child. So when those men came through Utah, screaming out their hatred of us, some people became alarmed, some wanted revenge, others thought they were coming in advance of the army to slaughter us all."

"How is it you know the story so well?" I asked.

"Well, the thing stuck in my craw, you might say," Wade replied. "I don't like killing of innocents, and I will question any man. I did question one of the leaders of the church who came to London. He made no excuse for killing, but told me the other side, as I tell it to you now. Fear and hatred and revenge always end with violence and, later, with guilt. Yes, the Mormons were guilty of fear and haste, but not hatred. We never hated anyone nor persecuted anyone. Mistakes were made at Mountain Meadows. Some say Brigham Young never ordered anyone killed but that others were hasty and took it upon themselves to kill those people. There have been inquiries. There will be more. I hope justice—whatever that is—will be done and the thing put to rest."

We kicked out the fire and lit a lantern. As we walked, the lantern light made whirling shadows in our path. Wade Ferguson sighed deeply. Then he said, "Some of our group are going on ahead. Supplies are low, and the nights are already cold."

"Who is going?" I asked, alarmed that we might be caught short of rifles and men.

"Some of the young, single men who have horses, and younger couples without children and wagons to slow them down. Go ahead with the others, Clem," Wade urged me. "Look, you can take one of the mules. We will catch up with you in Salt Lake City."

"No." I shook my head. "I would sorely miss Sister Candace's apple cobbler."

Wade turned to me. With the lantern between us, I could see the gleam of his eyes. He grinned and clapped me on the back. We both knew Candace had run out of apples weeks ago. "Very well, then. You might help Lucy with the mules. Her ankle is not yet healed."

"You knew about that?" I exclaimed.

He smiled. "It is my business to know what ails my family."

So I went with Lucy, and we talked to keep our minds off our travail. I told her about Pa, how I aimed to go to the gold fields to find him, perhaps even to San Francisco. I tried to picture San Francisco for her from the articles I had read at Libby's house. "Hotels and taverns and even a playhouse!" I said.

"What is a playhouse?" Lucy asked, turning to me from astride the mule.

"Why, it is a theater. And players come there to sing and dance and tell stories."

"Stories," Lucy murmured, smiling slightly. "Tell me a story, Clem."

And I told her the story of Oliver Twist, as well as I could remember it, drawing it out so that it might last until we came to our destination.

At the end, I had no energy left for stories. As we were crossing the last ridge, the air turned chill. Sleet swiftly rained down upon us, the pieces of ice cutting into our faces and hands. Our wagons lurched. The animals stood stoically in the wind and sleet, blinded by the cruel, cold fog.

We stopped, unable even to circle, and we stood in a long line, our wagons buffeted by the clattering sleet. After a time, Lucy and I saw Ellen stumble from her wagon. In her arms was the small bundle, rigid and unyielding. "Lucy! Lucy!" she called out. "It's Wilbur—oh he's gone!"

Lucy cried out sharply, then ran to Ellen. Together the two women stood in the fog and sleet, holding each other, the dead baby between them.

We had traveled two or three hours, and the day was warm, with a hint of breeze cooling the mountains. We began a gradual descent, thinking it just another approach to another mountain. We had eaten biscuits and the last of the dried buffalo. I had found some berries and shared them with Lucy and the children.

"Is Wilbur in heaven?" they continually asked. "Is he now with God?"

"Certainly," I answered. "Brave little soul," I added. I regretted having had any complaint about his habits, and I remembered how I had held him, sopping wet and odorous. Now, I wished I could do it again.

Our wagons creaked and swayed through the brush, over stones and gullies. Suddenly a kind of hush fell over the hillside, as if the very sky had opened, and a voice proclaimed, echoing Brigham Young, "This is the place. This is the right place."

I stared, blinked. At that moment I knew this scene would be locked in my mind forever.

Below us stretched a vast plain, its fields of corn and wheat, pumpkins, squash, and beans making a patchwork pattern of various hues, various shapes, all ordered by fences and irrigation ditches. My breath caught in my throat and my heart pounded. How could it be? A vast city had been created here in the wilderness, in the desert, and it flourished. Yes, I could see from here that it flourished, with woodsmoke rising from chimneys, animals small in the distance yet thriving, grazing, working. At the center was a large building that I would later know as the Temple, not yet completed but well on the way. Extending from the Temple, streets were laid out in a grid pattern. Each house was surrounded by the same size plot of land for privacy and for growing vegetables. Beyond the city were mountains, rings of huge mountains, some dusted with snow. The city below seemed to live in the palm of some great, protective giant.

"This is the place," murmured Lucy, standing beside me. I looked, and beside her stood Wade and Ellen and Candace, and all their children and the other travelers. They stood silent, gazing at their Zion.

"Remember this moment, children," said Wade. "When you are old, when you tell your grandchildren, remember how it felt to gaze for the first time upon Zion, our home, which our Heavenly Father prepared for us. Let us give thanks."

———◆—◆———

There was a rare kind of order and security in this city by the Salt Lake. Everyone, equally, received land, a house, an opportunity to be part of the community. Brigham Young himself had laid out the streets of the city, and he had established rules, declaring, "Those who do not like our looks and customs are at liberty to go where they please. But if they remain with us they must obey the laws sanctioned by us. There must be no work done on the Sabbath." Each family was urged to be industrious in cultivating fields and raising children who would become fine citizens, opposed to drunkenness, idleness, and profanity.

I thought of friends I had made in the taverns and on the road. Few would be tolerated here. I wanted to be good, but I wasn't sure I fit here, either. Often I did not feel saintly, or think saintly thoughts.

Wade Ferguson took me in, and we began building his house. He would finish three rooms before winter and complete the rest next spring.

"We can build on an extra room for a friend," he told me. "Look, Clem, you've become like one of the family. Why don't you stay here with us and make your home? Soon you'll have a wife and a house of your own. We would be proud to have you among us."

"I thank you kindly, sir," I said. "But I must go on to find my pa."

"How will you go, then?" he asked. "Soon the mountain passes will be snowed in and dangerous."

"I thought, if I could take the stagecoach . . ." I began.

Wade nodded. "If you would help me for the next month with my house," he said, "I shall pay you wages enough to take the stage to California."

<hr/>

When the time came, once again I experienced a dismal farewell, at the same time trying to be jovial. "I'm going to go look for some lice!" I yelled to the children, waving my cap. "Be good! Be well!"

Ellen gave me a scarf. Candace packed a bag of cookies for my trip. Lucy only nodded and tried to smile, then ran back to the house. As the coach pulled away, however, I saw her standing in the road, waving good-bye. I wished we could have been better friends.

CHAPTER 22

I Land in California, Find the Gold Fields, and Look for Pa in San Francisco

Dust is what I remember the most of that stagecoach ride, dust and constant arguments accompanied by swaying and lurching until my bones rattled in their sockets and my teeth clattered in my head.

Nine persons were squeezed into that small space like ointment in a tube. On top was luggage—none of it mine, as I had lost my possessions in various catastrophes—plus a traveler or two who squeezed in beside the driver, the shotgun rider, and the bags.

Of our company, two were Mormon men going to California to buy cattle and horses. Riding on top most of the way was a gambler, who tried to entice the others to wagers, including me. I kept my money in my pocket and my tongue quiet in my head.

There were two ladies coming west to join their husbands. They talked constantly, calling each other Dearie, and complaining about everything under the sun, including that heavenly body itself. It was too hot, too cold, too moist, too dry. Their perfume billowed through the coach, mingling with the dust from the road, making me want to puke.

A banker from Boston came on behalf of the railroad line. He smoked incessantly. His emaciated associate coughed with every puff of the smoker's pipe and every bend of the coach. A German man laughed and thumped his cane heartily at any comment, determined to be jolly despite the fact he understood not a word of English. "Ho-ho"—*thump, thump*, as the talk turned from outlaws and Indians to religion and politics, two topics that no traveler should address, at least not in an overcrowded, overheated coach.

"Election's this month. Hope you all know how to vote—begging your pardon, ladies. Anyone who doesn't vote for Lincoln is a fool."

"You think Lincoln's going to make it? I doubt it—too opinionated."

"A leader needs to have strong opinions—you want a yellow-belly for president?"

"Ho-ho"—*thump, thump*.

"Comes from the backwoods of Illinois. So unpolished. Well, Dearie, if I were voting—"

"Lord preserve us from such times as the need for ladies to soil their gloves with ink!"

"The United States is not a monarchy. We don't need a dictator telling us what to do and what to believe. We need someone to enforce the will of the people."

"And what is the will of the people? They all want different things. The Mormons want multiple wives, for instance. Isn't that right? Don't you fellows take to having several wives at once?"

"Now, now, let's not—"

"Let the truth be told! Mr. Lincoln doesn't care a pin about polygamy. All he can think of is the Negroes, getting them free. Well, for my money, polygamy is worse than slavery. It pollutes the very air—"

"Speaking of air—if you would ram that confounded pipe up your gullet!"

"Ho-ho." *Thump! Thump! Thump!*

The only reason they didn't come to blows is that the coach was lurching so, and we were crowded in like posts in a logjam.

I heard the two Mormon men speaking softly together, comrades in a hostile setting. "If Lincoln wins, the South may secede. The union will be weakened. If he loses, slavery continues and spreads."

"We will not have slavery in Utah. And if the South secedes, we may go our own way too. Why not? We possess our own goals, our own kingdom."

"Well, don't argue with them, I beg you. We are without law and order here on the road, and that one looks trigger-happy."

We rode through the night, only changing horses and drivers. The stage stops were small holes of debris, with hard biscuits and slops of soup to eat. I longed for the days of fresh buffalo meat and Libby's savory bread and Candace's cobblers. But then I thought of how I'd nearly starved after being injured, and I was thankful for anything that came my way.

I had lost most of my possessions—the books, the photograph of my parents, and most of the drawings I had made. They either drowned in the river crossings or became obliterated by dust and dirt. What remained were about half a dozen sketches, one of Sara, Gabriel's wife, and several I made on the trail. When I left Salt Lake City, Wade gave me a piece of oiled cloth to keep them in. Now I took stock of my possessions and came out with these few drawings, the clothes on my back, the boots on my feet, and the knife in my pocket—plus a few dollars left after the stagecoach fare.

I could not stop my thoughts, compounding now as I drew nearer to my quest. I imagined finding Pa, perhaps rich now from a strike just recently made. "Clem! I struck it rich, boy, and now I was just about to send for you and your ma. What a wondrous thing to have you here! Fellows, look, it's my boy! Remember, I told you all about my son, Clem."

Or he would have left the gold fields, discouraged and broke, working as a digger for the railroad or setting explosives into the hills. Perhaps he had lost a finger or a foot—my poor father, wounded and destitute! He did not want to be a burden to his family. Bravely he carried on alone, hoping to better himself before he came to find us. I would take care of my father and be a comfort to him.

All day and half the night such stories wove their way through my thoughts, bending, lurching, changing with every shift of the wheels.

It took eight days to reach Sacramento, as the coach lost a wheel midway and we had to wait out repairs. Then there was rumor of Indians on the loose, looking for booty. Of course we carried a chest of banknotes and other valuables, thus our route went roundabout to avoid trouble. By the time we dragged into Sacramento, I was sore in every muscle and limb, most especially my ears, which rang and burned from all the squabbling and gossip.

The commerce of Sacramento was centered on the gold fields. Sutter's Fort, once a prosperous settlement called New Helvetia, had been a famous inn and refuge for travelers. At one time I suppose it had been beautiful, with flowers and pleasant rooms, its own armory, well-appointed kitchen, and guest rooms. In the yard stood a large mounted cannon. Now the place was overrun with seedy-looking miners in from the fields. They slept everywhere, in the yard, on the floor, two or more to a bunk.

I walked about, dazed and discouraged. Where were the oranges growing on trees, the lemons and the figs? I had expected to see nuggets lying in the streets. I hiked over to the gold fields, to the shabby tents and rude huts where the miners lived. Mud ran in rivulets down the scarred hillsides. Cook fires dotted the flats. Dirty clothes hung on lines between trees. Foul smells greeted me as I wandered about, cautious of the holes and tunnels that had been dug everywhere amid the clutter of abandoned tools. There were pockets of uproar and rowdy dealings—smoking and card games and swearing, with plenty of whiskey going down. Once or twice a woman's face peeped out from behind a dark window. A few children ran about. But it was not a place for families, and most of the men were grizzled and worn, far removed from female niceties. Everyone carried a pistol and a knife.

I found the courage to saunter up to one group of revelers. "Anyone here know Pierre Fontayne?"

Their bloodshot eyes looked me over. They shook their heads and coughed. "Nope. Nope."

I pulled the battered drawing of Sara from my pocket. "How 'bout this woman? Has anyone seen her around?"

They shook their heads and mumbled, "No."

I wandered from place to place, asking, describing, finally coming upon a shack with a tin roof, which bore a sign in green-painted letters: GENERAL STORE.

Inside were bins of food, stacks of canvas and hides, shovels, picks, nails, blankets, pots, and lumber. I went up to the counter, where several men lounged, smoking and picking their teeth, most of which were mossy and nearly destroyed.

"Anyone here know Pierre Fontayne?"

"Nope. Nope."

"That Frenchie?" An old-timer tottered toward me, his rheumy eyes fastened on my face. "He was here a while ago. Can't say just when. Lose track of time in these diggins."

"He was here!" I wanted to grasp the man's hands, but it would have been like embracing a mule that had wrestled with a skunk.

"Used to talk politics all the time, talk about alerting the people. Didn't go over much here, fellows bent on finding gold, don't care about such as politics."

"Where did he go?" I asked, with that strange feeling of falling, falling into an abyss.

"Frisco, I suppose. That's where those fellows go when they want to talk politics."

"Frisco?" I repeated.

"San Francisco," said another, looking up from his task of picking mites out of a bin of oats.

"Much obliged!" I shouted, and I left them in a hurry, clutching the few dollars that remained in my pocket.

I discovered that I could ride to San Francisco with a rancher delivering apples the next day. He would take a passenger for a dollar. It was nearly the last of my funds, a fortune, to be sure, but I had few other choices. I bedded down in a field under an apple tree. At dawn I was awakened by birds pecking at the apples, dropping them down upon me. I rose, aching yet oddly refreshed. At an inn I spent a few pennies on coffee and a huge cinnamon bun, then found my driver and mounted to sit beside him.

"You're the first," he said, "so you can sit up front. Two other fellows are riding in back with the apples."

I considered myself lucky.

"Have a little smile?" he asked, offering me a drink from his small bottle.

"No, thanks," I said, glad that he thought me man enough to want whiskey in the morning, but sick at the thought of drinking it. My stomach was rolling over anyhow, with worry. Where would I begin? How might I find my pa amongst all those millions of people? And if Pa was dead, what would become of me? If he was alive, would he want me? This was the first time such a thought had come to me. Maybe my father did not want me with him. I tried to push down the thought, but it stuck, and when we stopped for lunch, I could not eat for worry.

In my state of nerves, I was only dimly aware of the fields of wheat, apple orchards, and vineyards. The land was green and golden, while in the East fierce wind and snowstorms would already have struck, and people would be fighting to keep warm. There was a fragrance about California, difficult to define, a combination of greenery and blossoms and sunshine. I wished I could revel in this beauty.

I laid my head back and slept, awakening as we came in sight of the bay. "How many people live in San Francisco?" I asked.

"About half a million, I guess."

"Oh. That's better," I said.

"How's that?"

"Better than the million I thought of. I'm aiming to find my pa."

"Good luck."

I dug into my pocket and brought out my drawing of Sara and showed it to the driver. "Have you seen this woman around?"

He shook his head and grinned. "You sure lost a lot of folks, haven't you?"

I told him she's the wife of a friend, and somehow I yearned to be back with the bullwhackers.

We rode in silence for a time. "What's your pa do?"

"Don't know. Maybe politics."

"Well, then, you want to go to the wharf. That's where all them fellows are yelling and hollering and preaching all the time. That's where the life is."

"Much obliged," I said, "if you could take me there."

"I'll point you there," he said. "You can find it, easy. Surrounded by water, ha-ha!" He took a swig and laid on the whip, so that we careened up the last hill and down again, around the bend, and there she was. San Franciso.

It was midafternoon, and the sun shone in a haze all about, landing on the water in silver streaks. Never had I imagined such a place, vibrating with sound and motion, more alive even than Saint Joe. White clouds blew across the sky, and that blue sky touched the blue-gray water so that it seemed I stood at the very edge of the world.

I ran in the direction my driver had pointed, ran through the muddy streets, past the rows of wooden houses set steeply into the slanted hills, down again, down toward the wharves from which came sounds and sights all mingled and frenzied. Oh, the variety of people assembled here! Italian fishermen were bringing in their glittering catch, shouting as they hoisted up their nets. They whistled and sang out to one another, stowing the fish into huge metal lockers, throwing buckets of fresh water upon them, letting the slime and the seawater spill into the dirt.

In the harbor steamers hissed and boomed. On the docks cargo came banging down—boxes of goods, machine parts, and clothing from the East, honey and molasses and spices and salt. Onto the ships were hoisted lumber and pelts and hides. Boxes of produce waited on the dock, oranges and lemons, apples and grapes. There were huge clipper ships, small sailing vessels, and paddleboats bound for the rivers up north.

The racket of river traffic almost drowned out the closer bellowing of cattle. Sheep grazed on the hillsides and waited in nearby pens for transport. Mangy, feral-looking cats prowled everywhere, eating fish entrails, leaping onto cartons and casks.

I walked and walked, listening to the many languages, hearing the varied sounds from taverns and shops and warehouses. Never had I seen so many different types—muscular Negroes loaded the ships, their arms like tree limbs, firm and strong. Chinese men with long braids and tunics hurried about with poles laid across their backs, baskets of wares hanging down at their sides. There were dark-haired Spaniards with wide-brim hats, trading livestock and grain. I heard German and French and other languages mingled together. The ironmonger and the stone mason had Irish names, O'Sullivan and O'Leary and Finley. I passed fisheries and meatpacking houses, the Polish sausage maker, the Swedish hatters, the Jewish tailors. A huge refinery sent billows of smoke into the air. On a corner a large marquis proclaimed, THEATER, LOTTA CRABTREE, THE LOVELY YOUNG ENTERTAINER—TONIGHT!" From inside came laughter and violin music, rehearsal for the evening performance.

A poster caught my eye, and I stopped at a window under a sign, GROSSMER, LITHOGRAPHY. Inside, stuck on the walls and lying on tables, an array of sketches depicted San Francisco and Sacramento, clipper ships, and an old hotel. My heart leaped at the thought of my own art, and how it would be to have my pictures printed. All I had seen was still vivid in my mind—the wagons and horses, the magnificent monuments, canyons, and forests and rivers—I would show the trail with its hardship and its raw beauty.

I stepped inside, awed by the sights and the smells of this craft. A man wearing a dark green smock turned to me, flustered and harried. "We are about to close," he said. "Come back tomorrow."

I nodded, straining for a last look at a scene of deep canyons and horses.

"You like these pictures?" he asked, leading me to the door.

"They are wonderful," I said. "I have just come across the plains, and I—"

"Come back tomorrow," he repeated, and I left, dazzled by what I had seen and at the thought of what I might yet do.

A gusty wind came up. I heard foghorns and the crying of seals in the distance. Everything smelled different, saltwatery and fishy and moist. I shivered, for the air became very cold.

I walked on and on, and I began to feel like a fool. In a city like this, how could I possibly find anyone? Pa and I could likely pass each other in the street and never know it. What on earth made me think we might find each other in the same place at the same time? It was not like home, wandering into the general store, where everyone knew the entire population and could direct a visitor to a person's door. What in the world had I been thinking of?

And yet—and yet—there was something marvelous about having come here, so far, to the very edge of the continent, to see the ocean pushing up against the pilings and the sand.

I walked on past hotels and cabarets, saloons, shops, and office buildings—the assay office, steamship company, the Wells Fargo office, Irish-American Benevolent Society, a French hospital.

I stopped short, walked up to the massive door, and pushed it open. Inside, at a long table, sat a nurse going over some registers. Again, I felt foolish, but I had to ask.

"I am looking for a Frenchman," I began.

"*Oui*. Is he ill? In this hospital?"

"I—I hope not. It is my father. I have come from—well, from far away. His name is Pierre Fontayne. I thought maybe you . . ."

"The printer. The newspaperman. Yes."

"You know him?"

She shrugged and smiled, showing a dimple. "Everybody knows. He makes a newspaper in French. He calls it *Le Pilote*. Like on a ship, you see? The first, the one who steers the ship, who knows the way to go."

"I see," I said faintly. My hopes had landed, at last, in this place, but I felt weak, scarcely able to go on.

"You would like something to drink, perhaps?" the nurse asked, frowning.

"Yes—no. Do you know where this newspaper office is?"

"Market Street, I think, two blocks from the pier. You can ask. Everybody knows *Le Pilote*."

She went with me to the door and pointed the way. "There. Not very far. You will find it."

I thanked her and set out. By now the sun was going down, tinting the sky golden pink beneath a blanket of dark blue and lavender.

Candles glowed in windows. As evening fell, so too came the more riotous laughter, shouting, and whistling as men completed their work and looked for leisure. Never had I seen so many buildings crowded together, and people hurrying to and fro, lanterns swinging, going about their business quite as if it were bright daylight.

Several times I stopped to ask directions, then found myself in front of a two-story frame building with a sign, MERCER MERCANTILE. Beside it was a narrow bookstore tucked into an alcove, a pharmacy, and then a small sign with a painted arrow pointed down a row of steep steps into a basement room, *Le Pilote*. I was beyond excitement now. My mind had gone numb. Only the fierce pounding of my heart gave reality to this moment, so long awaited.

I stood there, looking down through the iron grate, squinting into a shadowy doorway, listening for sounds, but none came. Slowly I descended. I peered inside to see a small pot-bellied stove, a long table, a dark iron machine, and several chairs. At the stove stood a man. I saw the long pigtail and the tunic. My breath froze in my throat. Surely this was the wrong place.

I rapped softly at the door.

The man turned and, seeing me, looked startled, almost angry. Words rang out, unintelligible, high-pitched.

I knocked again. The door was pulled open. The man, holding a pot in his hand, eyed me suspiciously.

"Good evening," I said in my most formal manner, nodding. "I am looking for—"

"What is it, Wang?" said a voice. And I recognized the voice, but not its owner for he was hidden in shadows and shorter, smaller by far than the father I remembered. But the voice sent waves of feeling through me. The room seemed to rock and sway. I reached out, but there was nothing to hold onto.

He stepped forward into the light. "Yes? Is there something I can do for you?"

I stood there staring at him, seeing the difference in the way his mouth moved, the familiar set of his shoulders, the lift of his brows, the cigarette between his fingers, the thin trail of smoke around him. "Father," I said. "It's me. Clem."

CHAPTER 23

I Make Some Important Decisions about the Rest of My Life

In the moment of silence that followed, a hundred thoughts and visions crowded into my brain, and probably into his, too, for Pa gasped, and took a step backward, as if he had been shot, then he recoiled and came toward me.

"Clem! Is it really you? Wang, it is my son. Come in. Sit down. How did you get here? How did you find me? But it is impossible—Clem!"

I could not sit, I could not move. I had lived this moment in my mind a thousand times. I had imagined unbridled joy, a wild embrace. Instead, I only stood there, trembling.

"Sit down, Clem!" my father called out. "Wang, bring him a bowl."

"Yes, yes," said the Chinese man. He walked in a strange, jerky fashion, as if he had pebbles in his slippers.

I sat down at the table. Weariness made me dizzy. I wished for a glass of water but could not ask.

"Chili," said my father, setting down a bowl of steaming stuff with a spicy smell. "Beans and peppers and onions, quite the thing in California. Mexican influence, you see."

"Chili," I repeated.

"Some bread?" asked my father, roving about the room, as if a loaf had hidden itself somewhere on purpose.

"Yes, please," I said. Wang poured coffee into a mug and set it down before me.

My father found the bread, took his time cutting several slices, and brought it to me on a chipped porcelain plate.

"Clem." He sat down opposite me. I saw now that his mouth had two teeth missing. It gave him a crooked and impoverished look.

Wang came and stood before me, hands clasped in his sleeves. He faced me solemnly, then nodded deeply and said, "Your father big man in San Francisco. Own big printing press. Make big newspaper every week. Very big."

Wang proceeded toward the monstrous machine, and I heard the ping and clang of metal parts coming together.

"He is setting the type," said my father. I glanced up at him and saw an expression of pride mixed with apology. "It took every penny I could scrape up," he said. "I bought it from a man called Stegemeyer. Went back home to New York. I'm still paying him back."

I stared at the machine, imagining all the money that must have gone into this venture. If only some of that cash had come to us in a letter, along with a few words of cheer. What a comfort it would have been. We sat together at the table, Pa and I. My mind spun with emotions, all mixed in perplexity—anger, sorrow, dismay. How could he sit here so calmly, offering me chili, when the world seemed utterly changed for us both?

"We are waiting for election news," Pa said. "I think Lincoln will win. Then we will write about him in the paper. It will be a good thing for him to win. We have been printing articles. Everybody knows about my newspaper."

Pa broke off. His eyes searched mine, and questions shot from his mouth. "How did you get here? How did you find me? Did your mother send you?"

"Ma died," I said, "over a year ago. And the baby with her."

"The . . . baby? There was a baby?"

"Of course there was a baby!" I screamed. "We named her Joy May—" My voice broke.

He stood up now, gasping, his hand to his chest. "I—I swear I did not know about a baby."

"How could you not know?" I cried.

Pa sank down, head in his hands, his face hidden. His shoulders shook. When he looked up, his face looked crumpled and strange.

"Clem, listen, these are things—you do not understand. You were so young, still a child. Died? Your mother *died*?"

"Fever and ague," I said. "I buried them on the knoll. Then I had to leave the place. I could not keep it up by myself."

"No, no, of course not. But how did you find me?"

"Why didn't you write, Pa?" I took a sip of the coffee. It was bitter and strong.

"Where would I send a letter? How? You must understand. When I got here I was sick, so weak I could not walk. I had nothing. All my money was spent on river crossings and supplies. I met a mountain man and gave him my last dollar for a pelt. I was freezing in the nights. My horse died on me. I lay there, and some trappers came along—wild men they were, and I was afraid for my life. But I went with them. What else could I do? I was lucky. I could have died. In the end we had to walk for nearly two weeks. We had nothing to eat. I became dazed. My teeth fell out." He opened his mouth and pointed to the gap. "Scurvy," he said. "I had boils on my skin." He shuddered. "You do not want to hear this."

"I can hear it," I said. "I also had some problems."

"I went, of course, to the gold fields. I told you I would go!"

"Yes, you told us. And you said you would send for us."

"Do you know what life is like in the gold fields? Murderers and thieves—I saw a man hanged one afternoon. *Hanged*, for taking another man's claim. He cried and begged, it was a mistake, he said.

No matter, they hanged him. Oh, the fights, the terrible things I saw. They would cut your throat as soon as give you a piece of onion. My health was poor, Clem. I could not tolerate it. And the new companies were coming in with their large machines, drilling for gold, making tunnels and shafts. How could I do this? I had no tools, no equipment. I had not the strength. I came too late, too late! All the easy gold was gone, all the big nuggets, the pans full of gold from the river."

I took up a spoon of chili, put it into my mouth, but I could hardly swallow. My throat felt dry and parched. Though I had not eaten since early morning, I could not eat now.

I told him, "Ma said you would come for us."

"Your mother was a good woman."

"Why did you leave us?"

"She wanted me to! Clem, you were so young. You do not understand. Sometimes people—married people—need to have their own life. She did not want to go. I had to see if I could make something of myself."

"You told me you were coming back," I cried.

"What else could I tell you? You were a child."

"Now I am not a child," I said. My heart beat furiously. I stood up, and we both saw that I was nearly as tall as my father. I wanted to grab him, shake him, make him care! I cried out, "I came to find you. I thought you might be sick or in trouble, maybe even dead."

"What if I *were* dead?" Pa asked. He rolled up a cigarette, licked the edge of the paper, pressed it down, put it into his mouth, and lit it with a match. Smoke circled around his head. "Would you cry for me?"

I looked at him, stunned not by what he said, but by what he failed to say, to ask, to wonder. I might have been a stranger stumbling in, someone who wanted and needed nothing more from him than a bowl of chili and a piece of bread. I wanted to run out, to leave him sitting there, but a terrible tiredness held me fast.

"Well, now you are here," he said. "When you set out, how did you know you would find me?"

"I didn't know," I said dully. "I just took my chances."

"What route did you take? How did you manage?"

"Walking. Riding. You know. It's a hard trail."

"Yes. A hard trail. But now you are here."

"Yes."

"I have not much space," he said. "But we will find a pallet for you, a bed. How old are you now, Clem?"

We were interrupted by a shrill cry. "The Pony! The Pony!"

Pa ran out, Wang rushing behind him, hands tucked into his ample sleeves. There was a commotion of people, horses, shouting and stamping, and the shot of a cannon. *Boom, boom!* Women laughed and screamed. Men raced through the streets.

"He's won! Lincoln has won!"

"Hurrah! Hurrah, boys, I'll buy the drinks!"

Bells rang out. In the pandemonium I went back into the cellar shop. I found a straw pallet in a corner and sank down into it, too dazed and weary to celebrate, to think, or to care.

I had found my father, but he was not the same man who had left me. Or perhaps he was, and I had never really known him at all.

———◆◆◆———

Pa spent the whole night and half the next day composing, editing, setting type for his paper, all about Abraham Lincoln, the new president of the Union, and what his election meant to North and South, to East and West, to American and foreigner alike.

People came and crowded into the small cellar, men wearing waistcoats and silk ties and white linen shirts and beaver hats. There were several women, a teacher, a poet, another who headed the Ladies' Improvement Society. They talked and laughed and took notes. They all called my father "Pierre," and none had trouble saying his name.

Important men spoke with my father about what it all meant. I stood leaning against the wall, watching. Pa was in his element, smiling, smoking, pondering, explaining. He had shelves full of books and magazines and papers. Outside the world of the merchants moved along. Down in the cellar the lamps glowed late into the night while my father held everyone in conversation. Later they went down by the wharf for ale and a look at a cabaret. This was the pattern day after day, night after night.

In a back room curtained off into two parts, Wang and my father slept on iron cots. Pa had met Wang after an accident that left Wang crippled in one foot and unable to work any longer building roads. Somehow the two became friends, helping each other to survive. Wang was clever and had learned the printing trade in China. Pa was eager to take up his career as a newspaperman. It was a perfect union of two souls cut away from their past lives. Wang had left a wife and three daughters in China. He sent them half his pay every month by steamer.

As the first week passed, I walked the streets of San Francisco, gazing at the faces of the people there, trying to understand what had happened. Often I longed to stop a stranger, man or woman, and to ask them, "Do you have a son? If he were gone from you for years, would you care? Would you be glad to see him again?" I imagined their replies, exclamations, astonishment, pity.

After several days, days when my head throbbed and my throat ached with untold anger and grief, I realized that I did not want pity. Perhaps it was the sight of all those people going their way, healthy or sick, tired or worried—no doubt all had had their share of bad luck. Still, I heard fishermen whistling, dock workers joking, young men calling out to girls, laughing, and I knew I did not want pity. Perhaps it was the vision of Libby, after all, that pulled me up. All alone in that desolate prairie, with children to raise and needing to make a living, she could still laugh and be a friend. And then there was Molly, game to try anything, even to go west, without any shoes, without any money, but only her own free spirit. And there was Gabriel, hunted and beaten, but man enough to carry on and to search for his Sara, to keep his dream of having a home. And Hank had set out on his own, beholden to nobody but himself.

I can't say when it dawned on me, exactly, but somehow I put away anger and blame and picked myself up with a certainty. I was going to be my own man. I was going to keep my promises.

I had been there just over a week when one afternoon a lady came by, dressed in a rose-colored gown of watered silk, with felt hat to match. "Pierre, I have not seen you for ages!" she cried. Seeing me, her eyes widened, her mouth fell into a pout. "Who is this? You have taken a new assistant?"

"My son, Nelda," said Pa. "My son came all the way from Missouri to find me. What do you think of that?"

"Oh, what a fine, brave boy he is, and so very loyal. What is your name?"

"Clem," I said.

"Clem? Not a French name, is it? Very American. So, Pierre, I had no idea you would have such a grown-up son. And he is handsome, like his father. And now, are you staying here to help your papa with the newspaper?"

I looked at the two of them, the odd, almost amused looks on their faces.

"No," I said. "I will stay the winter and work with Mr. Grossmer, the lithographer."

"Oh? You have spoken with him already?" my father said. "And you did not tell me?"

"I spoke to him yesterday," I said. "I showed him my sketches. He said I might work with him doing scenes of the trail for posters and magazines. He has a place in his shop where I can sleep. It is very crowded here."

"Well, if it is what you desire . . ." Pa said. He scratched his head and smiled, turning to Nelda. "You see how it is. Our children grow up, and we must let them go their own way, follow their own desires."

"How true," said the woman.

"Come spring," I said, looking into my father's eyes with neither fear nor anger, "I will make my way back to Missouri."

"Back?" Pa exclaimed. "You would go back? Why?"

"There are people I need to see," I told him. "Things I must do." I thought of Molly and Gabriel, Bud and Libby. "And then," I said, "maybe I will return to California. I would like to return with a friend."

Nelda laughed softly. "I think your son has a sweetheart, Pierre."

Pa laughed too. "Like father, like son," he said.

Unwittingly, I shook my head, but I don't think Pa noticed.

I turned away and went out into the streets, feeling the San Francisco air blowing its freshness all around me. Beyond, I saw the masts of ships. On the hillsides I saw the fir trees and white tops of Conestoga wagons.

New feelings of freedom and happiness surged through me. I had done what I set out to do. I had found my father, and more. If I'd stayed back in Missouri, I'd be poorer for it.

Grossmer, the lithographer, had been skeptical when I first approached him. But as I spoke of my desires, he sat and listened, watching me closely, and at last he nodded and said, "You have taken the trail, and you have passed its tests. An artist needs to experience life. It is not enough to copy what the eyes see. The heart must know. Do you understand?"

I nodded and showed him the drawing of Sara.

He gazed at it for a long moment, then said, "A fine face. A strong woman. We should render it on metal to keep."

He shook my hand then, and I knew I could stand alone, not in anyone's shadow. And I thought back on all of it. If Pa had not gone off the way he did, I'd never have met all those people who now were part of my life and my destiny. I'd never have seen the West or set eyes on this city of San Francisco, which in these past days of torment and wonder I had come to love.

As I walked the streets I made a vow to myself. I would work all winter and earn my way back to settle old scores and to find Molly. I would bring her to this city at the edge of the sea. How her eyes would sparkle and dance at the sights!

In my mind I sang the song I would bring her:

> *"Molly! Do you love me?*
> *Tell me, tell me true!*
> *Molly! Do you love me,*
> *Love as I love you?"*

Somehow I knew it in my bones: Molly would come with me to California, and I would never, never leave her.

ABOUT THE AUTHOR

Sonia Levitin is the highly acclaimed author of many books, including *Journey to America*, *Nine for California*, *Boom Town*, and *Taking Charge*. Her numerous awards include the Western Writers of America Spur Award, the National Jewish Book Award, and the Mystery Writers of America Edgar Allan Poe Award. Ms. Levitin lives in Los Angeles, California.